"Like Conan Doyle's London, the Lockridges' New York has a lasting magic. There are taxis waiting at every corner, special little French restaurants, and perfect martinis. Even murder sparkles with big city sophistication. For everyone who remembers New York in the Forties and for everyone who wishes he did."

—Emma Lathen

"This husband and wife team is unexcelled in the field of mystery writing when it comes to a completely entertaining crime story."

—*St. Louis Post-Dispatch*

"Among the smoothest of the old professionals."
—Anthony Boucher,
Ellery Queen Mystery Magazine

Pam and Jerry North made their first appearance in *The New Yorker* in the 1930s. In 1940, Richard Lockridge's first book-length mystery, *The Norths Meet Murder,* was published. Richard and Frances Lockridge went on to write forty-nine other Mr. and Mrs. North books, as well as numerous other mysteries. The Norths became the stars of a Broadway play and a movie as well as a long-running radio program and popular television series.

Books by Richard and Frances Lockridge

Murder Comes First
Murder Within Murder
Death Takes a Bow

Published by POCKET BOOKS

Most Pocket Books are available at special quantity discounts for bulk purchases for sales promotions, premiums or fund raising. Special books or book excerpts can also be created to fit specific needs.

For details write or telephone the office of the Vice President of Special Markets, Pocket Books, 1230 Avenue of the Americas, New York, New York 10020. (212) 245-6400, ext. 1760.

DEATH
TAKES
A BOW

RICHARD AND
FRANCES LOCKRIDGE

PUBLISHED BY POCKET BOOKS NEW YORK

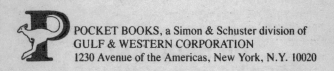

POCKET BOOKS, a Simon & Schuster division of
GULF & WESTERN CORPORATION
1230 Avenue of the Americas, New York, N.Y. 10020

Copyright 1943 by Frances and Richard Lockridge; copyright
renewed 1971 by Richard Lockridge

Published by arrangement with J. B. Lippincott Company

All rights reserved, including the right to reproduce
this book or portions thereof in any form whatsoever.
For information address J. B. Lippincott Company,
10 East 53rd Street, New York, N.Y. 10022

ISBN: 0-671-44337-2

First Pocket Books printing December, 1982

10 9 8 7 6 5 4 3 2 1

POCKET and colophon are registered trademarks
of Simon & Schuster.

Printed in the U.S.A.

1

Mrs. North was consoling. It wasn't, she pointed out, as if he really had to make a speech. Not a real speech. There was no sense in his carrying on so, and not eating any dinner.

"Actually," she explained with the air of one who has often explained, "actually all you do is tag Mr. Sproul. Then he's it and you just sit down and look interested and try not to wriggle. And don't pull at your hair."

Mr. North felt in his jacket pocket. The notes—notes which now represented, he dimly felt, all that he knew or would ever know about anything—were still there. This was reassuring, but it also reinforced his horrid conviction that this was real. In—Mr. North looked at his watch—in fifty-seven minutes he would have to stand up before five hundred people and open his mouth while five hundred mouths remained closed. He shuddered and took his hand away from the notes.

"Michaels should have done it," he said, angrily. "Why me, for God's sake?"

"Five minutes," Mrs. North said. "Or ten at the outside. You could do it standing on your head."

That, Mr. North assured her, would give just the touch. That would make it lovely.

"Mr. Gerald North," he said, "of the firm of Town-send Brothers, introduced Mr. Victor Leeds Sproul,

5

noted author of *That Was Paris,* while standing on his head."

"There, dear," Mrs. North said. "What's five minutes?" She paused. "He didn't go to Paris while standing on his head," she added, reflectively. "That came afterward. Is he really good, Jerry?"

"He's wonderful," Jerry told her. "He's immense. Five big printings. Total sales ninety-three thousand as of yesterday. He's colossal. Townsend Brothers loves him. Fifty-three minutes."

Mrs. North told him to try not to think of it. Or to think that, in an hour, it would all be over. Except, of course, Mr. Sproul, who would be beginning.

"Think how good you'll feel then," she said. "Duty done, audience contented, Mr. Sproul in full flight."

"And," Mr. North said harshly, "the platform covered with old vegetables. Thrown at me. Or me still standing there with my mouth open, trying to think of something to say. Or forgetting Sproul's name—Victor Leeds Sproul. Victor Leeds Sproul. Leeds Sproul Victor. Oh, God!"

"Five minutes," Mrs. North said, looking worriedly at her husband. "Only five minutes, Jerry. Not as long as we've been talking about it." She sighed. "Not nearly as long," she added. "And it isn't as if you hadn't done it before. You're a very good speaker, really. Once you get started."

Gerald North put out a cigarette, reached for another, fingered his notes instead. He held his hand out and watched it tremble. He besought Pamela North to look and she looked and said, "Poor dear."

"Once I get started," he repeated. "But you can't get started in five minutes. I'd rather talk half an hour. An hour, even. I'd rather be Sproul."

"No," Mrs. North said firmly. "Over my dead body."

For now, Mr. North pointed out. Not permanently. He would rather be Sproul making a speech of an hour than North introducing for five minutes. Because five

minutes was too long or not long enough; in five
minutes you could only talk at an audience, and nothing came back, because the audience hadn't the faintest idea who you were or what you wanted it to do;
because in five minutes you could not catch your
second fluency and had only to rely, frantically, on
what you had written down. And because you were
too scared to see what you had written down.

"Even fifteen minutes is better," Mr. North said.
"Oh, God!"

He stood up and looked around the living room.
Toughy raised an inquiring head from the chair cushion
on which he had, no doubt only momentarily, allowed
it to relax. He made the interested sound of a loqua-
cious cat which observes things in progress.

"Look at him!" Mr. North commanded. "Does he
have to make a speech before five hundred people,
introducing Victor Leeds Sproul? He just *lies* there!"

Mr. North glared at Toughy, who repeated his earlier remark.

"I'd like to be a cat," Mr. North said. "Just sleep
and play and be fed. Where's Ruffy?" He looked
around. "Off sleeping somewhere," he answered himself, bitterly. "Does she have to make a speech?" He
looked at Mrs. North. "Do you have to make a
speech?" he demanded. "Does anybody else in the
world have to make a speech except me?" He stared
around wildly. "Why me?" he demanded of the world
and, it seemed probable, its Creator.

"There, dear," Mrs. North said. "It's only five
minutes."

Mr. North glared at her.

"Five minutes!" he repeated. "Is that all you can
say? Five minutes?"

"Ten at the most," Mrs. North said, serenely. "After all, you've done it before." She paused. "And
always made just the same fuss about it," she added.
"And afterward never could understand why you were
so worried. I'd think you'd learn."

"So help me," Mr. North told her, "this is the last time. After this it's Michaels or nobody. Or all the Townsends—or—or anybody. But never me. So help me."

"You know there aren't any Townsends," Mrs. North told him. "Since 1873."

"Eighteen seventy-four," Mr. North told her. "Old Silas."

"And Michaels would have, only he's in the army," she pointed out. "He's being a captain."

"And if," Mr. North said, "he can see one bit better than I can I'll—"

"Jerry!" Mrs. North said. Mrs. North was firm. "There's no use going over that again, darling. It's just one of those things. You can't help it, and they can't help it and so you buy bonds and—and introduce Victor Leeds Sproul, so he can tell people about how lovely Paris used to be and make them want to make it that way again and—" She broke off.

"All right, baby," Mr. North said. "I'm sorry. I'll go make my little speech."

Mrs. North smiled at him.

"After all—" she began. Mr. North held up his hand.

"Don't go on," he warned. "Don't say—'after all, it's only five minutes.' Just don't."

Mrs. North smiled again. She said, all right, she wouldn't.

"And don't come," Mr. North said. "Don't get a taxicab after I leave and show up at the Today's Topics Club and think I won't see you in the audience. Because I will. And forget everything I was going to say. If anything." He looked at her. "Promise, Pam?" he said. There was a note of entreaty in his voice.

"Jerry!" Pam said. As she said it she looked, with sudden anxiety, at the little ball watch which hung around her neck. "Jerry, you've got to *go!* It's—it's after *eight!*"

There was no difficulty in distracting Jerry. He

looked at the watch on his wrist and shook the wrist and looked at it again. "Ten of," he said. "That's what mine says. Do you suppose—?"

"You mustn't take the chance," Pam told him. "Maybe it stopped. Jerry—you'll have to run! Have you got your notes?"

He felt again, although the touch of the folded sheets of paper was still reminiscent on his fingers. The notes were there. He picked up his top coat, spread on the sofa beside him, and Ruffy tumbled off, landing on her feet and making cat comments. But she saw her brother in his chair and went over quickly. She jumped up beside him and fell to washing his face. He closed his eyes in ecstasy.

"Ruffy," Pam North said. "You *are* a fool. Make him wash himself!"

Ruffy did not pause. Toughy opened one eye partially and looked at Pamela North and there seemed to be a kind of amusement in the amber eye. He closed it again and Ruffy washed behind his ears.

"I've got to go," Gerald North said. "I've got to go and make a speech."

The horror of the situation, now all at once so immediate, overwhelmed him. "I've got to go *now!*" he repeated, in a kind of horrified disbelief. "It's almost *now!*"

That, he thought as he went down the stairs to the street door, and out into the street, was the thing about agreeing to make speeches. You agreed absently in August, when it was suggested to you—when it was only suggested, and yours to take or leave, when you could get out of it easily. You said, perhaps, "Sure, I'll introduce the bloke. Now, Miss Casey, if you're ready—" And then, instantly, it was October and the speech was now. Because time before speeches—even speeches of only five minutes—did not flow smoothly and evenly along, as time sometimes did. Time tricked you, giving no warning. A week before the speech, the speech was still almost as remote as it had been in

August; even on Thursday a speech to be given on
Friday was comfortably distant. It was not until Friday morning that you discovered you could eat no
breakfast. And then it was Friday evening and you
were on the sidewalk of Greenwich Place, alone in a
hostile world, in which no one of all you saw bore your
dreadful, immediate burden; a world divided between
people who did not have to make a speech in half an
hour—less, maybe—and you.

Gerald North caught a glimpse of the Jefferson
Market Clock between two buildings. It said five of
eight. Sometimes, he had heard, they let the condemned man give the signal to the fire squad. Or was it
the headsman? The condemned man lifted his hand—
and what whirling anguish went on in the still living
brain as it commanded the hand to rise was something
it was not comfortable to imagine. Gerald North imagined it. He lifted his hand and a taxi in the stand at the
corner came to life. It leaped the intervening quarter
block and engulfed Gerald North. Clutching the sheaf
of notes in his inner pocket, his mind a cloudy swirl,
the man who was about to make a little introductory
speech rode northward along Fifth Avenue, toward his
doom.

Normally traffic would have held them up, but that
night there was no traffic. The cab dashed through the
half-lighted streets like a meteor. It whirled east at
Fifty-seventh, and up Madison, and the lights were all
green before it. It did not break down. It did not careen
into another car, wrecking itself and providing Mr.
North with welcome lacerations and contusions which
would make the giving of speeches impossible. The
driver did not get arrested for exceeding the speed
limit, nor was he held up by altercations with a traffic
policeman until it was too late to reach the Today's
Topics Club—why, Mr. North wondered dimly, not
Today's Topics Clubs? Or even Klubs? The cab
swirled up to the club's dignified four-story building,
which looked so oddly as if it must house some lesser

department of the government, and stopped. Mr. North, dazed now, got out and paid. He saw people going into the main entrance—people who were going to hear a lecturer, and the introducer of a lecturer, and had bitter, rapacious faces—and shuddered. He went into the smaller, narrow door reserved, on such nights as these, for the condemned. He entered the small elevator and was jerked to the third floor. He turned right down a cold, white corridor and came to a door marked: "Speakers' Room." With a shudder, Mr. North opened the door.

Of the three people in the room, Mr. North knew only one, the lion himself. Victor Leeds Sproul wore dinner clothes as if they were tweeds, and as if they were intended to be tweeds. One felt, instinctively, that if any disparity existed, it was the fault of the man who had first decided that dinner clothes were not to be made of tweed. Mr. Sproul was merely correcting an ancient error. When Mr. Sproul wore a dinner jacket, it became of tweed, and had better.

Mr. Sproul was taller and broader than ordinary. He, standing and putting down a glass on a polished table created to add impersonality to the detached surroundings of a speakers' room, loomed above Mr. North. He also loomed on either side of Mr. North. And if Mr. North, faced in the immediate future by an audience, lacked confidence, Mr. Sproul had confidence enough for two. It was clear that Mr. Sproul was going to enjoy lecturing, not only this evening but during the tour which stretched ahead.

Mr. Sproul was the lion and looked it. He was more impressive, more assured, even than Mr. North remembered him from meetings during recent weeks—meetings at the office, when Mr. Sproul, sitting beside Mr. North's desk, seemed somehow to leave Mr. North sitting beside it; meetings for luncheon, at which Mr. Sproul somehow became the host and made Mr. North feel at home. (He had managed, somehow, to make Mr. North feel at home in his own club, where before he had always felt a little away from home.)

He loomed above Mr. North now, with reddish hair bristling in suitable profusion, and reached out a hand.

"*Mr.* North!" he said, and somehow made it sound like the tag line of an anecdote. It was as if Sproul had been telling a story to which the entrance of Mr. North was the pay-off; as if Mr. North had entered only to pay off, only to complete a story already told. Mr. North felt, as he had felt before, as if he were essentially a figment of Mr. Sproul's imagination.

And yet, he thought, saying "Hello, Sproul," to the lion, Mr. Sproul did not really have a great deal of imagination. As Mr. Sproul's publisher, Mr. North could take his oath to that. There had been novels from Mr. Sproul and, without knowing the people Mr. Sproul had known, you could be almost certain that people Mr. Sproul had known appeared almost verbatim in the novels, which had, without being particularly interesting, a feeling of obvious reality. You could almost see the people whose lives Mr. Sproul had borrowed squirming uneasily on the pages to which Mr. Sproul had pinned them.

They had, since Mr. Sproul had spent so much of his life in Paris, been novels with a Paris background and, chiefly, they had been about people who had spent most of their lives in Paris but had been born elsewhere. There was a novel about a Parisian actress, born in Budapest, who had an affair—an *affaire,* really—with an American born in Sioux City. There had been a novel about a dancer, born in Warsaw, who had had an affair with an Englishman born in Shanghai, who succeeded where another American, born in Buffalo this time, had failed. The novels were extremely continental. They were not, however, extremely successful.

Townsend Brothers had, in fact, been considering the polite relinquishment of Mr. Sproul as an author when *That Was Paris* came along. This one was not a novel. As nearly as anything, it was biography, but it

was a biography of a city as well as of Victor Leeds
Sproul, and it came in time to be the obituary of the
city and of a period. And it caught on; prodigiously it
caught on. And Victor Leeds Sproul, in no wise astonished, found himself sharing with Elliot Paul the role of
a beautiful city's biographer. Mr. Sproul's book glit-
tered rather more than Mr. Paul's, being set in more
tinseled places, and it was not so real, but it served.
Townsend Brothers beamed on Mr. Sproul and forgot
that they had been thinking of polite relinquishment.
And Y. Charles Burden sent Mr. Sproul a telegram. A
few days later, and this was indeed tribute, Mr. Burden followed his telegram, although in the ordinary
course of events Mr. Burden's telegrams were not
harbingers but summonses.

Mr. Burden was lean and saturnine and by common
agreement—an agreement to which Mr. Burden was
vociferously a party—the best lecture agent in the
business. Mr. Burden took on only winners. Mr. Burden was a winner himself, and looked it; he was a well-
groomed lion in his own right. Confronting his ele-
gance, most prospective clients quailed and grew
small, realizing that they, by comparison, were pathet-
ically unfitted for the exposed life, to which Mr. Burden was, so regally, summoning them. This attitude on
the part of clients comported with Mr. Burden's de-
sires, making it easier to apportion what Mr. Burden
called the "split." (Now and then, thinking it over
after contracts were signed, Mr. Burden's more per-
spicacious clients suspected that they were what had
been split.) Mr. Burden offered, when the prospective
client was softened by his presence, a forty-five–fifty-
five cut of fees, the fifty-five going to Mr. Burden. In
exchange, he pointed out, he paid all expenses, except, of course, hotel bills and meals. And, naturally
enough, travel expenses too trifling to be itemized, like
cab and subway fares, and railroad fares of less than a
couple of dollars. It surprised Mr. Burden's clients
somewhat, afterward, to discover how frequently

they, if resident in New York, were booked for lectures in New York.

But Mr. Sproul, and this Mr. Burden admitted on confronting him, was a bigger kettle of fish. Mr. Sproul was de luxe, and Mr. Burden told him so. Mr. Sproul was suitable for a grand tour, opening in New York at Today's Topics Club and going on across the continent by easy and profitable stages. And Mr. Sproul would get a sixty-forty split.

"Sixty," Mr. Sproul had said—he had told Mr. North of this with beaming amusement. "To me."

Mr. Burden had been startled and hurt; had almost heatedly described overhead and permanent organizations and the high cost of riding on trains. Mr. Sproul had been expansive and assured, and had actually got fifty-five per cent. He was pleased, and his pleasure had seeped through his account of the interview. Mr. North did not tell him that Mr. Burden had, on occasion, been known to pay sixty, but this small fact Mr. North had treasured.

He treasured it now, looking up at Victor Leeds Sproul and waiting for Mr. Sproul to get around to introducing him to the two women. There should, Mr. North realized, have been only one woman—the program chairman. That would be—Mr. North searched his memory madly for a name which had been there a second before—that would be Mrs. Paul Williams. It was she who had suggested that, on this first lecture, so widely advertised and so, in all respects, important, a representative of Mr. Sproul's publishers might care to be on hand and introduce the lion. This suggestion had brought Mr. North to his present state, and during the negotiations he had received several letters of confirmation from Mrs. Williams and written several letters, also of confirmation, to her. He had also spoken to her early that day on the telephone, further confirming the already woefully confirmed.

"I'm Mrs. Williams, Mr. North," she said now, still confirming. Mr. North retrieved his hand from Mr.

Sproul and accepted the hand of Mrs. Williams. Mr. Sproul looked on with the air of a man who has made things right.

Mrs. Williams was, Jerry North estimated, in her middle thirties. And the word for her was "trim." Slightly taller than most women, she was trimmer than almost any. Her blond hair, swept up at the sides of her head, was perfect in its contours. Her figure was— Mr. North thought for a phrase—beautifully held in. Looking at her, you thought, with a sudden recollection of things past, of corsets. And yet she was not obviously corseted; it was more as if she were corseted by will power. She was, Mr. North decided, a businesslike lady and kept everything under control.

And then, murmuring a blurred "how do you do?" Mr. North was conscious of the first oddity of what was to become so odd an evening. Mrs. Williams was looking past him and a little upward, and Mr. North realized that she was looking up at Victor Leeds Sproul—looking at him with an expression which Mr. North found unexpected, but could not analyze. Involuntarily, Mr. North turned a little and looked, in turn, up at the lion of the evening. The lion was amused. He was looking at them with amusement. It was that amusement, Mr. North decided, which had momentarily disconcerted Mrs. Williams, who probably was difficult to disconcert.

If she was disconcerted, her recovery was instant. She looked at Mr. North, now, and said, with just that hint of disclaimer which detached politeness suggested, that she really felt as if she knew Mr. North.

"We are so delighted that you came, Mr. North," she said. "Yourself. And I am so glad the firm agreed with my thought. I'm sure that Mr. Sproul is pleased, too."

"Least they could do," Mr. Sproul said, but he said it jovially. "Eh, North?"

Mr. North said something about its having been a very happy thought. He looked at his watch.

"We'll give them another five minutes, I think," Mrs. Williams said. "They expect it. And would you like to have me introduce you, Mr. North? Just a word, of course."

"I think," the other woman in the room said, in a husky, attractive voice, "that somebody ought to introduce *me*. Don't you?"

This last was evidently to Mr. North. He turned, smiling.

"Loretta Shaw," Sproul said over their heads. He said the name as if it should be obvious. "Mr. North. From my publishers, Retta."

The girl, too, seemed amused, but her amusement was different in quality from Sproul's. She seemed amused at herself and at Mr. North and at all of them. Mr. North looked at her, which was enjoyable. She was slender and quick and vivacious and had dark-brown hair. She did not look corseted; she was, on the contrary, noticeably pliant. The pliancy was unobtrusive, but inescapable; no man looking at her could miss it. Mr. North, pleased—and for a moment almost forgetting the ordeal ahead—did not miss it. He wondered who she was.

"Just heartening me up, Retta is," Sproul explained. "Came around to see that I hadn't fainted, or done a bunk or—what do we Americans say?—scrammed. A friendly thought."

"And," Loretta Shaw said, "obviously unnecessary. I should have known, Lee. Takes more than an audience to—to frighten Victor Leeds Sproul."

Mr. North had a feeling she had first intended to finish her sentence differently—less amiably. But it was a fugitive feeling, based more on something in the air than in the girl's voice or manner.

"Tourists," Sproul said, with easy contempt. "American tourists. Here or there, what difference does it make?"

"Lee!" the girl said. "If you feel that way, keep it to yourself. Don't be—condescending."

She spoke now, Mr. North was sure, as if she had a right to caution. She looked up at Sproul and shook her head. There was admonition in the gesture.

"That's all over, Lee," she said. "Try to remember. This is New York. This is where we all live—where you live."

Sproul answered her in French, too rapidly for Mr. North's ears and memory. She smiled and, Mr. North thought, smiled involuntarily, against her own judgment. She answered in English, rejecting shared secrets.

"Be careful," she said. "Tell him to be careful, Mr. North. Mrs. Williams."

Mrs. Williams's voice was corseted, detached.

"I am sure Mr. Sproul will be—tactful," she said. "But he will find that ours is a very—mature audience. I have no doubt that it will understand Mr. Sproul."

It was, Mr. North thought, an odd word to use, as she used it. She gave it a rather special flavor, as if it meant more than it seemed to mean. She had, he decided, grasped Victor Leeds Sproul rather more completely than most people did in a short time, and she could not have met him more than once or twice in the course of her confirmations. She seemed to have hidden views concerning him. But then, Mr. North reflected, the outward contradictions of Mr. Sproul were not really difficult to grasp. And Mrs. Williams, although it was hard not to think of her as prim, was evidently not without comprehension. And judgment. It never paid, Mr. North thought—thought under the nervousness which was again taking possession of him—it never paid to take people as being altogether what they looked to be. Still, he added to himself, that's about the only thing we have to go on.

He looked at his watch again, and Mrs. Williams looked at hers, and this time she nodded. She went to a door opposite that by which Mr. North had entered, and instantly Mr. North guessed what the little door was. It was the little green door at Sing Sing. He took a deep breath, adopted an expression—of which he was doubtful—and prepared himself. Mrs. Williams smiled back at them encouragingly and opened the door. Mr. North heard the other door, now behind them, close, and was conscious that Miss Loretta Shaw had quitted their doomed procession. Mr. North stepped aside and let the lion precede him. The lion followed Mrs. Williams. As Sproul passed him, Mr. North looked up into the large face, wondering if, now that the moment had arrived, trepidation would make its impress even on Victor Leeds Sproul.

It had not. On the contrary, Sproul looked elated and a little flushed. He beamed down at Mr. North, and beamed excessively; he snapped two large fingers and, as he passed, murmured "tourists" and seemed to be laughing. Mr. North hoped that he had not had one drink too many to bolster himself for this crucial first stage of the de luxe tour. But the worry, at the most hardly palpable, passed instantly. Mr. North could not spend time worrying about Mr. Sproul; Mr. North had barely enough time left to worry about himself. Because, as he had feared, the little door— which was, he noticed, only symbolically green— opened directly onto the stage.

The muscles at the back of Mr. North's neck tightened as he looked out over the auditorium. It was filled, all right. There must be, Mr. North thought, nearer a thousand than five hundred. The tight muscles pulled Mr. North's head back. He was aware that a fixed smile had settled upon his lips—fixed and, he was convinced, fatuous.

"They'll wonder who I am," Mr. North thought. "They'll know her, and they've seen pictures of him and who, for God's sake, am I? What's been rung in on them?"

There were three chairs behind a lectern. There was a big chair in the middle, with a high back, and smaller chairs on either side, with lower backs. The big chair for Sproul, the papa bear. The little chair further on for Mrs. Williams, the mama bear. The little chair nearest for Mr. North, the rabbit. Oh God, thought Mr. North. He felt in his pocket for the notes.

He pulled the notes half out and pushed them back. What difference would notes make? He couldn't read them, obviously. They would be only a confusing blur, and this was as well, because—and now he realized it—what he had written on them, those few words which were to guide him, were beyond belief asinine. To utter them would make him at once pathetic and absurd. And they were the only words he knew!

Because now, as Mrs. Williams rose and went to the lectern and rapped on it, Mr. North's mind was blank. It was not merely blank in the ordinary sense; it was blank like a doorway opening on nothing. Mr. North opened the door of his mind and looked in and it opened on nothing. Even consciousness of his own identity seemed to have vanished; the world was an empty dream, with the trimmings of a nightmare. Mr. North searched desperately in his mind for an inkling of anything—he was to introduce somebody for some purpose—a man named Victor—Sproul Victor. I—

"And now," Mrs. Williams said, her voice corseted with assurance, "I am happy to introduce a representative of Mr. Sproul's publishers who will, I am sure, have something to tell us about their very successful author. Mr.—Gerald North."

Mrs. Williams turned and smiled at the blank which was Mr. North. He felt himself smiling back. He felt himself rising and walking to the lectern. He felt himself reaching for the sheaf of notes in his pocket and watched himself spreading them out on the lectern. He knew he was raising his head and looking out over the audience and smiling faintly, and he heard his throat clear itself.

And then, of course, that miracle occurred which always occurred; that miracle which, even when he was blankest, Mr. North had always realized would probably happen. Mr. North returned to himself. He saw the audience as a collection of reasonably friendly people, waiting without bias for him to speak; he heard the rustle behind him of Mrs. Williams sitting down and another sound which was, he supposed, Mr. Sproul shifting his feet. He could even, in the instant before he began to speak, hear Mr. Sproul breathing— breathing, it seemed, a little heavily from excitement. So it had got to Sproul, Mr. North thought, pleased— and now, almost amused, Mr. North had been through it and come out on the other side; Mr. Sproul was in it now. Before him, not any longer before Gerald North, loomed that awful moment of arising and that perilous step from seat to lecturing position.

Mr. North began to speak. He watched the people at the rear of the shallow balcony to make sure that they could hear him; he begged them not to be frightened because of the notes, promising them that he would not use them. "Consider them," he begged, "only as a straw which I have put ready to be clutched."

He would not, he promised, delay them. He might tell them one small story about Mr. Sproul. He told them one small story about Mr. Sproul and paused, with a half smile which meant that they might, if they wished, now laugh. They laughed. He capped their laugh with an inflection, and they laughed again.

"When you come down to it," Mr. North thought, "I'm really pretty good at this. Too bad Pam can't hear me."

He looked out over the audience and for a moment confidence caught in his throat. Pam could hear him all right—assuming his voice was carrying to the fifth row on the side, as presumably it was. Pam was sitting there looking interested and when she caught his eye she smiled and nodded. Dorian Weigand was sitting beside her, and Pam turned to Dorian and made a tiny gesture of lifted eyebrows toward Jerry and Dorian smiled at him. Mr. North hesitated, fractionally, and went on.

He had talked, now, for a little more than five minutes. He rounded it off. They had come to hear Victor Leeds Sproul, not to hear his publisher—obviously biased in Mr. Sproul's favor. "Our bias toward anybody who sells a hundred thousand copies is boundless," Mr. North assured the audience, which smiled. He had come, Mr. Sproul had, to tell them about a beautiful city which no longer was; about a gracious thing which had been killed. How ruthlessly, how barbarously killed they needed neither Mr. North, nor even Mr. Sproul, to tell them. But Mr. Sproul could, better than any other man of whom Mr. North could think, tell them something of that gracious life—of that ancient civilization—which now had ended but which might, they all hoped, one day rise again. And now it was his very great honor to introduce to them—

"Mr. Victor Leeds Sproul, distinguished author of *That Was Paris*. Mr. Sproul—"

Mr. North turned, smiling, with a half gesture toward the big man in the big chair. And for a second he waited, still smiling, his back half to the audience. And then, in a tone only a little raised, he repeated: "Mr. Sproul."

He repeated it because it seemed that Mr. Sproul had not heard. Mr. Sproul sat in the chair and did not move, and he seemed strangely relaxed, except that he was breathing very noisily. For a horrible moment it occurred to Mr. North that Mr. Sproul had gone to sleep.

But Mr. Sproul had not gone to sleep, and that realization was more horrible still. Mr. Sproul was in a coma and, at that moment, while Mr. North watched, the body moved a little and the eyes, which had been closed, opened. Then the mouth opened, too. But no words came out of it; never any more would words come out of it. The body, already slumped, relaxed just perceptibly and Mr. North, frozen incongruously with his smile and his half beckoning gesture, knew sickly what had happened.

Mr. Victor Leeds Sproul was no longer breathing noisily. He was not breathing at all.

2

For an instant after he realized this, Mr. North's inviting hand remained extended, mutely inviting Mr. Sproul to arise and lecture. Then Mr. North became conscious that his simple gesture had become grotesque. He let his arm fall. His eyes left the flushed face of Mr. Sproul and went to the face of Mrs. Paul Williams, who had left her chair and was standing beside him. Mrs. Williams' face was white and horrified.

"He's sick!" she said. She spoke in only a normal voice, but it carried through the auditorium, grown suddenly silent. "Isn't he sick?" This was to Mr. North. He looked at her.

"I don't think so," he said. "Not any more. A few minutes ago he was—sick."

She stared at him, and there was horror in her eyes.

"Yes," Mr. North said. "I'm afraid so."

His voice was lower, but not too low to carry. There was an odd sound from the audience; it was as if the audience sighed. And then, somewhere in the rear, a woman screamed. It was not a loud scream; it lay between a scream and a sob. And then the silence broke into fragments and the audience was alive, moving, uneasy. And Mr. North turned to it.

"I'm afraid Mr. Sproul is—unwell," he said. "If one of you is a doctor—?"

23

A middle-aged man rose in the third row and sidled toward the aisle. Mr. North caught his eye and the man nodded and came to the platform. There were no stairs, but it was a low platform and the man put one hand on it and half climbed, half vaulted up. He went over to Sproul and bent over him and felt his wrist and stared into his eyes. He leaned down and sniffed at the full, parted lips and stood up and looked at Mr. North.

"He's dead, you know," the man said. He looked at Mr. North, feeling evidently that there was more to be said. "Klingman," he added. "Dr. Klingman." It was obviously self-identification. Mr. North nodded.

"What—?" he began. Dr. Klingman shook his head.

"I'd have to examine him," he said. "Asphyxia, from his appearance. But what would asphyxiate him? Poison. A drug—opium. Or cerebral hemorrhage. Or something the matter with his brain. You'd better call somebody. Somebody in authority. I—"

A high, angry voice broke in. It came from the door leading to the stage from the speakers' room, and it preceded a tall, evidently angry man. He was a high, lean man and apparently about seventy, and his voice crackled in the upper register.

"Well!" he said. "What's this? What's *this?* Something the matter with him?"

The tall old man was obviously annoyed. He seemed to be addressing, chiefly, Mrs. Williams. At any rate he was looking at Mrs. Williams. He was looking at her angrily.

"Mr. Sproul seems—seems to have been taken ill, Dr. Dupont," Mrs. Williams said. "The doctor"—she gestured vaguely toward Dr. Klingman—"the doctor thinks he's dead."

"I don't think it," Dr. Klingman said. "He *is* dead. Completely." He looked at Dr. Dupont, whom he evidently knew. "Very unfortunate, Doctor," he said. "Very irregular." There was, in spite of everything, the faintest touch of raillery in the physician's tone. The tone accepted and lightly ridiculed the older man's annoyance at so improper an interruption to orderly procedure. Then Mr. North placed the tall man. Dr. Dupont, scholar not medico, was president of the Today's Topics Club. He ran it, Mr. North remembered hearing, on the highest plane of the intellect, and with notable asperity. He was not, Mr. North supposed, a man to countenance such extravagances as seemed to have occurred.

"Irregular?" Dr. Dupont repeated. "Unfortunate!" He glared at the physician. *"Irregular!"* He spluttered slightly. He turned his glare to Mr. North.

"Have to get him out of *here,*" he said. Mr. Sproul became, ludicrously, matter out of place, through the fault of Gerald North, who had put him there. Mr. Sproul became, it was clear, a responsibility solely of his publishers. Of Mr. Sproul, as such, Dr. Dupont washed his hands. He looked severely at Mr. North. Mr. North was conscious of annoyance.

"We'll have to get the police," he said. "It will have—to be looked into." He was conscious of a certain inadequacy in the words. "The doctor says it may have been poison," he added. "You can't move him around."

"Certainly you can't leave him *here,*" Dr. Dupont said, with asperity. "In front of all these people." He looked at the people. "Most of them members," he added. His tone was accusing.

They couldn't, Mr. North repeated firmly, do anything else. It was a matter for the police; it was a matter to be left in abeyance for the police. If Dr. Dupont liked, Mr. North would notify the police. Or Dr. Dupont could. But somebody had better. Then Mr. North thought of something and started for the door leading to the speakers' room. Halfway he turned.

"Nobody should touch it," he said. He said it loudly, so that the restive audience could hear. "It's a matter for the police."

That, he thought, ought to give Dr. Dupont pause; it ought to make an auditorium full of people sentinels over the body of Victor Leeds Sproul, protecting it from molestation by the weight of public attention. Assuming that anybody wanted to molest it. Meanwhile, Mr. North wanted to get into the speakers' room.

He entered by the door from the stage as Y. Charles Burden, elegant and saturnine as always, but now evidently in a hurry, entered by the door leading from the corridor. Mr. Burden confronted Mr. North.

"What the hell?" Mr. Burden inquired. "What the bloody hell?"

"Our man's dead," Mr. North told him. "No tour. No more books. No more Sproul." Mr. North looked intently at Mr. Burden. "Probably," Mr. North added, "somebody killed him. In front of all of us."

As he spoke, Jerry North was looking quickly around the room. He knew what he was looking for, but he did not see it. There should be a glass. Or glasses. Sproul had put down a glass as Mr. North entered, before they went onto the stage. He had been drinking something out of it. Had he been drinking alone? Mr. North's memory gave no answer.

"Damn!" said Y. Charles Burden, emphatically. "Booked through to the coast, too." He looked at Mr. North, and his glance, too, was accusing. "And back again," he added. "To the coast and back again."

"All right," Mr. North said. "And we had him under option. For the rest of his life." He looked at Burden and half smiled. "Which ought," he said, "to let us out—you and me, I mean . . . when the police come."

"Police?" Burden repeated. He thought it over. "Naturally," he said. He appeared to think. "Make quite a story," he said. "I wonder—" He did not wonder audibly. Mr. North could follow without words.

"Grist," he pointed out, "in its fashion. Grist for the Burden mill. Lend a certain touch of drama to the lecture business, in general." He paused, reflecting in his turn. "Start quite a run on the bookstores, too," he added. He looked at Burden, and was horrified at both of them.

"Can't help thinking of things," Burden said. Even he sounded defensive. "Got livings to make, both of us. Sorry about the old boy, of course. Still—there you are." He looked at Mr. North reflectively. "As a matter of fact," he said, "I used to know him pretty well at one time. In Paris. A funny sort of bloke, really."

"Was he?" Mr. North asked. "Funny enough to get murdered? That kind of funny?"

Slowly Burden nodded.

"I shouldn't wonder," he said. "I shouldn't wonder at all. However . . ."

He adopted an expression of worried decorum and went past Mr. North and through the door leading to the stage. After a moment, Mr. North followed him. The moment convinced Mr. North that there were no drinking glasses in the room, and that there was nothing apparent in the room to put in glasses if glasses were at hand. Mr. North went back to the stage.

There were more people around Sproul now. The physician and Dr. Dupont were still there, and Mrs. Williams was sitting in a chair, looking as if she were near to fainting. And there were several new men and a new woman on the stage. These were, it could be assumed, other officers of the club, sharing Dr. Dupont's perturbation loyally. And in the auditorium the members of the audience were, for the most part, standing up, and moving toward aisles. Without asking anybody, Mr. North went to the lectern and struck it with the little wooden gavel Mrs. Williams had used when first the audience was invited to come to order. There was a pause in the movement of the audience.

"Mr. Sproul is dead," Mr. North said, astonished instantly at his own bluntness. "He died here on the platform and it will be necessary to call the police." He waited. They were listening, now.

"I don't know any more about such things than any

of you," he went on, not altogether truthfully. "But I imagine that the police would like everybody to remain here until—until they've looked into things. You'll have to decide for yourselves, of course. But I think you should have in mind that that would be what the police would want. Dr. Dupont is going to call the police now, and they should be here almost at once."

Mr. North paused and regarded the audience, which regarded him. There was no telling what the audience would do; probably it would merely go home, except for its more curious members. And it was not, certainly, his responsibility. He had, he was pleased to think, put it up to Dr. Dupont.

It was evident that Dr. Dupont also thought so. He looked at Jerry North without affection.

"High-handed," he said. Mr. North was surprised and oddly pleased. It was an apt way of putting it. He smiled at Dr. Dupont.

"Somebody," he pointed out, "has to do something, Doctor. I thought you wanted me to get him out of here."

Dr. Dupont made a noise. It was partly a snort and partly a sound which might be spelled "grumpph!" It was pleasingly old school; it sounded like the Union Club on the subject of the man in the White House.

"Well," Mr. North said, "are you going to call the police, Dr. Dupont?"

"He doesn't need to," Pam North said. She was standing just below the platform, where it met the auditorium. "We did it. Or Dorian did, really. Because of Bill. I thought she was the one, really, because he's her husband. After all."

Everybody looked at Mrs. North, who was pleasing to look at. She wore a red woolen dress and a black felt hat with a red feather, and she was carrying a black fur jacket affectionately in her left arm. She held her right hand up to Jerry.

"Pull, darling," she suggested. She smiled at him.

"You were very good, Jerry, really and you needn't have worried at all. Only it was sort of wasted, wasn't it?"

Jerry reached down a hand. Pam rose to the low stage. Dr. Dupont stared at her, with a slight air of unbelief.

"The speech, Doctor," Pam explained. "Jerry's, I mean. Because of Mr. Sproul." She looked at Mr. Sproul. "He doesn't look awful, does he?" she said. "You can't believe it, really— It's not as if he were hanged."

"Pam," Jerry said. "Quit it. You're—"

"Jittering," Pam said. "Of course. I keep thinking—"

"Don't," Jerry told her. But he thought, too, of a man they had both seen slowly turning at the end of a rope and the nerves tightened in the back of his neck. He shook himself and tried to shake off the thought.

"Dorian called the police?" he asked, bringing them back to the concrete. "Just now—oh—"

Dorian was coming down the center aisle. She didn't look like the wife of a policeman. And she looked puzzled.

"They're coming," she said, when she saw Jerry North looking at her. "Only—they already knew. Bill had left to come up. Somebody had telephoned before. Somebody with a funny voice, Mullins said. Mullins was rounding up the squad. A high voice and rather strange English. The—the voice reported that Mr. Sproul had been murdered."

She was at the platform now. She did not offer to climb up.

"Has he?" she asked. "Been murdered?"

She looked intently at Jerry North and the others on the stage.

"Nonsense," Dr. Dupont answered. He looked with determination at those around him, and then at the restive, puzzled audience. "A sensational rumor," he

announced. Everybody stared at him. He stared them
down, or tried to stare them down—first those on the
stage, then those in the audience.

"Mr. Sproul is merely unwell," he said, in his high,
cracking voice. "Dr. Klingman will bear me out."

He gazed at Dr. Klingman; his gaze held command.
Dr. Klingman's face held a slight smile.

"Unwell?" he repeated. "Really, Dr. Dupont—that
is a matter for a metaphysician. On our—plane—on
our plane, he is dead. Quite possibly he has been
murdered." He looked with a barely more perceptible
smile at the tall president of the Today's Topics Club.
"I am sorry," he said. Again his voice held a note of
raillery. "It is an annoying fact."

Dr. Dupont looked disappointed in Dr. Klingman.
He shook his head sharply, admonishingly.

"Natural causes," he commanded. "If he is—*very*
unwell, it is obviously from natural causes."

Pam and Jerry stood side by side and looked at Dr.
Dupont. Everybody looked at Dr. Dupont. Then, from
the audience, there was an unexpected sound. Somebody had laughed, nervously. Pam saw that Dr. Dupont's tall, spare figure was shaking. His hand, half
raised in what might have been a gesture of command
to somebody, shook perceptibly. Pam spoke, and her
voice was unexpectedly quiet and steady.

"Doctor," she said. "Sit down, please. This has
been a shock. You must—catch him!"

Others had seen it almost as quickly. Dr. Klingman,
who was nearest, caught the tottering, tall old man and
eased him gently down to the floor of the stage. Dr.
Dupont's eyes closed and almost immediately re-
opened. They looked up at Dr. Klingman.

"The club," Dr. Dupont said. "What will they say
about the club?" Now there was something pathetic
about the dictatorial old man. But Pam North stared at
him, and then at Jerry.

"He takes it very hard, doesn't he?" she said.
"Harder than you'd expect. He was—he was almost

hysterical, wasn't he? Before he started to faint. Isn't that odd?"

It was odd, Jerry North thought. But it was oddness of a kind hard to identify. It might be that Dr. Dupont was merely an odd man, and then it was meaningless. For them, and, when he came, for Lieutenant William Weigand of the Homicide Division. But it might be, as easily, that Dr. Dupont was himself not particularly an odd man, but a normally quite predictable man who suddenly found himself in odd circumstances. The circumstances were odd, certainly. But did they have for Dr. Dupont an additional, personal, oddity? That would be one for Lieutenant Weigand.

Pam and Jerry North were standing near the front of the stage, and stage left. Dr. Dupont, now sitting up gingerly in the supporting arm of Dr. Klingman, was between them and the chair in which Victor Leeds Sproul still sat, as if lolling there. Beyond Sproul and those clustered around him, looking diagonally up-stage, was the door through which Jerry North and Mrs. Williams and Mr. Sproul had entered hardly half an hour before. Mr. North, wondering about the odd-ity of Dr. Dupont, looked at the door abstractedly. His gaze was so abstracted that it was several minutes before he saw that the door was opening. It opened inward, toward the speakers' room beyond. Mr. North was at first vaguely puzzled by an incongruity before he realized that the lights which had been burning in the speakers' room were no longer burning—that the door was opening inward on shadows, with a darker, human shadow in the doorway. The shadow kept back, so that the lights from the border above the stage fell on it only slightly. It was a dark, small shadow. It seemed to be a little, dark man; a little, dark, surrepti-tious man, staring out of an unlighted room at the scene of a murder. And then the shadow disappeared and, slowly, the area of darkness on which the door had opened grew narrower. The little dark man had seen whatever it was he wanted to see, and was withdrawing as inconspicuously as he had appeared.

That, Mr. North thought, was measurably odder than the behavior of Dr. Dupont. That needed looking into. Mr. North, forgetting the several occasions on which he had looked into odd matters and lived—once by a fairly narrow margin—to wish he hadn't, moved without announcement toward the door. He felt, strangely, that he was moving invisibly across the lighted stage, so evidently was the attention of everyone fastened on Sproul and the group around him. Even Pam seemed not to notice that he had left his place beside her.

The door closed fully, but without sound, just a moment before Mr. North reached it. Mr. North pushed it back cautiously, standing on the stage and letting it swing away from him. He could look into and across the room, and see the door on the far side which led to the corridor beyond. That door was closing, biting away a sector of light which had, only a moment since, entered the darkened speakers' room from the lighted hall outside. The little dark man was going away from there.

If Mr. North was to see the little dark man and inquire about his interest in the taking off of Mr. Sproul, it was evident to Mr. North that he would have to hurry. He stepped quickly into the gloom of the little speakers' room and started across it toward the other door; he took two steps and the second brought his shin sharply against the edge of a chair. Mr. North gave tongue, leaned slightly forward to move the chair, and felt a sudden, crushing weight descend on his left shoulder. Falling with it, Mr. North knew that he had not run into anything this time. Something had run into him.

His shoulder was numb, but as—half from the impact, half defensively—he let himself drop to the speakers' room carpet, Mr. North was thankful. Because the blow had been aimed at his head, and only the chance that he had leaned a little forward and to

one side after his encounter with the chair had saved
him. It was better, Mr. North decided, lying for an
instant motionless, to have a numb shoulder than a
numb head. Of course, the second might come.

Mr. North was twisting himself up, hands out pro-
tectingly, demanding that his eyes accustom themselves to the faint light, when the door leading to the
corridor opened again. It had been a blind before, Mr.
North supposed. Perhaps it was a blind this time—an
invitation to Mr. North to rise hopefully and undertake
pursuit, and make himself a better target than he made
crouched between a chair and what was evidently a
desk. Mr. North waited an instant.

Apparently it was not a blind this time. A small man
went through the door. He was a clear, black shadow
this time, moving with speed and moving quietly. He
was a little, dark man, all right. He was also a man who
did not want to tell Mr. North, or presumably anyone,
why he had been peering out of a dark room at the
scene of sudden death. At the scene, Mr. North was
now more than ever convinced, of a sudden murder. A
peculiar enough murder, when you came to think of it;
one which could hardly have been accomplished more
publicly. If this was the murderer, now departing
through the door as Mr. North worried his way up
between desk and chair and prepared to follow—if this
was the murderer, he had developed a new, and apparently uncharacteristic, desire for privacy.

Mr. North was up and the numbness was going out
of his shoulder. It had not, he thought, been as hard a
blow as it felt to be. Even if it had landed where it was
unquestionably aimed, he might have escaped with a
bad headache. The little dark man lacked thorough-
ness—or perhaps did not wish to be thorough. Possibly, Mr. North thought, opening the door which the
little dark man had closed behind him, his assailant
limited himself to one murder an evening. Or possibly
merely to one an hour.

Mr. North came to the corridor. It was bright and

empty. At one end it ran to a flight of stairs leading downward; at the other it ran to what was evidently another corner at right angles to it. There was nothing to indicate which way the little dark man had gone. But the turn to the right, leading to the intersecting corridor, led evidently to more immediate concealment. The stairs were broad and led downward in full sight to the floor below—and there was no sound of anyone hurrying down them.

Mr. North turned right and began to run, trying to run lightly. A few strides brought him to the crossing corridor. He looked quickly to right and left. Toward the right, the transverse corridor led straight, evidently to the other side of the building. It must, Mr. North decided, run behind the stage of the auditorium; probably it gave, part way down, some means of access to the backstage area. But the little dark man had had his look backstage. Presumably, now, he merely wanted to get away. If so, the shorter stretch to the left would look more promising. Mr. North, hoping—or hoping he hoped—that he was right, took the turn to the left.

He reached the end of the corridor branch and heard something. The corridor ended in a flight of stairs, narrow and metal-edged. The stairs mounted at right angles to the corridor, to the right. Somebody was running up them.

Mr. North reached the lowest step in time to see movement at the uppermost. The little dark man had come this way; the little dark man was, not quite so silently as before, going this way. Mr. North went after him, reaching the top of the flight rather winded. He reached another corridor. The place was a labyrinth. And this corridor was lined with office doors and it came over Mr. North, gloomily, that the little dark man might be in refuge behind any of them, assuming he found any of them unlocked. Mr. North tried the nearest; it was unlocked. It led into a kind of class room, planned evidently for small discussion groups.

There was a little platform at one end, and on either side of the platform was a door. And the little dark man, if he had chosen this particular room, might now be behind either of the doors. But he might equally well be in any of the other rooms along the corridor. And as Mr. North searched any one room—this one, for example—the little dark man had only, if he chose, to return to the corridor and go back down the stairs. Only by the sheerest fluke of luck, Mr. North realized, would he now be able to catch the little dark man and make inquiries of him. Mr. North felt his shoulder. Mr. North did not feel lucky.

In any case, Mr. North thought, the thing to do is to tell Bill. And Bill can catch the little dark man as he tries to get out. That was the thing to do all along.

He had been impetuous to no purpose, Mr. North decided. Probably even now the little dark man was sifting out of the building and into the unsiftable mass of New York's population. The thing to do was to tell Bill Weigand about it as quickly as possible.

Mr. North left the room hurriedly, without further investigation. He trotted, feeling a need to rectify his now obvious error hastily. When he came to the stairs he ran down them, and then he trotted to his right along the corridor. He came to the intersection of his corridor with that which had a door to the speakers' room, turned briskly to the right and encountered a large, somewhat padded object. The object said "ouf!"—Mr. North bounded slightly.

"Well," the object said, "where do you think you're going, buddy? Trying to get away from something?"

The object was dressed in blue and wore a badge on its left breast. The object, under more favorable circumstances, responded to the name of Patrolman Byrnes, had three children, the eldest five, and lived in outermost Queens. But now Patrolman Byrnes, assigned to keep people from wandering in corridors outside the auditorium in which, it was probable, murder had occurred, was not responsive. Patrolman

Byrnes looked at Mr. North with dislike and some triumph.

"I—" Mr. North began.

"Hold it, buddy!" Patrolman Byrnes directed. He took hold of Mr. North's shoulders and pushed Mr. North from him. Then he drew Mr. North back sharply. Mr. North's head bobbed. "Don't try any funny business," Patrolman Byrnes advised. "Tell it to the loot."

He took Mr. North firmly by his shoulders, turned him around and, now using only one hand, propelled him up the corridor to the door leading into the speakers' room. He propelled Mr. North through the room and through the door leading onto the stage.

Mr. North, who had left the stage unnoticed, returned to it with publicity. Patrolman Byrnes gave Mr. North a final shove and released him. Mr. North staggered and caught himself.

"Why, Jerry!" Pam North said. "What ever in the world?"

Bill Weigand, standing with several other men beside what had been Mr. Sproul, looked up at Mr. North and started grinning.

"Bill," Mr. North said. "Tell this—"

"All right, officer," Bill Weigand said. He grinned at Jerry. Feebly, Jerry grinned back. Detective Sergeant Aloysius Mullins, standing a little behind Weigand, beamed—at least Jerry preferred to think it was a beam. Patrolman Byrnes looked puzzled.

"All right, fella," Sergeant Mullins informed the patrolman. "This guy's Mr. North. He's a pal, see?"

Byrnes looked stubborn for a moment.

"He was runnin'," Byrnes said. "He looked funny to me."

Pam North and Weigand and Mullins, and Dorian Weigand who had joined them when her husband arrived, looked at Mr. North and smiled. Probably, Mr. North thought—and a hand went up to his now doubly damaged shoulder—I look funny to all of them.

And then he realized that he had made his unimposing entrance in full view of the audience—the audience before which he had recently performed so satisfactorily. He looked at the audience, which had not grown perceptibly smaller. The audience looked back at him. Some of its members had no expressions which could be diagnosed. But there could be no doubt that several of its members were grinning.

3

Thursday, 9:10 P.M. to 10 P.M.

Detective Sergeant Mullins nudged the group on the platform away from the big chair behind the lectern and the sprawled body in it, and the police photographers moved in. There were two of them and they ignored the audience, talking jargon between themselves, but talking it a little more audibly than was their custom. Even police photographers, Pam thought, watching them, played up before an audience. They shot the body from the sides and from above, they pictured it in relation to the lectern; one of them backed out and took a wide-lensed view of as much of the stage as could be got in, with the body at its center.

Lieutenant William Weigand, watching with a kind of attentive abstraction, also listened to Mr. North. Mr. North told him about the little dark man who had run so fast and Bill Weigand agreed that it was odd and cried out to be looked into. However—

"You'll admit, Jerry," he said, "that you can't give us much to go on. By way of description—little and dark. Little I'll give you; dark perhaps only because you saw him in the dark. It would take in thousands."

"Obviously," Jerry agreed. "Millions. But if you saw a little dark man running out of the building you could stop him."

Bill Weigand agreed with that, and that they would.

38

For the moment, at any rate, they were stopping anybody who tried to leave the building—running or walking, tall or short, without regard to color. But that, obviously, had a time limit.

"There're five or six hundred out there," Weigand pointed out, waving toward the audience. "Some of them left before we came. We can't hold the rest." He looked at the audience. "Or want to hold the rest," he said. "Our man wasn't killed from the audience."

He looked at Jerry, consideringly.

"As a matter of fact," he added, "we don't know he was killed at all. It's even money, or thereabouts, that he merely up and died. Thrombosis. Apoplexy. Cerebral hemorrhage. Klingman says he can't tell."

"He also," Jerry North pointed out, "says it could have been a drug. A narcotic—opium or something."

That, Weigand agreed, was what kept them there. That was why they took pictures; why—now Weigand nodded—they took fingerprints of the body. Two men were rolling the dead fingers on pads; rolling the inked fingers on slips of paper, clipped in order. The men finished as Jerry and the lieutenant watched.

"O.K.," one of the men said. "What else, Loot?"

Weigand hesitated. What else indeed? There was no weapon to be powdered and examined, no heavy object or light object which might have played a part. Jerry, considering too, jerked his head toward the door which led to the speakers' room. Weigand nodded and gave directions. Everything, he told them.

"Perhaps your little dark man will show up," he said to Jerry. "Perhaps—"

"There ought to be a glass in there," Jerry North told him. "He was drinking out of one. Before we came out here."

Weigand was interested. Jerry told him what he remembered, or thought he remembered. It was, he agreed, only an impression. He told of looking for the glass after Sproul died and failing to find it. He thought of something.

"Maybe the little dark man was looking for it, too,"
he suggested. Bill Weigand nodded. Again, he agreed,
it was interesting. It might be more than interesting
when they knew where they were. The detective's
eyes roved over the scene as he talked to Jerry, noting,
sorting, rejecting. Dr. Dupont was sitting in a chair,
now, with Dr. Klingman beside him. Dr. Dupont was
staring at the floor. Mrs. Williams was standing off to
the side and Dorian Weigand was near her, but they
did not seem to be talking. The photographers were
packing equipment; the fingerprint men were crossing
toward the speakers' room door. Sergeant Mullins
exercised general supervision, waiting.

It was the lull, Weigand thought. It might be the lull
before the storm; it might be a lull which would merge
into a larger lull. The machine was set up, the materials which would be fed into it stacked in readiness.
Only the switch needed to be thrown. Had Sproul been
killed? Or had he merely, if publicly, died? It was an
appropriate time for the entrance of science.

Science, taking her cue, entered in the shape of Dr.
Jerome Francis, assistant medical examiner. He came
through the door from the speakers' room and
sneezed.

"Damn that powder," he said. He looked at
Weigand, and then at Sproul.

"What," he said, "have we here?"

Weigand asked him what he thought.

"Corpse," Dr. Francis told him, succinctly. "And
you want to know when he died. Down to the half
minute."

"We know when he died," Weigand said. "He died
when North here finished introducing him." Bill
Weigand looked at Jerry North. "No necessary connection," Weigand added, reassuringly. He turned
back to Dr. Francis. "He died just as he was about to
make a speech," he told the assistant medical examiner. "But we don't know of what."

"Probably," Dr. Francis told him, crossing to the

body, "probably the intervention of Providence. It could happen oftener."

Dr. Francis looked down at the body. He looked at Klingman, still beside Dr. Dupont; to the eyes of another professional, in professional attendance.

"You examined him, Doctor?" the assistant medical examiner asked. Klingman nodded, and moved a step nearer. The two physicians withdrew into the medical world, symbolically taking the body with them. They nodded over it. Klingman pointed at the eyes and Francis nodded. Francis flexed the dead fingers, and Klingman nodded. The lay world waited. The physicians nodded again, now evidently in agreement, and unexpectedly shook hands. Dr. Francis came over to Weigand and Mr. North, who waited anxiously.

"Well," Dr. Francis said, "he's dead, all right."

"Good God!" Bill Weigand said. He looked at Dr. Francis without approval. "Do tell," he said.

"Dr. Klingman and I find ourselves in agreement," Dr. Francis went on. He was very grave—it seemed to Jerry North that there was a faint touch of amused malice in his gravity. "We agree he might have died of a lot of things."

"You're a big help," Bill Weigand assured him. "Both of you."

"Mark it 'suspicious death,' " Francis directed. "That's my report."

Bill Weigand looked at the doctor carefully.

"And—?" he prompted.

"Look for somebody who gave him an overdose of morphine," Dr. Francis said. "Without quoting me. Or find out that he took an overdose himself."

"Addict?" Weigand wanted to know.

"No," Dr. Francis told him. "I shouldn't think so. On the contrary." He looked at Weigand, seriously grave now. "You want me to guess, Bill?" he inquired.

"Right," Bill Weigand told him. The physician nodded.

"For a guess, then," he said. "He was one of those people who are abnormally susceptible to morphine. Maybe there was something wrong with his arteries. Maybe he was just naturally sensitive. Susceptibility varies a lot. Maybe somebody knew that and gave him a dose of morphine, figuring it to kill him. Maybe somebody didn't know it, and gave him a dose of morphine figuring to put him to sleep. Maybe somebody didn't want to hear him make a speech." He looked thoughtfully at the detective. "I've heard guys—," he offered.

Bill Weigand and Jerry North smiled in appreciation of the hinted jest. When the smiles ran their brief course, Bill Weigand took it up again.

"Probably morphine," he said. "Right? Probably— how long ago? How long ago was it given?"

Dr. Francis shrugged. That was where susceptibility set in. Suppose the normal person took morphine by mouth. In half an hour, more or less, he might feel mental exhilaration and physical ease; objectively, his pulse would quicken. He might appear elated; might grow talkative. This condition would pass, but how soon it would be hard to guess. Susceptibility again. Then he would go to sleep, and sleep would become a coma, and, if nobody did anything, he might die. If he had taken enough morphine. He might die in a couple of hours, he might live ten hours.

"But—," Jerry said.

"Right," Weigand said. "He walked out here less than an hour ago. He died within a quarter of an hour." He looked at Dr. Francis.

"It could be," the doctor said. "We're granting remarkable susceptibility. Like that of a child. Or of a person with arteriosclerosis. Or some other circulatory trouble. Or both together—a naturally highly susceptible person *with* circulatory trouble. In other words, a special case."

"But a possible case?" Weigand said. "Right?"

"We think so," Dr. Francis said. "I told you it was a

guess. Maybe he died of a blood clot on the brain. Maybe somebody held a pillow over his head and suffocated him. Medically. But somebody would have noticed if Mr. North, here, held a pillow over your corpse's head. Not very private up here, was it?"

"Somebody would have noticed," Bill Weigand agreed, gravely. "We can count out the pillow, or poison gas." He stared over at the body of Victor Leeds Sproul. "Natural causes," he said, thoughtfully. "Or morphine? Anything else?"

Conceivably, Dr. Francis told him. Opium, of course. But that was morphine all over again. Possibly cocaine, although that, in view of Sproul's behavior before he died, was not indicated. Call it suspicious, he repeated. Work tentatively on the assumption of an overdose of morphine, not self-administered—unless they had a suicide on their hands. Assume peculiar sensitivity on the part of Sproul, wonder whether he had displayed it in the past and recovered and left a confession of weakness as a small, curious fact in the mind of someone unidentified.

"How much morphine?" Weigand asked. Francis shrugged. Susceptibility again. Addicts could stand a lot; people had died from less than a grain. Grown people; children from less still. If injected hypodermically, the drug might give three times the effect, in a third the time of the same quantity taken by mouth. Also it might not.

He was helpful, Lieutenant Weigand told him bitterly. It would be impossible to get on without him. Francis ostentatiously snubbed the sarcasm, and said he was very glad. He said he would now help further by having the body taken away and opened up. Then he might know something. He'd run LeFort's test and if it was morphine they'd know. Meanwhile—

Far be it from Dr. Francis to tell the Lieutenant his business. But if he were detecting, he would be interested in anything Sproul had had to eat or drink within a couple of hours of his death, and in the persons who

gave it to him. He would report "suspicious death"
and go on the assumption of "homicide."

Bill Weigand nodded and stood for a further moment
in thought. Then he said, "Right" and "Thanks." He
crossed to the lectern and rapped on it with the gavel.
Everybody looked at him.

"As you've gathered," Lieutenant Weigand told the
audience, "Mr. Sproul has died very suddenly. The
police are in charge and I see nothing to be gained by
keeping you here. So most of you may go. But I want
to talk to any of you who knew Mr. Sproul personally—knew him here or in Paris, recently or even a
number of years ago. I'll ask any of you who did know
him, even slightly, to remain. Is that clear?"

The members of the audience looked as if it was
clear enough.

"Right," Weigand said. "I might add that we have
the means of making a fairly complete check on those
who did know Mr. Sproul, so I'd advise anybody who
might think he was saving himself trouble by not
admitting acquaintanceship to abandon the idea. Is
that understood?"

It seemed to be. Weigand looked at the audience
with grave severity, hoping that nobody would suspect
how hard it would really be to sift out such of Sproul's
acquaintances as did not elect to be sifted. He held
them a moment and turned away. The audience began
to eddy out. Weigand wondered if Sproul's murderer—always assuming a murderer—was in one of
the eddies. He wondered—yes, already there were
counter eddies pressing against the departing. The
press was coming in, with cards in its hat-bands and
folds of copy paper in its hands for notes and— It
made Weigand think of something. Sproul probably
had notes.

He crossed to the body and ran long, nervous fingers
into the inside coat pocket. Nothing. He felt a side
pocket. Something. A sheaf of folded papers. Weigand
flipped the fold open. He had Sproul's notes for the

first lecture of his de luxe tour. They began without preamble:

"Tell you Paris meant to me. One American. That way what meant ENTIRE WORLD. Paris symbol of civilization in peril—little ways men lived there—big things happened there—things tourists saw—residents saw—right bank, left bank . . . try picture what world has lost—"

The notes went on, but Bill Weigand broke off. They would come later, for what help they might be. But before words written down, dead now as the man who was to have spoken them, came people. Bill Weigand turned to the people.

And Pamela North looked at the watch which dangled around her neck and said, unexpectedly and quite clearly, "Oh!" She crossed to Jerry, still looking. "Oh!"

"Jerry," she said. "The girls!"

"What?" Jerry said. "What girls?"

"The nieces," Pam said. "What girls did you think?"

"I didn't think any girls," he said. "I forgot all about them."

"One of us," Pam said. "The Penn Station in—in five minutes, really. But they'll be late, of course. They're all late, nowadays."

It puzzled Bill Weigand, through his major puzzlement.

"Nieces?" he said.

"Trains," Pam told him. "The war, somehow. They're coming to visit us, because their mother is going to the hospital and their father can't get away. The war, you know."

Bill Weigand sorted it out. Trains—no, nieces— were coming to see Pam North because, obscurely, of the war. They were going to be late in arriving, also because of the war. But Pam went on. She was addressing both men now—Jerry and Bill Weigand.

"I hate to," she said. "Leaving you with it. But I'll come back and help as soon as I put them to bed. Martha is going to stay and look after them anyway."

"Listen," Jerry said, "I thought—are you sure about their ages?"

"Of course," Pam North said. "Little girls. I'm sorry about the murder, but I'll hurry." She looked at Bill Weigand. "I wish you could wait for me," she said. "But I suppose you can't?" Bill smiled at her and shook his head.

"Do you think—?" Pam began again, and stopped because both men were grinning at her, and because Dorian had come up and was smiling at all of them in an amused way.

"We'll do our best," Bill Weigand told her gravely. "Naturally, it will be—"

"You?" Pam said. "All of you." She looked around the stage, and seemed a little wistful. "What a time for nieces!" she said. "I wish—"

She did not say what she wished. She looked around again and accepted the situation with evident decision and went to the edge of the platform. She put a hand on the edge and dropped down without waiting for help and hit solidly and said "Ugh!" She did not pause, however, and went up an aisle, rubbing the dirt from her left hand with a handkerchief.

Mrs. North's steps were brisk but her spirit was reluctant. Here, she thought, is what looks like being one of the best murders we've ever had and I've got nieces. Little nieces. The thought filled her with rebellion.

"It's always women," she thought and the taxicab driver, pushing the door open from inside, looked at her.

"Huh?" he said. "Where'd you say, lady?"

Pam realized that she had thought out loud again and sighed. Apparently there was, after all, nothing to be done about it. She couldn't even be scared out of it, she decided. "Like hiccoughs," she thought and, hearing the words, realized that she had done it again. She looked at the taxi driver a little anxiously and discovered that he was looking at her wildly.

"Listen, lady," he said. "I heard you. Do you want to go some place, that's all I wanta know? Or do you just want to talk about hiccoughs?"

"I'm sorry," Pam said. "It comes over me sometimes. I plan not to but I do in spite of it. Penn Station."

"Do what?" the taxi driver asked.

"Penn Station," Pam said. "Talk to myself."

"I don't get that about hiccoughs," the driver said, in a rather gloomy voice. "Which side?"

"Hiccoughs?" Pam North repeated, in apparently honest puzzlement. "Both sides, usually. Right in the middle, really. What about hiccoughs?"

"What about—" the driver began, reaching back to push down his flag and stopping, bemused. "How should I know what about hiccoughs, lady? They're your hiccoughs."

"I haven't got the hiccoughs," Pam said. "I want to go to the Pennsylvania Station."

The driver turned around and stared at her.

"Listen, lady," he said. "Can we just start over? You get into the hack and you say—what do you say, lady?" His voice was beseeching.

"Oh," Mrs. North said. "I was thinking about the murder. Pennsylvania Station."

"O.K.," the driver said. "Pennsylvania Station. What murder? Murder!"

It seemed to reach him slowly.

"Back there," Pam told him. "That's why all the police cars. And if you've got to talk, can't you do it while we go? Because they're little girls and I've got to meet them. It's always the woman who has to; while men do interesting things."

"Your—," the taxi driver began. He lapsed, staring straight ahead for a moment. Then he shrugged, lifting both hands from the steering wheel. He lowered his

right hand to the gear shift level, still staring ahead,
and pulled. There was a grinding clash which seemed
to please him, and the cab started. The driver stared
straight ahead, a little wildly. Mrs. North dismissed
him from her mind.

It was true, she thought (and this time she thought
silently) that when there were dull things to do, women
were ordinarily chosen. If it came to a choice between
murder and nieces, men got the murder and women
got the nieces. And you couldn't deny that murder was
more interesting than nieces. Murder was tremen-
dously, engrossingly interesting.

Realizing how interesting it was, Pam North felt a
little worried about herself. Probably, when you came
down to it, it wasn't good for you to be so interested in
murders. "Habit-forming," Pam thought. You started
out able to take murder or leave it alone—never
dreaming of taking it, really. And one murder led to
another, and it became—well, a sort of game. And it
should never be a game; not really a game. Or, she
corrected, not essentially a game, because it would
always be in the nature of things a kind of game. A
dreadful kind of game, at bottom, but still a game. It
would be—Pam tried to think of a simile—it would be
like tennis, if, after the set was over, the loser was
shot. That would make tennis a rather horrible game,
but it would not keep it from being a game. The strokes
would be the same, the maneuvering for position, the
sparring for openings. Watching it, you would still be
watching a game. Only you would care more.

And would it, Pam wondered, be morbid to watch
tennis of that sort? She grabbed the handstrap at the
side of the cab, which seemed to be going very rapidly,
even for a cab—which seemed to be progressing toward the Pennsylvania Station with a kind of despera-
tion. The driver was certainly in a hurry to get there,
Pam thought, in parenthesis. But would it be morbid?

I don't really know what being morbid is, Pam
thought. Of course you're more interested in things

which are important, like life, than in things which are not really important, like tennis cups. Is that morbid? And you are more interested in murder than in nieces, and there is no use pretending that you are not. Because, Pam told herself, murder is always important. Maybe it is the most important thing in the world, because it is the most final thing in the world.

"You can't be interested in life without being interested in death," Pam told herself and realized that, this time, she had again thought out loud. She realized it because the driver bent a little lower over his wheel, as if he were shrinking from something. She was sorry she had spoken aloud, but after all it was true. That was one reason why almost everybody was interested in murder—everybody who was alive. It was because, however you thought about it, it was in itself a thing of major importance.

It isn't morbid, Pam thought. Not really—not being interested in it isn't. People always are, as long as they're interested in anything—anything human. Some people pretend not to be, but it is either pretense or they aren't interested any more, in anything. Even uninteresting murders are interesting and you read about them in the newspapers. You read enough, anyway, to find out that the details are not interesting. But you read that much, always, because murder is interesting. It is horrible and frightening and dangerous, and perhaps it is morbid. But it is interesting.

"And," Pam thought, "what really is morbid is not to be interested in things which are interesting."

The taxi driver spoke. His voice was uneasy, tentative.

"Which side, lady?" he said. "Penn or Long Island?"

"Oh," Pam said. "It doesn't matter, really. I'm meeting . . . Either side—Penn, I guess. Or right in front."

"Thanks, lady," the driver said. "Right in front all right?"

He seemed to be a very odd taxi driver, Pam
thought. He wasn't like most taxicab drivers, really.
He was—sort of subdued. Which was inappropriate in
taxi drivers. The cab stopped and she left it and paid
her fare and looked thoughtfully at the taxi driver. He
was inappropriate, although he looked appropriate
enough. It was—

The word "appropriate" seemed to have done
something to her mind; it had stirred her mind and
found a lump in it, of which Pam had not a moment
before been conscious. It was a lump of something she
ought to remember, or think about; it was a lump of
something odd, not yet arranged in its proper place—
not yet resolved by her mind. It was a lump about
something else which had been inappropriate and not
what she expected, although both what had been at
odds with expectation and what the expectation had
been were only uneasy feelings, not ideas.

It did not, Pam thought, walking along the arcade of
the Pennsylvania Station toward the stairs leading
down to the concourse, apply essentially to the taxi
driver. He was clear in her mind, and he was inappropriate, and that was that. This was either before the
taxi driver, or was to come after him. The inappropriate thing was either in the past or in the future—
something which had been wrong, or something which
was going to be wrong. Like going to the Penn Station
to meet people coming in at the Grand Central. Although it wasn't that, because the girls were coming
from Philadelphia, and that was Penn Station. So it
couldn't be that.

It was in the past, Pam decided, and, because it was
now bothering her noticeably, she went into the past to
look for it. It felt like being in the very recent past—
today's past, probably. She went over her day—over
breakfast with Jerry worrying about his speech, and
over luncheon with Dorian at the French place in
Radio City, where they had taken up the outdoor
tables and were laying a kind of floor, probably for the

ice skating which ought to begin before long, now; over cocktails at Charles with Jerry and dinner afterward at home—dinner early because of the lecture, and with Jerry still not eating anything much, and turning every topic of conversation into something about the introductory speeches he had to deliver. (Jerry is so foolish about things, Pam thought. He's so sweet, really.)

There was nothing inappropriate in the day up to then, or at the Today's Topics Club. Nothing until Jerry had turned, after a really very nice little talk, and invited Mr. Sproul to get up. And Mr. Sproul hadn't got up—that was inappropriate, all right. Pam thought about it, going down the stairs, and shook her head. That was a big thing; this which bothered her was a little thing. It wasn't about Mr. Sproul—or, anyway, not about Mr. Sproul's being dead. It was a little thing, perhaps afterward, which was at odds with expectation. It was—Pam tried again to make it come clear—it was as if a picture you had once seen and now saw again had subtly changed in the meantime; it was as if the tree in the right foreground had turned, between the two times of seeing, into a bush.

Pamela North went through the doors which always seemed to her to open by magic, and in whose opening she never trusted, always reaching out hands to push just as the doors receded of their own miraculous accord. She went downstairs to the arriving train level, still trying to identify the discrepancy which continued to bother her.

It felt right, she decided, for the discrepancy to concern one of the people she had encountered on the platform after the murder—or encountered somewhere between the time that Mr. Sproul failed to stand up and the time she got into the taxicab to come and meet her sister's little daughters. It felt right that she had met one of those people before, or seen one of them before, under conditions which did not accord with the conditions under which she had seen them this evening. If she had, for example, seen Dr. Dupont turning cartwheels in a vaudeville show, that would account for it. "Although," Mrs. North admitted to herself, "a little extremely." If she had seen that other doctor—the *real* doctor—acting as a traffic policeman on Fifth Avenue, that would explain it. Or if she had seen the woman who had preceded Mr. North at the lectern, and was presumably the program chairman of the club—Mrs. Williams or something—performing as a ballet dancer, that would be the sort of thing it was.

But it was not any of these things, and it was not, Mrs. North decided, anything she was apt to get straight until something else resuggested it to her mind. Eventually, perhaps, something would happen which would throw an oblique light on her puzzlement and give sudden illumination. Or it might be, of course, that nothing would happen until the puzzlement had slowly faded away.

She was ten minutes late for the train, Mrs. North observed as she passed a clock. But on the other hand, she saw on the arrivals blackboard, the train was twenty minutes late for itself. She lighted a cigarette and waited, wondering about Mr. Sproul. Red caps went down the stairs, which meant the train was coming. Mrs. North could have gone down; but she decided that that way there would be greater danger of missing the little girls. She could stand here, between the two stairways—the Pennsylvania Railroad had certainly arranged things awkwardly—and look in both directions and pretty soon see them.

The stairway leading to the rear of the train probably was the better bet, she decided, because her sister would have sent the little girls in a Pullman, and asked the porter to look after them. So she stood nearer the stairway leading to the rear and looked down it and saw people beginning to come up.

She could not see any little girls coming up the stairway, so she hurried to the other and looked down it. More people were coming up it, including what was evidently a large part of the army, and no little girls. "Damn the Pennsylvania Railroad," Mrs. North said, and dashed back to the other staircase. Still no little girls. She took a place between the staircases and vibrated her head as rapidly as she could, making her neck hurt. Still no little girls. And now the stream of arriving passengers was reduced to a trickle—two trickles, specifically. Mrs. North began to be worried.

And then there was a glad young voice behind her. It said:

"Auntie Pam! Auntie *Pam!*"

That was one of the girls. Margie or—or the one you mustn't call Lizzie, but must remember always to call Beth. Somehow they had got around her.

Mrs. North turned quickly, with a welcoming smile. There were no little girls. There were—

One of the two young ladies confronting Pam North beamed and gamboled forward.

"Auntie Pam!" she said. *"Darling!"*

Mrs. North gasped. They were not little girls; they were almost grown up girls. And attached to each, with a kind of firm hopefulness, was a sailor. The sailors were looking at Mrs. North with anxious doubt, like uncertain puppies. They were very young sailors.

"But not *that* young!" Mrs. North thought a little frantically, as she started foward. "Not nearly young *enough!*"

"Children!" Mrs. North said. For the first time in my life, Mrs. North thought, I sound like a mother. *"Margie! Lizzie!"*

"Beth," said the foremost of the children, and she let her sailor slip away to meet, it was evident, this new and greater emergency. *"Beth,* Aunt Pam." There was a kind of wail in her voice. "Not *Lizzie!"* She blushed furiously, then, and looked back at her sailor in evident anguish. The sailor, however, merely looked uneasily at Pam North.

4

Bill Weigand watched Pamela North drop to the auditorium floor and go off to meet her nieces. He turned back to the platform, counting off. There was the dead, Victor Leeds Sproul. There were the quick—Gerald North; Dr. Klingman, who still hovered over Dr. Dupont; Dr. Dupont himself, who at first glance seemed somewhere between the quick and the dead; the woman who, Weigand gathered, had introduced Mr. North so that he might in turn introduce Sproul, thus earnestly duplicating efforts; a very well finished off, rather saturnine man at the moment unidentified; two men without distinguishing characteristics who presumably were somehow connected with Today's Topics Club; Sergeant Mullins and assorted policemen.

It was a mixed bag, Weigand thought. There was no particular reason to think that the cat in it was a murderer, or even that there was a cat. But detectives must start somewhere. Weigand looked the catch over speculatively, wondered about Mr. North's little dark man and where he was and who he was and if he had anything to do with anything, and let his glance fall on Dr. Klingman. But he already, through Dr. Francis, knew what Klingman could tell him as a physician and it was not clear that Klingman had any other capacity. Weigand looked at Dr. Dupont and decided he had to

54

start somewhere, and that the tall old man might as well be the where.

He took a step toward Dr. Dupont and the well finished, saturnine man intervened. He stepped forward briskly, a man who knew what he was about, and confronted Bill Weigand. Weigand stopped and looked at him.

"Y. Charles Burden," the saturnine man said.

"I don't know," Weigand said. "Why?"

The saturnine man smiled faintly.

"I'm used to that one," he said. "Very used to it. I am Y. Charles Burden. The 'Y' stands for Young, which my misguided parents thought to be a suitable name for an offspring."

Mr. Burden stopped, leaving it up to Weigand if he wanted it.

"Very interesting," Weigand told him. "I am—"

Mr. Burden did not think it necessary for Weigand to finish.

"A detective," Mr. Burden told him. "Heard about you. Read about you some place." He looked Weigand's spare figure and thin face over with interest. "Ever lecture?" he inquired. "Might go, you know. Secrets of the police; famous murders I have solved; how to catch saboteurs. Very interested in saboteurs, people are just now. Naturally."

"And I, just now, am interested in a murder," Weigand told him. "This murder. Have you anything to do with it?" He considered Burden. "You'd be his lecture agent, probably," he said. "Right?"

"I was," Burden said. "I certainly was. Booked him from coast to coast—and back. Can you picture what this means—cancellations, substitutions, program chairman frothing, re-routing all over the place?" As he spoke his tone grew accusing; he ended in a stare which seemed to hold Weigand responsible. Weigand merely looked at him, blandly. When Burden seemed to expect an answer, Weigand told him that it was unfortunate.

"Murder usually is," Weigand said. "Inconveniences a lot of people. Friends, relatives, business associates, the police. To say nothing of the corpse. You have something to tell me? Right?"

Burden shook his head quickly.

"Just placing myself," he said. "I saw you looking at me and thought you probably were wondering. Thought I'd clear it up."

It was the evident conviction of Mr. Burden that people had only to look at him to wonder about him. He did not suppose that any gaze, even one of pure chance, could remain utterly indifferent after it had encountered Mr. Burden. And probably, Weigand thought, he's right. And he was the first end of the tangle to come to hand. Weigand decided to pull.

"Right," Weigand said. "Cooperative of you. And, so long as you have, we may as well find out what you can tell us. About Sproul—in case it turns out he was murdered. You knew something about him, of course?"

Y. Charles Burden nodded. That, he indicated, was obvious. He amplified. He knew that Sproul had written a book that was a hit, he had heard that Sproul could talk on his feet and that he had manner, he knew that he could sell Sproul to women's clubs.

"From coast to coast," Weigand prompted. Burden, relaxing, grinned. He said, "Precisely."

"That's all you knew?" Weigand pressed. "What you'd heard of him, which made you think he'd be useful in your—your list?"

"Stable," Burden said.

"Right," Weigand said. "That's all you knew about him?"

Burden seemed to hesitate, although Weigand was convinced that he had expected the question, planned how to answer it, probably introduced himself to Weigand to bring it up. Y. Charles Burden was not, Weigand thought, a man who did things on the spur of the moment. But now he gave every evidence of making up his mind on the spur of the moment.

"As a matter of fact," Burden said, "I did once know the guy. Years ago, here in New York. But too long ago to matter—before he went to Paris. And I knew him in Paris for a while, in the old days—1928 or thereabouts. When everything was high, wide and handsome and the boys and girls were living on the fat of the Left Bank." Burden smiled slightly in reminiscence. "I came back in '29," he said. "With my tail between my legs. Sproul stayed on, of course." He abandoned the softness of remembrance. "However," he said crisply now, "I never knew him at all well. And I don't know anything that will help you."

Weigand told him that one couldn't tell. It was impossible to guess, at this stage, what would help. It might help, however, to know what kind of a man Sproul was, even in the old days. It was a starting point. While they waited.

"While we wait," Burden repeated. Weigand nodded. He seemed to grow very confiding.

"Actually," he said, "we don't know that there's a case here. It's merely what we call a suspicious death. He may have died naturally, he may have poisoned himself, intentionally or without meaning to. And he may have been murdered." He let Burden take it in, feel himself a confidant of the police. "By the way," Weigand said, as an afterthought, "did he ever take drugs, that you know of?"

Burden shrugged. Then he shook his head.

"Not that I ever heard," he said. "Or noticed. And he never mentioned it. I don't think he did in the old days, because he would have mentioned it. The boys and girls went in for the vices, sometimes—and usually wanted the credit. Sproul was a chaser, and he drank a good deal of brandy from time to time—made a fetish of brandy, you know?" He looked thoughtful. "Always gives me a headache, for some reason," he

added, contributing an interesting fact. "But I never
heard anything about Sproul and drugs. Over there or
here in the Village before he went abroad."

He ran down, but waited.

Weigand had imperceptibly drawn him aside; now,
nodding, he took advantage of the pause.

"We may as well sit down somewhere," he suggested. "In that little room over there, perhaps." He
pointed toward the door to the speakers' room.

"Why not?" Burden said. "Although you've got
what I know. However—anything to help."

He preceded Weigand to the speakers' room, stood
while Weigand switched on a desk lamp, then sat down
and offered cigarettes. Weigand took one. For a moment, neither said anything.

"It's a damn shame," Burden said suddenly. "A
Goddamn shame."

"Murder is," Weigand agreed. "Or, if this isn't
murder, why death is. Tell me more about Sproul when
you knew him."

Burden disavowed information of importance, but
talked willingly. As he talked, Weigand, sorting and
accepting, making allowances here for the kind of man
who was talking, trying to discount prejudices without
discounting facts, began to draw in his own mind an
outline of Sproul alive. It was a first step, something to
go on.

Sproul was, it appeared, around forty-five when
death caught up with him. He had come from somewhere in the West, showing up in the Village a year or
so after the other war. Burden, who had also showed
up in the Village, thought he had met him then, but
found the memory vague. At least, he had known
people who knew Sproul, who was then only Vic
Sproul. Then, a year or so later, he had disappeared
from the Village and was supposed to have gone back
home.

"People came and went in those days, you know,"
Burden said. "I did myself. It wasn't the old, old

Village even then, you understand, but it was more than it is now. Or less, depending on how you look at it. You got the feeling that you knew 'everybody,' in which you didn't count the people you didn't know. I mean the people who just lived there and went about their ordinary business. The people you knew—the people Sproul and I knew—were the people who sometimes called themselves 'Villagers' and who usually called other people 'Up-towners.' They were also sort of interested in writing or painting or making linoleum blocks or something. They came and went—beat it back home and earned some money or got some given them; came back and stayed a while. You remember?"

"I was an up-towner," Weigand said. "But I got the picture. And Sproul came and went?"

Sproul had. Several times, Burden thought. He was sure that he had known Sproul in, he thought, 1924—known him as an individual, not only as a name which was known, vaguely or sharply, to most of the rather amorphous group. Sproul had been writing then and seemed to be in funds. This puzzled everybody, because Sproul was a great one for the misunderstood writer and the crass public.

"We didn't know it then," Burden said, "but what he had was his tongue in his cheek. Even then. Because he was making a pretty fair living writing for the pulps and the rest was—well, so much hog-wash. He just thought it was funny to pull our earnest young legs." Burden smiled at a memory. "As probably it was," he said. "As probably it was. We grow up. But Sproul grew up earlier than most of us."

"He must have been around—what?" Weigand interrupted.

"That's right," Burden said. "He wasn't so terribly young, was he. Thirty, probably, this way or that. I was about twenty-five." He was reflective again. "But I must have been a lot younger," he said. "Or not so bright. I was pretty serious about it. No tongue in cheek. However—we all grew up." For a moment it seemed to Weigand that Y. Charles Burden was not altogether satisfied with his own growing up. The moment passed.

Burden had, it developed, been discussing Sproul's early practicality only a week or two before. After the contract for the lectures had been duly signed, and both Sproul and Burden could relax, Sproul had recalled the old days, laughed at what a credulous group they had made then, talked of his own less naive activities. He regarded it, Burden evidently had felt, as a big joke on everybody—as a kind of joke, somehow, on youth and youth's aspirations.

"He was a malicious sort of guy when he wanted to be," Burden said, as if he were only then discovering the fact. "He made a lot of fun of a lot of people and some of them must have squirmed. Even then. From all accounts, he kept at it in Paris."

In Paris, Sproul was a group center and everybody knew him. Again, "everybody" was a special group of Americans living in Paris, speaking French with some fluency and, usually, less exactitude, working on newspapers published there in English for the tourists, laughing at the tourists, studying art vaguely or working purposefully in American banks, enjoying the exchange advantage and the freedom.

"And," Burden said, "enjoying Paris, enjoying France. Which meant enjoying a kind of civilization we didn't have here. It was a good way to live for most of them; I liked it myself." He smiled at Weigand. "However," he said, "I grew up. Got ambitious. And came back."

Sproul was writing novels then, and having them published. But he lived considerably better than the novel sales would have suggested.

"Still the pulps," Burden said. "It wasn't so much of a secret by then. Sproul was—brazen about it. Ostentatiously brazen, as if it were a vice. And arranging, somehow, to make everybody else appear a little ridiculous."

He paused.

"That was the chief thing about Sproul, come to think of it," he said slowly. "He managed to make almost everybody he met feel, in the end, a little ridiculous. Even me—in the old days, of course. It was—a knack he had. And enjoyed. Yes—enjoyed very much. He was a peculiar person, in some ways."

Weigand said that Sproul sounded malicious. Burden nodded.

"More than most," he agreed. "Although aren't we all?"

There seemed to be no great reason for answering. Weigand digested what he had learned, wondered about its value and regarded Burden absently. The detective's fingers drummed gently on the desk by which he sat. Finally he said "Thank you."

He would, he said, want to look at any records Burden had touching on Sproul—contracts and the like. He would like to look over, or have looked over, any biographical material which might have been prepared in connection with publicizing Sproul's projected tour. But those things could be taken up in time, when they knew whether anything was really going to have to be taken up.

"At the moment this is all very speculative," he told Burden. "The blueprint stage." He smiled slightly at the lecture agent. "And we may never get around to build," he added. "No materials. Perhaps Sproul just died. Perhaps he will turn out to have killed himself. It's all very open."

Burden started to shake his head at the suggestion Sproul might have killed himself. Weigand watched him, saw him change his mind. It was impossible to tell why he had changed his mind; why, at first rejecting suicide automatically, he appeared to come to accept it as a possibility.

"You think he wouldn't?" Weigand asked. "Suicide, I mean."

Burden hesitated. He spoke slowly.

"I don't know," he said. "At first thought—no. But then it occurred to me—perhaps yes. I don't know why, you understand. It would be something I don't know about. But if he did decide he was finished—well, he might do it this way. Make as much trouble for everybody as he could; leave everything messed up. Figuring, maybe, that he'd have a chance to laugh. Somewhere else. When he got where he was going, if he went any place. He'd think it funny to leave me high and dry, and to make poor old Dupont ridiculous, and to leave North introducing a dead man. He was that kind of a guy."

It would, Weigand commented, be carrying things rather to an extreme. And Sproul, unless he was very optimistic, might be doubtful whether he would get to enjoy the joke.

"I don't mean that he would kill himself just for that," Burden clarified. "The chance of troubling people would be—well, call it an additional inducement. Assuming he had a major inducement."

"Right," Weigand said. His tone ended it. Burden got up and started toward the door leading to the stage. Then Mullins opened the same door and got ready to speak, but Weigand thought of one more question.

"By the way," he said, "did Sproul know a little dark man?"

Burden looked at him and said "What?"

"A little dark man," Weigand repeated. "Was there one somewhere in Sproul's life, that you know of?"

Burden said he didn't get it. There might have been a dozen little dark men in Sproul's life.

"How little?" he said. "How dark? A Negro midget?"

Weigand grinned and shook his head. Not quite that little, or that dark, presumably.

"I really don't know," he admitted. "I didn't see him, myself. But there seems to be a little dark man in the wood pile somewhere. Peering out, as nearly as I can gather. Mr. North saw him."

Burden said "oh" and shook his head. He continued to look at Weigand doubtfully. He said that he didn't connect Sproul with any little dark man in particular.

"Although obviously—" he began.

Weigand nodded and said "right." Probably, he added, it didn't come to anything. Sergeant Mullins moved aside to let Burden pass out to the stage.

"They're taking it away," Mullins said. "O.K., Loot?"

"Why not?" Weigand said. "We don't want it, do we?"

"I don't," Mullins said, flatly. "Not any part of it. It looks screwy to me, Loot."

"Does it, Mullins?" Bill Weigand said politely.

Mullins said "yeh." He looked at the lieutenant darkly. "The Norths are in again," he advised his superior darkly. "It's bound to be screwy."

Weigand nodded, abstractedly, admitting there was something in what Mullins said. Still abstractedly, he took from his pocket the notes Sproul had prepared against that evening's lecture. He nodded at them, glad he had them. They would tell him more about Sproul; they were bound to.

"And every man is the clue to his own murder," he remarked. Mullins stared at him.

"Huh?" Mullins said. "I don't get it, Loot."

Weigand told him not to bother. He laid the notes beside him on the desk, nodded to Mullins and told him to let them take the body. Then he said, "No, wait a minute," because he decided he would like to look at this guy Sproul again. He followed Mullins to the stage, went past the waiting men from the New York County morgue, and looked down at Sproul.

He was a florid corpse, was Mr. Sproul, and his hair bristled in an incongruously lively fashion. Weigand stared at the body and the body stared back; probably it was pure imagination to think that the body grinned in a kind of malicious triumph. That was just something which had already begun to happen to the face. Weigand shook his head at the corpse and said it could be taken away. The white-uniformed men from the morgue put it in the basket, neither roughly nor gently. They did not chuck it in; on the other hand they were evidently conscious that it was in no danger of breaking.

Somebody had pulled aside heavy velvet curtains which backed the shallow stage. Double doors opening into a corridor were revealed, and they stood open for the convenience of the men from the morgue. Abstractedly, Weigand watched the removal of the body. Less abstractedly, turning, he looked out into the auditorium. There was a little knot of people there, made up mostly of detectives. But there were strangers; those would be, presumably, people who had known Sproul and volunteered themselves as friends, in accordance with instructions. Weigand motioned to have them brought up and thought of something. He stepped quickly across the stage to the door leading to the speakers' room and pushed it open.

Then he stopped, because the room was dark. And he had left lights on. He went on, ducking quickly in case somebody was swinging. He crouched for a moment, listening, and heard only his own breath. Still in a half crouch, the furniture of the room charted in his mind, he moved to the desk, reached quickly and switched on the light. He moved to the side abruptly as he did so and nothing happened.

There was no one else in the room. But there had been. A glance at the desk proved that. The sheaf of notes which Weigand had laid abstractedly on the desk when he went for a last look at Sproul was not any longer on the desk. There was no use looking for them elsewhere in the room—on the floor for example—but Weigand looked swiftly, making remarks to himself about himself.

The notes were gone. Gone with somebody who wanted them as badly as Weigand did, perhaps for a more specific reason. Gone with somebody who was, it had to be admitted, more efficient at getting what he wanted. For the present.

Weigand spoke bitterly, and aloud, and yanked open the corridor door of the speakers' room. Not that there would be anybody on the other side, holding out the notes politely.

"Oh," the girl said. "Inspector!"

Weigand stared at her. She had been just coming in, apparently. Or had she been just going out, and heard him and thought fast. She was a slender, pliant girl with dark brown hair. And her face was drawn and unhappy.

Weigand was feeling abrupt. He sounded abrupt.

"Well," he said, "what do you want?"

The girl said she thought he had wanted her; wanted everybody who had known Victor Leeds Sproul. "Lee," she said. "Poor Lee. I was going to marry him."

"Were you in here before?" Weigand said. "Just now?"

"Not just now," the girl said. "Before Lee went—went out to make his speech. Then I went around to the auditorium to listen." She looked at Weigand. "To listen," she repeated. "To listen to Lee."

She looked as if she were about to cry.

"I'm sorry," Weigand said. "You're—?"

"Loretta Shaw," she said.

"I'm sorry, Miss Shaw," Weigand said. "But why didn't you wait with the others?"

She started to say "What others?" and said, instead, "Oh—Jean and the others. I don't know. They started to come for—for Lee and I couldn't just sit there. And then I remembered the corridor and this room and came this way. Wasn't it all right?"

"Did you see anybody outside?" Weigand said. "A—a little dark man or anybody?"

He was surprised that he spoke of the little dark man. But it seemed as if somebody might have repeated a trick.

The girl shook her head and said, "Nobody." She looked puzzled. "Mr. Jung?" she said.

"I don't know," Weigand said. "Did you see somebody called Jung?"

The girl shook her head again.

"I thought that was who you meant," she said. "He's a little dark man. Bandelman Jung."

Weigand said, "Who?" She repeated the name and spelled it. Weigand shook his head this time.

"Come in," he said. "Who is Bandelman Jung?" He listened doubtfully to his own voice. "It doesn't sound like a name," he said. "Who is he?"

He was, the girl said, coming in, a friend of Sproul's. She had merely happened to think of him, thinking it must be he Weigand meant.

"Bandelman Jung," Weigand repeated. "A little, dark man. Right? But you didn't see him just now?"

"I didn't see anybody," Loretta Shaw said. "Should I have?"

Weigand shrugged and said he didn't know. He said, vaguely, that he had been looking for somebody, but that it did not matter. He had Miss Shaw sit beside the desk and sat looking at her, as if he were seeing her for the first time. The lecture notes would have to wait.

She was going to marry Lee Sproul very soon, Loretta Shaw said. In a few weeks. As soon as he "made arrangements."

"What arrangements?" Weigand wanted to know. He watched her carefully. She hesitated and started to answer and apparently decided against it.

"Oh," she said, "things. You know—things."

Weigand didn't believe her and made a guess.

"I understood Sproul was already married," he said. He said it flatly. The girl looked at him and her eyes widened.

"No," she said. "Why, no."

Weigand let her have it that way. He asked other questions. She had met Sproul in Paris several years before; she had seen a lot of him then; she had returned to New York and then gone on to the West Coast. Recently she had returned, seen more of Sproul and decided to marry him. Her voice broke a little at the last.

"If you'd rather wait," Weigand offered. She shook her head and Weigand said "Right."

"Anyway," he said, "I'll have more to ask you later, if there is any need. This is merely preliminary. We won't bother too much with background for the moment. But you did see Sproul earlier this evening?"

She had. She had had dinner with him, along with several other people.

"We tried to get out of it," she said. "Lee and I did. But they were all old friends—from Paris, mostly. It was—well, a kind of celebration. Georgie said it was a launching and offered to break a—a bottle of champagne."

A sob broke her voice.

"It was—gay," she said. "We thought it was so gay. And funny. And now—"

Weigand made sounds which might comfort her. She looked up and tried to smile. She said she was all right, now.

"You and Sproul at the dinner," Weigand prompted. "And—who is Georgie?"

Georgie was George Schwartz, who had been on the Paris *Tribune* in the old days and was a copy-reader now on one of the morning papers and had been a great friend of Sproul's in the old days. "Poor old Georgie," the girl said. "He drinks so much," she said, explaining herself. In addition there had been the Akrons—Jean, who also had been in Paris in the old days, and her brother, Herbert, who evidently had not. Momentarily there was nothing to identify the Akrons for Weigand. There had been a man named Ralph White, also of the Paris-in-the-old-days group.

And Mr. Burden had dropped in at the end and had coffee with them.

It had been an early dinner, because of the lecture. They had eaten at Florio's in Forty-fourth Street and finished about seven-thirty. Or Sproul had finished then and gone on, leaving the others—except Burden—to finish their coffee and follow. They stayed about fifteen or twenty minutes, she thought; possibly longer. Then she had left the others, pleading she had to stop by her apartment for a moment, but really wanting to see Sproul again before he went on the platform.

"Why?" Weigand wanted to know.

Loretta Shaw shook her head.

"No reason," she said. "I just wanted to see him. It had been—oh, so gay and noisy at the party. I just wanted to see him a minute. Just the two of us. For—oh, so that we'd remember."

Weigand found himself thinking, suddenly, of Dorian. For reassurance, the girl meant. Or might mean. For a moment of being together, quietly without others. That was what she might mean. But you couldn't tell.

It had not, it developed, worked out that way. Loretta Shaw had come to the club and explained what she wanted and been told the way to the speakers' room. She had found the door unlatched and lights on, but nobody in the room. It was ten minutes, anyway, before Sproul came, and then he was not alone.

"Mrs. Williams was with him," the girl said. "The woman who was on the platform and introduced the other man. Mr. West."

"North," Weigand told her. She nodded. The man who in turn was to introduce Lee. That was it. Apparently Sproul and Mrs. Williams had met downstairs and not come up directly. She thought they had stopped for a drink. It had not been clear, or important, she said. But she gathered that they had sat for a few moments in the lounge downstairs, perhaps having a drink and, she supposed, meeting people. Then it had got too crowded—"too many damn people," Sproul had said, and they came on to the speakers' room. But apparently Sproul had not got his drink, or had not finished it, because a few minutes later a waiter had come with a fresh drink. She had been offered one and declined it; she thought Sproul was finishing his when Mr. North arrived. She did not remember whether Mrs. Williams had had her drink, or what had become of the glasses. It hadn't been—important.

"Is it now?" she asked, puzzled by the guiding questions.

Weigand spread his hands slightly. It could be; if Sproul had not died naturally, or taken something voluntarily—the girl shook her head anxiously at this—then he must have been given something. Morphine, they thought, in a large quantity.

"By the way," he said, "did he ever use morphine, as far as you know?"

The girl shook her head so that the long brown hair swayed.

"Never," she said. "It—it horrified him. So many people in Paris did, and it was something he couldn't stand."

Weigand repeated the words, "Couldn't stand?"

She looked puzzled.

"He thought it was a dreadful thing to do," she said. "It really—he was really serious about it. Because of what it did to people."

It sounded like a new side of Sproul. But Weigand let it go. After a moment, he let the girl go too, advising her to go home, taking her address, expressing sympathy. She went and Weigand looked after her and remembered the notes and swore. He went to the door and called Mullins, admitted without pleasure what had happened, and they went into it.

If it was the little dark man, he might be anywhere. No little dark man, identifiable as such, had left the building. Since they had heard of him. But the loopholes were large in that. The doors opening from the rear of the stage had been open for perhaps ten minutes before Weigand went out. Dr. Dupont and Dr. Klingman had gone out through them, hunting a place where the tall, old man could lie down and rest. Mullins thought that Mrs. Williams had also gone out, although she was now back on the stage, and that Mr. Burden might have. And the doors led into a corridor which connected with that from which the speaker's room opened. Mr. North had been right about that. So there was nothing to prove that anyone on the stage had not taken the notes, although it was difficult to see how they could have known Weigand would leave the notes available and unguarded.

"Why did you, Loot?" Mullins asked. His question apparently was serious and interested. Weigand stared back at him and advised him to skip it. Mullins said, "O.K., Loot."

"Presumably," Weigand said, after thinking it over, "whoever took the notes was an opportunist. Perhaps he came in for something else and was lucky."

"What else, Loot?" Mullins inquired.

Weigand asked to be told how he would know. He looked at Mullins without favor. Then the telephone rang.

"Jerry," the telephone said, "they've got sailors. *Sailors.* They're not babies at *all.*"

"No, Pam," Bill Weigand said. "They don't sound like it. This is Bill, Pam."

"But they can't be more than fifteen," Pam North said, "at the oldest, and the other one fourteen. It's just that they're mature. For their ages. You know what I mean, Bill? Is Jerry around?"

Bill Weigand said he knew what she meant. And that he would call Jerry.

"Because I need him," Pam North said. "I can't cope. It's so—sudden. And Martha won't be enough."

Bill Weigand thought of Martha, ample and dark and, on occasion, firm with the Norths. He thought

Martha might, on the whole, be enough even for nieces with attached sailors. But that was up to Pam.

"I shooed them," Pam said. "But you can't tell. There are such a lot of sailors. Not that they aren't nice. Jerry was one last time, you know. But that was before I knew him."

It was not entirely clear to Bill Weigand this time. He motioned to Mullins, held a hand over the transmitter and said: "Get North, will you, Sergeant?" Mullins looked perception and went out.

"Bill," Pam said, "are you still there? Before Jerry comes, I thought of something. The thing that was bothering me, you know?"

"No, Pam," Bill Weigand said. "Was something bothering you?"

"I told—no I didn't," Pam said. "I just told the taxi driver. Or did I? Anyway, there was something wrong. There, I mean. With the murder, or the people. And when I saw the sailors I remembered what it was. Because the sailors were the same sort of thing, in a way."

"Please, Pam," Bill Weigand said. "What is it?"

"Mrs. Williams," Pam North said. "She's so—proper and everything. But I remember we saw her one night at the Roundabout and she wasn't. Proper, I mean. On the contrary. So much so that we both noticed. With a man."

Weigand thought about it.

"Listen, Pam," he said, "you mean you're all steamed up because you saw Mrs. Williams at the Roundabout with a man? Just that? And she'd had a drink or two?"

There was a slight pause at the other end, and during it Jerry North came in, preceding Mullins. He gestured toward the telephone, but Weigand held up a hand, telling him to wait.

"It doesn't sound like much," Pam admitted. "Put that way. And I don't suppose it matters, or has anything to do with Mr. Sproul. But she was—like another person. The way she was looking at the man and—letting him look at her. It doesn't belong with Mrs. Williams and you always say discrepancies are important. Anyway, it worried me. You can forget it now, if you want to. Or talk it over with Jerry. Where is he, by the way?"

Weigand held out the telephone to Jerry North who took it and said "hello." Jerry listened for a minute or two, ran the fingers of his free hand through his hair and after a moment more said: "Good God!" He listened further and said "good-bye" gently and put down the telephone. He looked at Weigand, who grinned.

"Sailors," Jerry said, in a strange voice. "The nieces have got sailors." He stared beyond Bill Weigand for a moment and recovered himself. "I've got to get along," he said. "Pam's upset." He looked at Bill, seeing him. "Listen," he said, "couldn't you drop down after a while and—and—"

"Pam already has," Weigand said. "Shooed them. Do you want an armed guard? Or moral support?"

"Both, I expect," Jerry North said. He grinned, finally, in his turn. "The future is dark," he said and went out through the door leading to the corridor. Weigand, remembering that he wanted to check Jerry's impression of Mrs. Williams, started to call him back. He decided against it, smiled as he thought of the nieces, frowned when he remembered the notes, and sat for a moment drumming his fingers on the desk, Mullins watched the fingers. The rhythm was slow, as yet. That meant Weigand didn't see a clear road ahead. Things were still screwy, and getting screwier.

5

Thursday, 10 P.M. to 11:15 P.M.

Clearly, Lieutenant William Weigand decided, looking
at Mrs. Paul Williams and listening to her crisp an-
swers, Pam North had got her people mixed. It was,
admittedly, unlike her; Pam mixed words more often
than people, and it was never entirely certain that she
mixed words. But Mrs. Paul Williams was not the
woman Pam had seen at the Roundabout, evidently
the worse—or the better?—for alcohol, looking with
languishing eyes on an anonymous man. That went
against nature, or against Mrs. Paul Williams's im-
provements upon nature, which were manifold. Nature was never so trim as Mrs. Williams, so precisely
and confidently in place, so decisive. Mrs. Williams
had pulled herself together, now, and her togetherness
was almost alarming.

She introduced herself crisply when she answered
Weigand's polite summons, politely enough conveyed
through Mullins. Mullins came with her and brought
his notebook, leaving shepherding outside to Detective (First Class) Stein. She gave Weigand her name,
which he knew, as if she were disposing of a question-
naire. Only then did the name become faintly familiar
to Weigand. The familiarity was not decisive; it was a
name he had heard. Possibly he had heard of her
husband. His question was to satisfy his mind's vague
inquiry.

73

"Isn't your husband an attorney, Mrs. Williams?" he asked. "I believe I've heard of him."

"My husband is dead," Mrs. Williams told him, with something like severity. "*I* am an attorney."

Weigand said, "Oh."

"Corporation," Mrs. Williams added. "So you would not have encountered me in magistrate's court, Inspector."

"Lieutenant," Weigand said. He was puzzled. "You use your husband's name," he pointed out. "Possibly that confused me."

Mrs. Williams obviously thought that Weigand's questions were frivolous. Her tone said so.

"Obviously," she said. "I prefer to be Mrs. Paul Williams, although my husband has been dead for many years. My own name is Daphne. It is not suitable."

Weigand said, "Oh," again.

"And," Mrs. Williams said, "I have two children. Both daughters. The eldest is sixteen, the other a year younger. My husband died in 1927, a few months after our second daughter was born. And surely, Lieutenant, all this is beside the point."

Weigand had to admit that he had asked for it, although not for as much as he had got. But he did not look particularly disconcerted.

"Entirely, Mrs. Williams," he said. His tone left with Mrs. Williams responsibility for a spate of unsought information. She looked as if she were about to protest, so he continued.

"We are merely collecting information which may have a bearing on Sproul's death," he told her. "It is naturally necessary to talk to those who were with him immediately before his death. In the event that it becomes a police matter."

"Very well," Mrs. Williams said. "I met Mr. Sproul for the first time a week or so ago, when I had luncheon with him and Mr. Burden. At the Astor, for some reason. We talked about the lecture. I am program chairman of the club this season. I had not met him before. I met him for the second time this evening."

"Yes?" Weigand encouraged. He was entirely polite. Mrs. Williams was not engaging, but she was specific. A good thing in witnesses.

"He came to the club about a quarter of eight," Mrs. Williams said. "I had dined here and only just finished. One of the club servants said that Mr. Sproul had arrived and I went out to meet him. He said he was very early and something about having had an engagement which had not materialized. I said that it was very pleasant to see him, and something about how much we preferred lecturers who were early to lecturers who were late, and kept us worrying lest they had forgotten the engagement. I said we might go into the lounge and meet some of the members."

"Yes?" Weigand said.

"We went into the lounge," Mrs. Williams said. "It was about five or ten minutes of eight. I asked Mr. Sproul if he would care for a drink, and ordered him a brandy and soda. I had ginger-ale. I very seldom drink; never when I have responsibilities."

She looked at Weigand firmly. Weigand said she was very wise. She nodded.

"However," she said, "there were a great many people in the lounge and all of them wanted to meet Mr. Sproul and after a while I thought so many people might not be good for him. I find that lecturers usually like to have a few minutes of repose before they speak."

Weigand nodded.

"So I suggested he might prefer to go to the speakers' room and he agreed," Mrs. Williams continued. She was being a very good witness. "He left his drink after taking only a few sips and when I noticed this, in the speakers' room, I naturally suggested that he have another. He decided that he would and I called the bar steward, who sent up another brandy and soda. Miss

Shaw, who I gathered was an old friend of Mr. Sproul's, was waiting in the speakers' room when we got there. Mr. North came five or ten minutes later. We talked until it was time to go on the stage."

Weigand nodded. He said she was very helpful.

"During that time did anything odd happen?" he asked. "I don't know what sort of odd thing I mean. Anything you noticed. Did Sproul seem upset at all?"

"He seemed very gay," Mrs. Williams said. "In excellent spirits—quite unlike most of our lecturers, who are inclined to be—a little morose before they go on. I noticed that, particularly. But I can't say it was odd. Perhaps Mr. Sproul was always in good spirits. I was not familiar with his usual manners, remember."

The counsellor-at-law qualified, keeping the testimony neat around the edges. Weigand was appreciative.

"Did you have another ginger-ale in the speakers' room, Mrs. Williams," he asked.

"No," she said. "Why?"

"I don't know why," Weigand told her. "I wondered."

This struck Mrs. Williams, it was apparent, as irregular. It seemed to confirm a rather low opinion she had formed of Lieutenant Weigand, as a frivolous man. She stood up. Weigand stood with her.

"Yes," he said, "that is all, Mrs. Williams. Thank you."

She left and Mullins joined Weigand in looking after her.

"Quite a dame," Mullins said. "Quite an old dame."

Not so old, Weigand told him. Thirty-five, at a guess. "A very precise person," Weigand said. "We must try to be more precise ourselves, Sergeant."

Mullins looked doubtful, and finally said, "O.K., Loot."

So they had Sproul's activities charted from about 7:45 to the time of his death. Now they would work back. Then the telephone rang. Weigand said "Yes?" to Dr. Jerome Francis.

"It was morphine, all right," Dr. Francis told him. "A lot of it. Plus, evidently, a special sensitivity—what you'd call an allergy, probably."

"Would I?" Weigand said.

"Sure," Francis told him. "With Sproul a little morphine went a long way. The whole way. Partly because he had a mild heart condition. Partly because—well, his system just didn't resist morphine. And if you want to know why I can't tell you. It was just the kind of a guy he was."

Weigand assumed that Sproul wasn't, under the circumstances, addicted to morphine. Dr. Francis snorted mildly and said of course not.

"He'd have died first," Dr. Francis said. "Literally."

Weigand thanked the assistant medical examiner and cradled the telephone. So it wasn't natural causes. It was suicide or murder, and you could take your choice. And he, as the policeman responsible, had to take the choice and prove it.

"What've we got, Sergeant?" Weigand asked Mullins. "Did he jump or was he pushed?"

"Hell," Mullins said. "Who'd suicide before a mob? He was pushed."

Weigand found he thought so, too. He nodded.

"Can you picture our Mrs. Williams going all soft over some guy in a restaurant?" he asked. "And getting a little high in the process?"

Mullins said "Hell, no."

"Pam North thinks she saw Mrs. Williams doing just that," Weigand said. Mullins looked puzzled.

"Mrs. North said that?" he repeated. Weigand nodded. Mullins shook his head slowly.

"I don't get it," he said. "But if Mrs. North says so." He looked at Weigand. "Sometimes I get the idea Mrs. North ain't as screwy as she sounds," he confided. Weigand pretended astonishment. He said,

"Not really, Sergeant!" Mullins nodded. "Sometimes I do," he insisted. "But it's hard to see the Williams dame unlaxing."

It was, Weigand agreed. But it was merely an interesting side issue; one of those things which cropped up when you had to stir people around during an investigation. One of those oddities which had, in the end, nothing to do with the main issue, but which had to be noted down all the same, because you were finished before you knew what was important and what trivial. So—

It was almost an hour later, and Weigand sat staring at his notes—the cryptic, fragmentary notes which he kept for his own reminders, supplementing Mullins' record. Weigand stared at his notes and Mullins stared at Weigand. Finally Mullins said one word.

"People!" Mullins remarked.

Weigand nodded slowly. People indeed. People who had known Sproul and known one another; people who had sat and answered questions, telling what they wanted to tell but sometimes revealing more. The Akrons, brother and sister; George Schwartz, summoned from a copy desk, and flaring in sudden anger at a dead man; Ralph White, a large man who looked as if he lived on a small income and who had an odd, heavy expansiveness about him; Loretta Shaw again, to say, "So what?" to a question Weigand asked her; Y. Charles Burden, back unexpectedly and without summons, to give a warning which seemed at first glance to have no purpose, but which must have had. And finally Bandelman Jung of the unlikely name, who was, beyond question, a little dark man. But *the* little dark man?

"People," Weigand agreed.

"The Akron dame," Mullins remarked, a little querulously. "And her brother. If he is her brother."

Weigand nodded. She had been tall and almost sedate when she entered, had the Akron girl. Fair and tall, with a broad forehead and taffy-colored hair lying in braids, unfashionably but with effectiveness, around her head. She had been slow to answer and calm and she had known Victor Leeds Sproul in Paris. She had been living in Paris when he was there; she had returned, it became unexpectedly reasonable to suppose, when he returned. She had been doing nothing in Paris, except living there.

It was she, jumping down to the present, who had planned the dinner for Sproul which was in a fashion a reunion and, in a fashion, a celebration of Sproul's new career. A celebration in advance, of a career markedly aborted.

"Poor Victor," she said, sitting serenely. "Poor Victor. He was looking forward to it, I think."

Her voice was sober, as became a voice in the presence of sudden death. But it did not, it seemed to Weigand, reveal any sense of personal bereavement. Sproul, it appeared from words and tones, was a friend who had remained an acquaintance to Jean Akron; she was regretful at his taking off, but not greatly moved. She could remember nothing out of the way at the dinner; Sproul had seemed much as he always seemed. Certainly he had not seemed depressed. But he could always hide his feelings. It came over Weigand, listening, that each answer given by Jean Akron served to cancel the preceding answer; each sentence drew a line through the one which had come before. Was she careful? Or, as seemed equally probable, merely negative?

It seemed, Weigand suggested, looking for a spark, unlikely that Sproul would have killed himself when he was about to try something both new and, apparently, interesting and when he was about to marry. Miss Akron had known he was about to marry.

"Oh," she said, "we all knew that. Or that he said he was."

"Do you mean," Weigand pressed, "that you thought he really wasn't?"

The placid girl seemed faintly, but only faintly, surprised.

"Why, no," she said. "Why should I think that?"

(Mullins had looked at her then, evidently puzzled. He had lifted his head, and his pencil from his notebook, and stared at her. She had not seemed conscious of the stare.)

She knew Loretta Shaw, of course; she was very fond of Loretta. But she did not really know her well; they had met often in Paris, but had never been close friends.

"We are so different," Jean Akron explained. (Her tone might have thrown the onus for that difference on Loretta Shaw. But it might have implied no onus. Recalling, Weigand was not certain. But he was left, and of this he was certain, with the belief that Miss Akron had not really liked the slight, vivid girl who said she was soon to have married Sproul.)

Jean Akron had not—as now Weigand led her into the past—known Sproul before he went to Paris. Weigand looked at her, guessed her age as the middle twenties, and said "of course not." She had met him in Paris through her brother, who had known him somewhere in the United States—she was uncommonly vague just there—and had run into him when he was visiting her.

"When my brother was visiting me," she explained. "He didn't live in Paris, of course. He was there on business."

She did not know of any reason for anyone to have killed Sproul, if he had been killed. She knew Mr. Burden slightly and thought him a "very pleasant man" and added, with an inflection, "but so dynamic." She knew George Schwartz, then a name to Weigand, and Ralph White, another name. But she did not seem to know any of them well. Weigand let her go and had her brother in.

("If he is her brother," Mullins said, when Weigand,

reviewing for both of them, brought up his name.
Weigand nodded.)

It had seemed a question, certainly. Herbert Akron
was at least fifteen years older than his sister. He had a
sharp face and a high, domed forehead from which the
hair receded, shrinking back from the edge of a preci-
pice. He sat down, but sat restlessly. At almost every
pause he scratched the thin hair over his right ear, but
it was evident that he quieted no itch, except the itch
to move his hand. And almost from the start he began
to snarl.

He did not see, to begin with, what business
Weigand had bothering him. "Or Jean," he added.
"We hardly knew the heel."

"Heel?" Weigand repeated.

Herbert Akron's voice rasped as he described the
kind of heel.

"We never saw him," he asserted. But then he
admitted that they had seen him at dinner that evening.
They "couldn't get out of it." It did not appear why
they could not get out of it. "So we sat around
listening to the pompous fool tell what a knock-out he
was going to be in front of the women's clubs. He—he
gloated over it."

Akron's tone was contemptuous.

"And all the while he was planning to take poison,"
Akron added, making the act of suicide an offense
against the dignity of the Akrons. "Damned exhibi-
tionist."

It was interesting to search out the root of this
animosity. Weigand prodded around the base of Akron, looking for a lead. For a long time he was unsuc-
cessful. But he discovered other things, some of which
he wanted. He discovered that Akron headed a small,
but growing, factory in New Jersey, which made a
part—a very secret part, Akron indicated—for several
bomber factories. He discovered that Akron and his
sister shared an apartment on Park Avenue, not too far

up. And he discovered that Akron's tone changed when he spoke of his sister. It was hard, for a while, to put a finger on the nature of the change.

Now and then, it developed, Akron and his sister entertained in their apartment people Jean had known in Paris. Akron spoke of such entertainments, and of the people, with contempt.

"Something Jean wanted," he said. "A pretentious bunch, all of them."

Sproul was there sometimes.

"I thought you never saw him," Weigand said.

"As seldom as possible," Akron assured him. "Only when we couldn't get out of it."

But again it was not apparent what had kept them from getting out of it. It was not apparent, indeed, what had kept Akron from getting out of entertaining his sister's Paris friends. It was not clear why Akron's nerves were so on edge, why his voice rasped so. Unless edgy nerves and a rasping voice were part of Akron, as they might be.

"Of course," he said, "he hung around as much as he could. Everybody knew that."

"Hung around?" Weigand repeated. "Sproul hung around? You?"

The tone was not incredulous; the tone could hardly be said to exist.

"Jean," Akron told him. "There was no secret about that. But he never got anywhere. I kept an eye on him."

Weigand let his voice sound puzzled.

"I understood," he said, "that Sproul was engaged to be married. To a Miss Shaw—Loretta Shaw, isn't it?"

Akron sneered. There was, Weigand decided, no other word to fit it. Akron drew one corner of his mouth down in derision and let the other corner curl up. It was quite a face to make, Weigand thought.

"Eye-wash," Akron told him. "Sproul wasn't marrying anybody. Not the Shaw girl. Not Jean. He was a heel."

Weigand waited a minute.

"Did he want to marry Miss Akron?" he inquired.

Akron said, "Hell, no."

"Not *marry*," he added. His emphasis completed the remark. But he completed it in words. "A week end was about his speed," he said.

There was a kind of viciousness in his tone. "It sounded like his sister was his wife," Mullins said, summing up. "You'd have figured he was jealous."

(Weigand looked at him and smiled faintly. He did not answer.)

It had been then, unexpectedly, that Y. Charles Burden opened the door from the stage to the speakers' room and came in without apology. Weigand looked at him without friendliness. Burden looked at Akron, ignoring the detectives.

"You," he said. "Shooting off your mouth again, probably. Getting Jean into a mess."

Akron looked at him and his mouth twisted.

"Sir Galahad," he said. He stared at Burden. "I'll take care of my sister," he told the lecture agent. "I don't need any small-time Barnums."

"Listen," Burden said. He ignored Akron and was speaking to Weigand. "This guy's a nut, Lieutenant. Whatever he says about Jean, don't believe him. She hadn't anything to do with Sproul."

Weigand was interested. But his voice was mild.

"That's what he says," he told Burden. "And who sent for you, Mr. Burden?"

His voice was mild to the end. But the last question might have been put to a small, unruly boy.

"All right," Burden said. "But lay off her."

The last seemed more to Akron than to Weigand, but Weigand was included.

"Get out," Weigand said. "And stick around. Sergeant, see that Mr. Burden sticks around."

Mullins was up, and took Mr. Burden back to the door and out. Mullins' voice rumbled for an instant in instruction to Detective Sergeant Stein. Mullins returned.

"There's another heel for you," Akron said, with venom. "Another small-time wolf."

Weigand's voice was lighter, apparently friendly, seemed to be sharing a man-to-man situation.

"After your sister too, is he?" Weigand said. "But what can you expect, Mr. Akron? With a sister like that?"

Akron looked at him with no corresponding friendliness.

"A helluva chance," he said. "Burden or any heel like him. What do they think she is?"

Weigand refrained from telling him. Weigand said he might go. And he, unlike Burden, might go where he liked. It was kind of him to help. Akron went, after a hard look at Weigand.

"There's a guy'd like to kill somebody," Mullins said. "But why? Guys don't kill for their sisters, Loot?"

"They have," Weigand assured him, "to protect them . . . or something."

Mullins looked puzzled.

George Schwartz had come in ambling. He was very thin and well over six feet; his legs had an odd detachment of their own, and seemed to be leading the rest of Schwartz. Schwartz's face was broad and flexible, with high cheekbones and an extraordinarily mobile mouth. He did not, however, use it to sneer with. He smiled at the detectives and to Weigand said, "Hello, Lieutenant.

"The boys said you wanted me," he reported. "Took me right out of the middle of a piece about wills for probate. You picked a very fortunate time, Lieutenant."

Schwartz had been fortifying himself with a drink or two. But he was a long way from drunk on them.

"Not," he added, "that it wouldn't be pleasant at any time to hear that somebody had done in Victor Leeds Sproul."

"Why?" Weigand asked, with great simplicity.

And then, quite suddenly, the long, easy-going man was no longer easy-going.

"Because," he said, "Sproul was as unmitigated a bastard as I've ever known. He was—"

Schwartz seemed suddenly to blaze as he continued his description of the dead lecturer. It was a strange, unaccountable spectacle. Sproul was this and Sproul was that; he was a windbag and he was a crook; he weaseled in where nobody wanted him.

"Where?" Weigand put in.

"My life," Schwartz told him. "Everybody's girl. My girl's life; everybody's girl's."

He broke off, suddenly cooling. He looked as if he wished he had cooled earlier. But then he shrugged.

"What the hell?" he said. "You'd find out anyway."

"Sproul got my wife to leave me," he said. "Got her to divorce me, so he could marry her. Only he didn't plan to marry her." He paused again, and smiled a little crookedly. "It leaves a guy prejudiced," he said. "I was right prejudiced against Mr. Sproul."

"I see you were," Weigand said. "Who was your wife?"

"Loretta," Schwartz said. "Loretta Shaw she calls herself now. Loretta Schwartz as was."

"They're the damnedest bunch," Mullins said, rather helplessly. "A bunch of bed-hoppers."

Weigand nodded. He said the whole crowd seemed to get around.

The bomb-shell had been Schwartz's chief contribution. He had been at the dinner, getting time off.

"I sort of liked to watch that monkey," he said.

Nothing out of the way had happened at the dinner; everybody had been polite and friendly. Sproul had been much as he usually was. Schwartz was of the opinion that somebody had killed the lecturer, but evidently only on the basis that he needed killing. But if Sproul had contemplated suicide, he would have planned it as spectacularly as possible. He had known Sproul in Paris, where he was working with him for a time on the *Herald*. It was during those days, near the end of them, that Sproul had persuaded Loretta Schwartz to leave her husband and become Loretta Shaw, as preparation—so she supposed?—for becoming Loretta Sproul.

"And there's a guy with a grudge," Mullins said, when they came to George Schwartz in their checking over.

Weigand nodded.

"With grounds for a grudge, anyway," he agreed. "And obviously a man who is sore. But a murder grudge, Sergeant?"

That, they agreed, was what they didn't know. Not yet.

Schwartz's long, independent legs had carried him out of the little room off the stage of the Today's Topics Club and, after a pause, Loretta Shaw's slender, pretty legs had carried her in. They had carried her in decisively, because she was in readiness for the question. Inevitably, Weigand realized, she would be in readiness for the question. But that was no reason for not asking it.

"So you used to be married to Schwartz?" Weigand said. "And you ditched him for Sproul?"

"So what?" the girl said, very ready. "Is it something that never happened before?"

Weigand agreed that it wasn't. But he was not as amiable as he had been.

"Girls leave poor men for men with more money," he agreed. "Obscure men for prominent men. It happens."

The girl flushed, just perceptibly. But she entered no denial.

"So what?" she said.

Weigand shrugged. So nothing, of necessity.

"It would be simpler, however," he told her, "if people would volunteer information we are bound to get anyway. Simpler for them. It doesn't matter to us." He looked at her, deliberately and without expression. "We have plenty of time," he told her. "All the time in the world. If we need it."

"You're comical," the girl told him. "Completely comical."

Weigand was unperturbed. He even agreed that it was possible. As an individual, thinking what he was thinking, wondering in a new direction. But as a policeman—no.

"The police are not comic, Miss Shaw," he told her. "Don't fool yourself."

That, she told him, was what he thought. She had plenty of animosity. Now, she wanted to know, what did he do?

He smiled at her, indifferent to the bait. He did not answer directly, but said only that she could go. She would, he added, stay in town, because he would have other questions from time to time.

"Comical questions," he said. "Anything for a laugh. That's all, Miss Shaw."

She went. When her back was turned, Weigand nodded to Mullins, who went behind her to the door and nodded over her head to Detective Stein. Stein gave no sign of noticing, but as she went down the aisle toward the exit he spoke, casually enough, to Detective Flannery, who was a small man for a policeman and not conspicuous. Flannery put his hat on and went down the aisle too, like a man going nowhere in particular. Mullins, standing in the door, nodded approvingly and looked at a short list in his hand and said:

"Which one of you's White—Ralph White?"

A tall, plump man, with a heavy face shaped like a piece of dough, said he was White. Mullins jerked a directing head and White passed him and went into the little room. Mullins came behind him and said:

"Mr. Ralph White, Lieutenant. One of the guys who knew Sproul."

"Did you, Mr. White?" Weigand inquired. He was very pleasant again. His eyes suggested a chair.

White had a heavy, buttered voice; he reminded Weigand of somebody in the past and after a moment Weigand remembered who. It didn't matter, because the other man was dead. He had died rather suddenly one evening around eleven o'clock, in a manner he had been permitted to anticipate in a cell for thirteen months and seven days.

Which meant, Weigand reminded himself, nothing whatever about Mr. White. It was a type—the pompous and pontifical, who ran to fatness of person and of phraseology. This did not, Weigand told himself with increasing firmness, mean that representatives of the type ran also to murder.

"I had known Mr. Sproul for a considerable period," White agreed. "Our paths crossed."

"Did they?" Weigand inquired. He paused for a word. How would paths cross? "Intimately?" Weigand added.

White's heavy face produced a heavy smile. His large head shook itself.

"We were merely acquaintances," he said. "We frequented the same circles. In Paris, of course. From time to time we met. When I returned to America"— the voice ridiculed an action so gauche, but at the same time admitted its necessity—"when I returned to America, Mr. Sproul looked me up. We met here from time to time, as my work permitted."

The picture was of a Sproul suppliant, thankful for crumbs of time.

Weigand nodded gravely.

"Your work is—?" he said.

"I am an author," Mr. White told him, in a tone which faintly chastened. "A novelist."

Weigand nodded.

"I observe," Mr. White told him. "I fear I am

merely an onlooker, Sergeant. A looker-on and a noter-down."

Weigand did not question his demotion. His eyes warned Mullins, who would have questioned in his behalf. Weigand threaded his way through the verbal labyrinths of Mr. White's mind—learned that White had met Sproul for the first time in Paris, that he knew most of the members of the group in which Sproul had moved there, that he had dined with the rest before what was to have been Sproul's first lecture and, despite his authorial observations, had noted nothing of particular interest. He agreed with the rest about the facts of the dinner.

Throughout the questioning, White maintained an attitude. It was a little difficult to define. It included a suggestion that White was superior to the rest, who were scurrying small folk to be observed under a glass. It included a note of heavy malice and—unrecognized envy. The last was a guess by Weigand.

"Amusing people," White told him. "Amusing in their fashions." He smiled, as to another man of superiority. "All mixed up together, in devious ways, inspector. All very—emotional."

There was contempt in the voice which formed the word "emotional."

Weigand nodded, waiting.

"Rather impulsively sexed," Mr. White continued, and Weigand thought that no man could employ so many phrases without encountering one which was apt. "Impulsively sexed" was, Weigand suspected, apt.

"Sproul not the least," White continued, a little as if he were dictating a paragraph. "He—sought the favors of so many. Of Loretta Shaw, of Jean Akron. Of others, and often with success."

Was it an envious note again, Weigand wondered? Did men whose novels made no stir hate men whose novels shook reviewers of the *Times* and *Tribune* book sections? Did men who had, one might reasonably suspect, little success with women, envy men who had, one might again suspect, considerable? The answer to both speculations was the same, and obvious. Was it conceivable that such envy, curdling, might lead to hate and hate lead to murder? That depended, Weigand told himself, on the degree of the curdling. Mr. White was, he suspected, curdled to a rather marked degree.

"I don't like that guy," Mullins said when, reviewing, they came to him. "He talks like a book."

"On psychiatry," Weigand amplified.

Mullins looked blank.

It had seemed, when they let him go, that Mr. White had had nothing but his presence to contribute; Weigand ticked him off as a supernumerary. He wondered, indeed, whether they were not all supernumeraries—Mrs. Paul Williams, the Akrons, George Schwartz and Burden, as well as White. Were they there, as people so often seemed to be during an investigation, merely to fill in the back rows; merely to make trouble for detectives? Or did they fit, each in his inevitable place, in a mosaic which had led to violent, absurdly public, death? That was for them to know, Weigand realized, and for him to find out. Or for one of them to know.

And then Detective Stein opened the door and said, with no great interest, that a guy named Young was there and wanted to see the lieutenant. Lieutenant Weigand repeated the name inquiringly, heard the faint tinkle of a bell, and repeated it with a slightly different pronunciation. Detective Stein said, "Sure, that's what I said" and, on instructions, let in a little dark man. He was, Weigand was pleased to discover, neither a Negro nor a midget. He was only reasonably little and not much more than moderately dark. He had wide cheekbones, with skin stretched over them, and black hair; he was thin and straight and he had, rather surprisingly, quite ordinary brown eyes. They looked at Weigand with no perceptible guile.

"Jung," the little dark man said. "Bandelman Jung." He answered a question which he had no doubt discovered to be inevitable. "Eurasian," he said.

He had no accent. But he did not speak as if English were his native language. It occurred to Weigand that he probably would not speak any language as if it were native.

"You wish to see me?" Bandelman Jung inquired. He was polite with dignity.

Weigand went through routine. Jung had known Mr. Sproul in Paris, where he had also known most of the other members of the group; Mr. Jung was himself a "journalist," which seemed, on inquiry, that he had written Paris anecdotes for newspapers in a quite remarkably large number of places; he had come to New York after the Germans came to Paris.

"It became necessary," he said, simply, leaving the story behind to be guessed. His little reports from Paris had not, one could guess, pleased the new invaders of Paris.

He had looked Sproul and the others up and had seen them occasionally; he had not been invited to the dinner that evening; did not, until Weigand mentioned it, know about the dinner. He had dined by himself at a Childs' restaurant and then come to the club, expecting to hear his old friend Mr. Sproul speak about the fine days in Paris. What had occurred was very shocking.

The soft voice of Mr. Jung sounded shocked. Weigand's fingers gently drummed on the desk.

"What did you do afterward, Mr. Jung?" he asked. "After it appeared that Mr. Sproul had collapsed and would not be able to lecture?"

Mr. Jung looked surprised.

"I waited with the others," he said. "In the—the theater."

"You didn't leave the auditorium?" Weigand pressed.

"The auditorium," Jung said. "No."

Weigand pressed him. "Not for any purpose?"

Mr. Jung seemed to consider. His face lightened after a moment.

"But yes," he said. "I went into the—the hall, to a drinking fountain. I was thirsty."

"Nowhere else?" Weigand insisted. Mr. Jung allowed himself to look surprised. He shook his head.

That was futile, Weigand realized. Mr. Jung was not going to admit anything, if there were anything to admit. The detective tried a new tack. He became frank.

The reason he asked, he explained, was that a man who might be said to answer Mr. Jung's description had been seen elsewhere in the building—on the floor above, he thought it was. No doubt this man had quite proper reasons for being there; it was merely a side-issue.

"We like to clear things up as we go along," Weigand said, very frank and open. Mr. Jung nodded and smiled.

"But it was not I," he said. "I am sorry, sir. I went merely to the drinking fountain. Because I was thirsty."

"Right," Weigand said. "That means, of course, that you couldn't have been in this room, doesn't it?"

Did the quite ordinary brown eyes go blank for just a second, Weigand wondered. Or was it a trick of the light? You had to guess, while you listened to Mr. Bandelman Jung agreeing, with no perceptible change in tone, that he could not have been in the speakers' room, having gone no further than the fountain in the corridor.

"Then," Weigand said, "you wouldn't have seen this before, Mr. Jung."

He handed the little dark man a paper knife, part of an ornamental desk set on a desk which, it was to be assumed, nobody ever used. Mr. Jung took it by the dull blade, which was nearest as Weigand held it out,

and looked at it with a puzzled expression and handed
it back. Weigand held it, awaiting the answer.

"But no," Mr. Jung said. There was no doubt that
he looked puzzled. "Is the knife important, Lieutenant?"

Weigand let the knife drop to the table top.

"We don't know, as yet," he said. He was quite
truthful, this time. If the prints Bandelman Jung had
left on it matched any unidentified prints which might
have been found elsewhere in the room, the knife
might carry importance—carry it literally, on its dull
but polished blade. The knife might become important
to Mr. Jung, under those circumstances.

Mr. Jung, who still looked puzzled, went his way.
Weigand was still staring after him, wishing he had
held Mr. North to try identification of rear elevations
of little dark men, when the telephone rang. He agreed
that he was Lieutenant Weigand.

"Flannery," the voice told him. "The Shaw girl."

"Yes," Weigand said.

"She's over here having a cuppa coffee," Flannery
said. "I'm in a booth looking out at them. It seemed
like a good chance to give you a ring."

"Right," Weigand said. "Them?"

"The Shaw girl," Flannery told him. "And this tall
guy—Schwartz. He was waiting for her when she
came out and they both got in a cab. So I got a cab."

"Right," Weigand said again.

"So we came over here," Flannery said. "On Third
Avenue, for a cuppa coffee and a talk. In a booth. Shall
I stick with them?"

"Yes," Weigand said. "With them, and when they
separate, with her. Anything else?"

Flannery said he guessed not. Unless maybe the
lieutenant was interested in the Shaw girl's love-life.

Weigand was patient. Patient and interested.

"Well," Flannery said, "their cab was stopped by
the lights, see? And we had to come up alongside

because there was a place and it would have looked funny not to. Right?"

"Right," Weigand said. "And—?"

"So I looked in," Flannery said. "Just like a guy would. And baby!"

"Love?" Weigand said. "Love life in a big way?"

"Baby!" Flannery said. His tone held admiration. "What a clinch, Loot. *What a clinch!"*

Weigand cradled the telephone gently. He looked at it. He said, still very gently, "Well, well."

6

Thursday, 10 P.M. to Friday, 2:25 A.M.

Toughy and Ruffy sat shoulder to shoulder and looked at the nieces. The nieces sat shoulder to shoulder and looked at the cats. Mr. North returned from his study, where he had deposited a hat, and regarded the spectacle. Toughy and Ruffy turned simultaneous heads, noticed his advent and returned to their fixed regard of the nieces.

"They're—well developed," Pam had told Jerry North on the telephone. "You know what I mean? It seems to give sailors ideas."

Margaret and Elizabeth were, tangibly, well developed. Or—call it nicely developed. But now, away from sailors, they looked like nice little girls in their middle teens. They looked innocent. "They're really little girls after all," Jerry thought, greeting them. He remembered to call Elizabeth "Beth." The nieces said "How do you do, Uncle Jerry," very nicely. Then Beth said: "They're cute, aren't they?"

"Yes," Jerry said. "Hello Ruffy. Hello Toughy."

Ruffy, a small gray cat with a white collar, was always talkative. She spoke a little querulously to Mr. North, chiding him for his long absence. Toughy regarded him with baleful yellow eyes revealing the Siamese which had, a little mysteriously, invaded his blood stream. He flattened his ears, twisted his long, bushy tail and waggled the tail's tip.

95

"Watch him, Jerry," Mrs. North said urgently. *"Curtains!"*

It had been too much for Toughy and Mr. North realized this a moment too late. Toughy, the pleased center of all eyes, recognized his duty. Toughy would now entertain. Jerry North reached for him and Toughy trickled through his fingers. Toughy ran half way across the living room, leaped the other half, landed on the curtains and swarmed up.

"He can climb, can't he?" Beth said, with interest. "I think he's cute, don't you, Margie?"

"They're both cute," Margie said. "Very cute. Can he get down?"

Toughy had extended himself. Using spurs, he mounted the curtains to the top, scrambled around the corner to the valance board and gained the summit. He extended himself on the board and looked down, beaming. Then his beam changed to another expression.

"No," Pam North said. "He can't get down. He always forgets. Toughy, you're a fool cat."

"Yow," said Toughy. "M-yow. We-ah!"

"Is that good for the curtains?" Margie wanted to know. It appeared that she was the practical niece.

"No," Jerry said. "It raises—it is very bad for the curtains."

"I should think it would simply raise hell with them," Beth said, interestedly. "Leave little holes all over."

"Me-*yow!*" said Toughy, demandingly. Ruffy walked over and looked up at him. She looked back over her shoulder at Jerry North. *"Yow!"* said Ruffy, shortly.

"She wants him to come down," Beth advised. "She's afraid he'll fall. Are they—husband and wife?"

It was a delicate point, Jerry North thought. He looked at Pam.

"Well," Pam said, "they could have been. And, of

course, they're brother and sister too. It's—it's odd about cats. So, of course—"

She stopped, a little puzzled. You couldn't tell about little girls in their middle teens.

"Spayed," Beth said. She looked at her aunt with surprise. "Anyway, I should think so."

"Jerry," Pam said, "are you going to get the ladder?"

Jerry was glad to get the ladder. The ladder unfolded itself out of a chair and wobbled, but he still was glad to get it. He brought it out and climbed it and dislodged Toughy who, now terrified by the results of his own prowess, clung. He put Toughy on the floor and Toughy, with avid yellow eyes, crouched at the foot of the curtains and stared up at them.

"He's going back," Margie said. "I think he's cute."

But Ruffy went to Toughy and rubbed his nose with hers, in a friendly, warning fashion. He put an arm around her neck and began to wash her face. Beth said, "Oh, look! Aren't they—*cute!*"

Pam and Jerry beamed at their cats. Mr. North found his opinion of the nieces rising. They were, it was clear, perceptive little girls. And what lass didn't love a sailor?

"Jerry was a sailor the other time," Pam said. Mr. North was a little startled to encounter her just there, but it was a familiar surprise. The nieces looked at Jerry.

"Really?" said Beth, with an inflection. Margie was sensitive to the inflection.

"Beth!" she said. "It was ever so long ago. Years and years." She looked at Mr. North again. *"And years!"* she added.

"He tried to be again," Pam went on, to Jerry's uneasiness. . . . "But they said he was—"

"I should think so," Beth said. "But it was wonderful, Uncle Jerry. Perfectly wonderful." She looked at Jerry. "And cute," she added. "Terribly cute."

"They turned me down on account of my eyes," Jerry said coldly. He looked coldly at his nieces. "I'm eligible to the draft," he informed them. "They just haven't got around to me."

The nieces looked sceptical. Then Margie understood and nodded.

"It goes up to sixty-five now," she reminded her sister.

It was time. Mr. North thought to himself, that little girls—even nicely developed little girls—were in bed. In a moment he would be annoyed at them.

"I am in the second registration," he told the girls, with annoyed dignity. "There's nothing to keep me out of the army." He paused. "Except my eyes, perhaps," he added.

"And me," Pam said.

Beth nodded, consolingly. She said, "Of course."

"You're really quite young, Uncle Jerry," she said. "I mean, *really*."

"That's—" Jerry North began, with acerbity. Pam intervened.

"You know," she said, "I think I'm sleepy. And I'm sure Margie and Li—Beth are, aren't you, girls."

She looked at them commandingly and they exchanged glances. They looked at Mr. North and then quickly at each other, and then Beth said:

"Of course, Aunt Pam. Of course we are."

Then both girls looked at Jerry again. Their looks said that, at his age, he needed all the rest he could get. Their looks said that they were being considerate of the aged. Jerry got ready to speak, but Pamela cut in quickly. She said she hoped the girls wouldn't mind the guest bed being only three-quarters—"on account of the room," she added—and that she would show them where their towels were. She looked at Jerry anxiously, and he grinned at her. So that was all right. She took the nieces off.

When she came back, Jerry was stretched out in a

chair, his legs extended and a cigarette in one hand. He did, Mrs. North thought, look rather tired. She looked at him carefully. He didn't look at all old, she decided. Except, she added honestly, to the very young. Jerry's unoccupied hand hung down beside the chair and its fingers tickled Ruffy, who was lying on her back and wriggling in ecstasy. Ruffy stretched languorously and looked up at her favorite human with brimming eyes.

"Mrs. Williams!" Pamela North said suddenly. Jerry looked at her in surprise, saw she was looking at Ruffy, and looked at Ruffy too.

"Not really," he said. "How cute."

"Jerry!" Pam said. "After all they're just children." She paused. "Innocent," she said. "Really innocent. Even with the sailors. And with Ruffy it's cute, but Mrs. Williams— After all, Mrs. Williams hasn't been— I mean, it's different with humans. Not so—sweet."

Jerry North looked up at her, smiling.

"I saw Mrs. Williams," he assured her. "It must have been just a resemblance." He looked down at Ruffy, and into her liquid eyes. "It couldn't have been Mrs. Williams," he said, with more confidence. "I saw her."

"So did I," Pam told him. "At the Roundabout. The night you thought we ought to see some of the places people talk about so much. Like the Stork. And El Capitan."

"Morocco," Jerry told her. "I was there, and I didn't."

"You," Pam told him, "were looking at the girl without any clothes. The dancer. With the skinny legs."

"Well," Mr. North said, judicially. "Skinny?"

Pam looked at him.

"Of course," she said, "they do say it's the dangerous age. For men."

"Do they—Beth?" Mr. North said. "Or was it

Margie? And they weren't skinny. Just—slender."

"All right," Pam said. "Jerry—are the girls going to be all right? Or an awful responsibility?"

"All right," Jerry told her. "*And* a responsibility. They're sweet children, but they're curious. Naturally. Weren't you?"

"Terribly," Pam admitted. She thought it over, and looked worried. "From about ten," she said. "I sometimes wonder."

Jerry told her that she needn't. It was natural. And Beth and Margie were of an age to wonder, and reach out inquiring fingers toward the fire. And to draw fingers back and run back to childhood at the faintest actual heat.

"How do you know?" Pam asked. Jerry shrugged.

"I can't prove it," he said. "But that's the way they are. It sticks out all over them. Don't worry, Pam." He diverted her. "About Mrs. Williams," he said.

"Oh," Pam said. "She was like Ruffy." She looked at Ruffy, still languorous on her back. "In essence," she amplified. "She'd had some drinks and she was with a man she liked and—you know. She looked it. Only, more than most people. In public, anyway. Enough more to notice. And when I saw her today, it didn't seem possible. But it was, so there's something—something odd. A discrepancy. Isn't there?"

If she was right, Jerry admitted, there was a discrepancy. If she was right, Mrs. Williams was not what one at first sight guessed her to be. But that was all it came to. It had nothing to do with them.

"Or with Sproul," he added. "Unless Sproul was the man?"

"Oh no," Pam said. "It wasn't Mr. Sproul. It wasn't anybody—anybody concerned, I mean. It was just a man. Rather good looking, with a straight nose and broad shoulders and—"

"Well," Jerry North said, "they do say it's the dangerous age. For women."

Pam made a face at him. She said that, being human,

a girl couldn't help noticing. She said she didn't really like straight noses.

"Yours is much better," she told him. "Why doesn't it matter? If somebody is strange—not what they should be—in a murder case, it always matters. Bill says so."

"All right, darling," Jerry said. "It matters, Mrs. Williams killed Mr. Sproul because she made calf eyes at a man with straight shoulders and a broad nose. And I'm going to bed."

Pam said she didn't see how he could, with so much going on, but all right and she would be along in a minute. Jerry went and as he undressed reflected hazily on his own psychological vagaries. Because, Jerry thought, I am not feeling at all the way I should expect myself to feel. I ought to be stirred up and excited, because of Sproul's murder, and I am merely tired and rather sleepy and—yes, relaxed.

Remarkably relaxed, Jerry thought, stretching out in the twin bed nearest the door. Which merely proved that a man's own nerves were shamefully egocentric and that they didn't, really, care at all what happened to other people. Whatever the mind may say, Jerry reflected, dreamily.

Because, he thought, my nerves are lying down and purring because the speech is all over. It doesn't matter how it ended, or what happened to Sproul, because my nerves don't give a damn about anybody but me. A nerve's love, Jerry thought; there's nothing in the world like the love of a nerve for its body. Whistler's nerve. It isn't that I'm callous, really, but just that my nerves don't care. If it came down to it, I'd make a speech every day to keep anybody from being murdered and anybody would, but that isn't what the nerves care about. The nerves are primo—prime—the nerves don't give a twinge what happens to anybody else and—

"What?" Jerry's mind came back, bumping, from the stream of sleepiness in which it was floating.

"Are you asleep?" Pam asked again. "Because if you are I don't want to wake you and I'll be very quiet. Only I want to know what you *really* think."

"Think?" Jerry said.

"You *were* asleep," Pam said. "Go right back."

"Think about *what?*" Jerry demanded.

"Never mind, dear," Pam said. "We'll talk about it in the morning."

Apparently Pam had come in and undressed while he was thinking about his nerves, because now she was in the other bed. Jerry sat up in his bed and looked at her excitedly.

"Think about what?" he demanded. "Think about what, for heaven's sake?"

"What?" Pam said, a little mistily. "Jerry. I was just getting set to sleep, like a bud."

"Bud?" Jerry repeated, running a hand through his hair. "What do I think about a bud?"

"Never mind," Pam said. "You're sleeping. I can tell. I mean sleep was setting like a bud; like a plant getting set to bud. We'll talk about it in the morning."

Jerry took a firm grip on himself, beginning with his hair. He spoke slowly and carefully. He said, "Listen, dear."

"Listen, dear," Jerry said. "I was asleep. You wake me up to ask what I think. Then you talk about a bud. Then you say wait until morning. What is all this?"

"Go to sleep, darling," Pam said. "You'll wake the nieces." Then she listened. Then she said, "Why, *Jerry!*"

Jerry turned on the light.

"What," he said, "do I think about what?" He said it with a kind of grim resolution.

"Oh," Pam said. "I've almost for—oh, Mrs. Williams, I guess. Do you think she murdered Mr. Sproul?"

"No," Jerry said. "I do not think she murdered Mr. Sproul."

"I do," Pam said. "Or maybe I don't, really. But I think she's eligible. Because of the discrepancy. But I want to go to sleep now. We'll talk about it in the morning."

"Pam," Jerry said.

"Please, darling," Pam said. "Not tonight. I'm just ready to fall off. Can't it wait until morning? Then we'll talk as much as you want to. About Mrs. Williams and buds and everything. I've had *such* a day, Jerry. Nieces and—everything."

The last word unexpectedly trailed off. Jerry waited a moment and realized there was no doubt about it. Pamela had, with the graceful ease of a young cat, gone to sleep while she was still talking. Jerry looked at her and thought she looked very nice and turned off the light and lay down. He lay very quietly, ready to welcome sleep. He lay for a long time, ready to welcome sleep, and listened to Pam's easy, sleepy breathing and waited for his nerves to relax. And he had never, he grimly discovered, felt more wide awake in his life. There was nothing to indicate that he was ever going to sleep again.

He did, eventually. Not really very long after the banjo clock struck two, in tones to waken the dead.

An hour or more earlier Bill Weigand swept his notes together, wadded them into a pocket and said they might as well call it a night. At that time he knew that Loretta Shaw had gone downtown to her apartment in Bank Street; that George Schwartz had seen her there and taken the subway back uptown, presumably for his long vacant chair on a copy desk rim, and that Mr. Bandelman Jung, with slightly suspicious skill, had lost his tail in the Grand Central Station. Or had he not been skilful, but merely done, unsuspectingly and by chance, one of the things with which no detective, however able, can single-handedly cope?

Bill Weigand took Dorian, who was waiting, and drove downtown in the Buick to their new apartment just off Washington Square, and within a block or two of the Norths'. Dorian's head subsided on his shoulder after a few blocks, and he looked down at her fondly and wished for a world in which there were fewer murders to distract a man from things which were really important. And he thought, ruefully, that when—and if—Deputy Chief Inspector Artemus O'Malley discovered what had happened to Sproul's lecture notes there might be, for him, markedly fewer murders. Then he brightened. Perhaps O'Malley would then approve his resignation, and he could take the intelligence majority which the army dangled in front of him. If O'Malley did, the Commissioner might make an exception to his stern rule that resignations from the force for army duty were unacceptable.

7

Friday, 3:15 A.M. to 10:20 A.M.

It happened, Bill Weigand afterward argued to himself, because it was too early in the case for anything to happen. It was after you had a line, when you were beginning to put the heat on, that, as a policeman, you needed to watch your step. Not when you had merely some rather confusing information about some people who had known a man who might have been murdered. Or maybe, Weigand had to add: it happened merely because he was himself half asleep. But however it happened, it was hard to forgive.

It began at 3:15 in the morning with a ringing which Weigand, inured as a general practitioner to inconvenient summonses, at first supposed to be related to the telephone. He reached the telephone with one hand, without waking up, and answered it before he realized that the ringing continued. So it was the doorbell. Weigand waited a moment longer and Dorian said, "Something's ringing, Bill."

"Right," Bill said, and climbed sleepily out of bed and groped for the door release button, in its unfamiliar location in the new apartment. He found it, started to press it, and remembered his own advice to the Norths, who lived in a similar walkup: "Always call down before you click."

"Hello," Weigand yelled into the transmitter embedded in the black box. "Who is it?"

The black box said something unrecognizable in an amorphous voice. *"What?"* Weigand called.

"Message," the voice said. "Headquarters."

Or that was, afterward, what Weigand thought the voice said. In any event, it was at the time as much as his own voice was worth to try for more specific information. He had followed advice; he had called before he clicked. He clicked and, two flights down, heard the outside door open. He waited, trying to come awake, during the time it would take a messenger from headquarters to climb to their floor. Then, as innocently as any civilian, Lieutenant William Weigand, acting captain in the Homicide Squad, opened his own front door and stuck his head out. He supposed, afterward, that he stuck his head out with some faint idea of confining the conversation to the outer hall, thus not disturbing Dorian more than needed to be.

There was no conversation. There was an explosion somewhere, and an instant of dizziness and not quite time for an instant of nausea. And then there was nothing. And then there was violent pain in the head, and a longer period of dizziness and the groping realization that he had been expertly knocked out by someone who had—yes, fingers confirmed the guess—laid a blackjack behind his left ear. Just hard enough, not quite too hard.

Weigand's mind swirled for a moment in darkness; darkness eddied around him. Then, when he knew he was conscious, the darkness remained. It was objective darkness. He was lying on a carpet. He was lying on the hall carpet in his own apartment and the hall was black.

Weigand staggered as he stood up and groped on a half familiar wall for a light switch, and then he remembered. Then, in a tight voice, he called "Dorian!" and, when there was no answer, *"Dorian!"* And then he thought he heard a moan.

The light came on. He was alone in the hall. He was

running the short length of the empty hall toward the bedroom, and terror was running with him—riding in his mind, clutching at his throat. *"Dorian!"* he called again, and his voice was desperate.

Dorian lay across her bed, slender and motionless, her curved body quiet under thin silk. Weigand was beside her, and fear was cold in his chest, before she moaned again. It was a faint moan, but it was a sound for which Bill Weigand would have prayed if there had been time for prayer. Then Dorian's eyes opened, and the green was clear in them, and they were puzzled.

"Bill!" Dorian Weigand said, and her tone was strange and puzzled. "Bill. What made you hit me?"

It was all right then, or in a few minutes it was all right. Because now Bill Weigand, without ceasing to be a terrified lover, became a reasoning policeman with an ingrained knowledge of contusions and lacerations, and almost a physician's knowledge of what to do about them first. Dorian had only a contusion. Somebody had laid a blackjack neatly, with just the force needed, behind her right ear.

"We're going to have a fine pair of headaches," Bill told her, holding her in his arms.

"Going to?" Dorian said, still a little faintly. "Going to? If it wasn't you, who was it?"

That, Weigand thought, becoming almost all policeman, was certainly the point. Who had walked into the apartment of a police lieutenant, knocked out the lieutenant and the lieutenant's wife, and proceeded to— But what had he proceeded to do? Bill Weigand laid his wife gently down on the bed again, turned on the lights and looked at her to be sure she was all right, and decided she was fine any way you looked at her, and searched the room with his eyes.

Apparently the invader who thought nothing of knocking out policemen and the wives of policemen had, thereafter, done nothing at all. The room showed no signs of any invader. Weigand looked puzzled, and felt puzzled, and stepped down the hall and turned on the lights in the living room. All was serene. His dressing-room study was likewise unmarked by invasion. He left the kitchen until later and returned. He said it was damned funny. He looked around the room again, and saw his suit jacket hanging on the back of a chair.

"Damn!" he said again, and crossed to it. He rammed his hand into the pocket where he had put his notes, and the hand came out clutching a sheaf of papers. Not even that—

Then the papers felt wrong and he looked at them. He stared at them unbelievingly and made low, angry sounds.

"What is it?" Dorian said, sitting up. "Ouch!"

"It will go away," Bill told her. "We'll try aspirin after a bit. The so-and-so took my notes."

"Notes?" Dorian said. "The ones you made tonight."

"Right," Bill said. "The ones I made tonight. But he made a fair exchange."

"Which is no robbery," Dorian told him. "Of what, Bill?"

"This," Bill said, waving it. "The notes Sproul made for his lecture. The notes somebody grabbed earlier when I was asleep at the switch." He stared at her unhappily. "Which," he said, "is where I seem to stay. Damn."

"Get me some aspirin, Bill," Dorian told him. "I can't think. Can you?"

He didn't, Bill Weigand told her, want to. He had no pleasant thoughts. He got the aspirin and a glass of water. They took aspirin and water. Weigand sat on the edge of the bed, holding the water glass angled in his hand, so that the little water remaining began comfortably to drip to the carpet. He shook his head, said "Ouch!" and remarked that he didn't get it.

"Somebody," he said, "goes to all the trouble of stealing the lecture notes. A little dark man, presumably. He finds out they aren't what he wants. So what does he do? Throw them away? No, he goes to a lot of trouble to see that I get them back, but in exchange he steals the notes I made this evening. Which won't do him any good that I can see. What kind of a murderer is that?"

"I don't know," Dorian said. "Maybe it isn't one. Maybe it's somebody who's just—sort of curious."

"He's sure as hell curious," Weigand said. "He's curious in a big way."

"Will your notes do him any good?" Dorian wanted to know.

Weigand said he couldn't think of any. They were merely jottings, taken to fix in his mind certain points he thought might prove important. They amounted to a kind of summary of the verbatim notes Mullins had taken. Gaining them did the intruder no good that Weigand could think of, and did him no harm.

"Beyond the considerable embarrassment," he said, grinning without great amusement.

They thought about it.

"All I can see," Dorian said, "is that it's somebody who wants to keep abreast of things. Know how the investigation is going, and what people say. And—" She broke off, and looked puzzled.

"And," Bill finished for her, "wants me to keep abreast of things, too. Or he wouldn't have returned the lecture notes."

"Maybe," Dorian suggested, "it's another detective. From a rival firm."

She said it lightly and then stopped rather suddenly and looked at her husband with an intent expression. He looked back, touched his bruise, reflective, and said, "Ouch!" Then he heard her.

"A rival firm," he repeated, and their eyes shared a theory. "Now do you suppose there's a rival firm interested in Mr. Sproul? Who just came out of Paris on the run?"

Then his eyes held a doubtful expression.

"It doesn't figure," he said. "Because this guy's

being helpful. To me. He wants me to read Sproul's notes." He looked at them. "So," he said, "I guess I'd better do what he wants."

Pamela North awakened first and reached for the watch on the table between the beds. The watch said it was 8:15. Pamela thought herself over and decided that she felt fine.

"I think I'll get up," she announced and waited. There was a little pause and then Jerry, from a long distance off, said, "Huh?"

"I think I'll get up," Pam North repeated.

"Do," Jerry said. "Come back in an hour and let me know how it works out."

"It's almost nine o'clock," Mrs. North told her husband. "Aren't you going in today?"

"Later," Mr. North said. "A good deal later, please. Because—oh, damn!"

"What?" Mrs. North said. "Damn what?"

"Sproul," Mr. North told her. "Or—I don't mean Sproul really."

"No," Mrs. North said. "That's out of our hands. You mean about Sproul."

"I'll have to tell them at the office," Mr. North said. "They'll be—"

"Interested," Mrs. North said. "Don't they read the papers?"

"—upset," Mr. North finished. "Obviously, darling. But they'll expect me to mention it. I mean, our most popular author dies on a lecture platform just after I've introduced him and I'll have to say something about it, obviously. Something like, 'By the way, too bad about poor old Sproul, wasn't it. You could have knocked me over with the gavel.' Something like that. Oh, lord!"

"What?" Mrs. North said, preparing to get up.

"The number of times I'll have to tell all about it," Jerry North said, with a slight moan in his voice. "From T. G. down."

"To Y. Z.," Mrs. North suggested, stepping out of pajamas and looking at herself in the long door mirror. "I'm gaining again, I'm afraid. What happened to A. B.?"

"Fired," Mr. North said, looking at her appreciatively. "I don't see it."

"Here," Mrs. North said, slapping herself there. "I always liked to think of A. B. up there, busy as—"

"All right," Mr. North told her. "Not before breakfast. Anyway, I think it's something to throw to the nieces."

"Oh, lord!" Mrs. North said. She stood on one foot, ready to put the other through her girdle, and stared at Mr. North. "I forgot all about them." She looked at him reproachfully. "I was feeling so good," she added. "And you brought up the nieces."

"Really, Pam," Jerry said. "I didn't."

Pamela North finished with the girdle, wriggling.

"They're nice, of course," she said. "And I love them. I guess. Only a whole day with the nieces. Fighting off sailors, probably. Why do you suppose sailors?"

"Sailors are fine," Jerry told her. "I was a sailor once."

"You must have been cute," Pam said. "I wish I'd known you then."

"Nobody knew me then," Mr. North said, morosely. "Even my best friends. They're nice girls, Pam. A little—well, maybe a little inexperienced. If they happen to run into a—well, a troublesome sailor they'll scoot for home. And most sailors will understand. Even if they do look older." He paused. "Beth particularly," he noted. "She's—appreciably older."

"Yes," Mrs. North said, "except maybe her mind. And you and Bill will be hunting murderers and I'll just be showing the nieces Grant's Tomb. Do you suppose they'll like Grant's Tomb?"

"No," Jerry said. "Try Twenty-one. Or the Algonquin bar."

"I always feel under water in the Algonquin bar," Mrs. North noted, finishing a second stocking and twisting to see the seam in the mirror. "And anyway, not bars."

Jerry said he supposed not and swung out of bed.

"I still think you ought to get cold," Mrs. North observed, looking at him. "No, I suppose not bars. What do you really think about my Mrs. Williams theory."

We hadn't, Jerry told her, been thinking about it at all. He would. He paused, clad now in shorts, and assumed an expression of thought.

"Not much," he said.

"No," Pam said. "It doesn't seem so good this morning. But still— Still, it was funny. And one funny thing leads to another."

Murder, Jerry pointed out, wasn't funny. Pam told him not to stickle.

"Strange," she said. "Abnormal. Twisted."

Jerry North really thought about Mrs. Williams. The word "twisted" seemed to have started him.

"Assuming," he said, "that you haven't made a mistake, that it was really Mrs. Williams you saw." He nodded at Pam. "And I think it was," he said, rather hurriedly. "I know you don't make mistakes, of that kind. Assuming it was Mrs. Williams, it does indicate that Mrs. Williams isn't what she appears to be."

"What she's arranged to appear to be," Pam told him. "Because if ever I saw a woman who arranged—"

"Arranged to appear to be," Mr. North agreed. "But it would be easy to carry the assumption too far. Anywhere you'd carry it, without knowing more, would be too far. Maybe she's just a girl with a yen, who has another side to face the world with. As per Browning. Maybe it's just another instance of murder—of any sudden, violent, interruption of ordinary things—cutting through lives and showing you cross-sections."

He looked at Pam, who was pulling her dress down.

It was a sheer woolen dress in pale orange. Or something Mr. North decided he would call pale orange. Pam looked at herself in the mirror.

"Probably," she said. "I smell bacon. Martha's here." She looked at Jerry thoughtfully. "Still," she said. "You'll have to admit that it's funny about Mrs. Williams. Whatever you say. It's a discrepancy."

Jerry said all right, it was a discrepancy. He plugged in his electric razor, and its buzz shut him off from the outer world. Pam watched him for a moment and went out of the bedroom. The table was set up in the dining room corner of the living room, and set properly for four. In the kitchen there was a reassuring sound of pans in action. Pamela looked in.

The nieces sat side by side on a single chair, which was the only chair available, and watched Martha, with anticipation. The two young cats sat on the floor, their tails wrapped carefully around them, and looked up at Martha hopefully. It was, Pam decided, a pretty picture.

"But tautological, somehow," she said. "They all look just the same, essentially. I'll certainly have to keep an eye out for strange dogs."

"Aunt Pam," Beth said. "It's raining. What do we do today?"

It was, Pam admitted to herself, a question. She found an unexpected answer.

"One thing," she said, "I'm going to take you to lunch at a very interesting place."

"That will be nice," Margie said, politely.

Nice wasn't, Pam thought, precisely the right word for the Roundabout. But it wouldn't be un-nice, at least for luncheon. It wasn't, of course, really a luncheon place. It was merely a point from which a wild goose chase might be started.

"But," Pam said to herself, "I've got to begin somewhere. Because I still think there's something in it."

She looked at the nieces. They were darlings, of

course. But they were obviously going to cramp her style.

Lieutenant Weigand drove to his office morosely, through driving rain. He wanted more sleep, his head ached and he felt peculiarly incompetent. He also felt a grumbling desire to get his hands on the man—little and dark, or large and pale—who had provided both the headache and the conviction of inadequacy. He picked up newspapers and carried them to his office and regarded them without favor. Even with the war, the sudden and mysterious death of Victor Leeds Sproul was being well noticed. Top heads, front page, even in the *Times*. That would make Deputy Chief Inspector Artemus O'Malley sit up and take notice.

Weigand sat down, rubbed his head reflectively and spread out the lecture notes which his assailant had left in exchange. Fair exchange hell, Weigand told himself. I owe him a large bump. He felt his bump. A very large bump, he told himself. The telephone rang. Weigand said, "Yes, Inspector," into it and went down the corridor to beard O'Malley. O'Malley said it looked as if he'd got into something.

"Again," the Inspector added, puffing a little. He regarded the lieutenant with accusation. "See those Norths are still around," he remarked. "Maybe we'd better swear them in."

It was, Weigand told him, mere accident. It simply happened. O'Malley said it seemed to happen a good deal. The thought evidently did not amuse O'Malley, who continued to look upon Weigand without affection. Then Inspector O'Malley rallied.

"All right," Inspector O'Malley said. "Got to get on with it, Lieutenant. Let's have it."

Weigand let him have it. He omitted the invasion of the night. There was no use upsetting O'Malley. When he finished, O'Malley looked at him and said, "What the hell?"

"He bumped himself," O'Malley announced. "Whoever heard of morphine in a homicide?"

Weigand pointed out that it was an odd way to commit suicide—an odd time and an odd place; an action oddly without reason so far determined.

"You think somebody got him?" O'Malley wanted to know. "It's a hell of a lot funnier way to kill somebody."

Weigand agreed with that. Still, considering everything, he thought it was murder. He realized that he was holding back; that he had been sure it was murder ever since things had gone bump in the night. But there are some things about lieutenants that inspectors should never learn. The inspector would not like to hear that somebody had entered Weigand's apartment, knocked out Weigand and Mrs. Weigand, and gone his way at leisure. It would arouse doubts in the inspector. It aroused doubts in Weigand.

"They're giving it a play," O'Malley noticed, waving at a newspaper on his desk. "Quite a play, considering. We won't look so bright if it turns out suicide."

O'Malley liked to look bright in the newspapers. He liked sentences which began: "Deputy Chief Inspector Artemus O'Malley of the Homicide Squad, in charge of the investigation of the death of Victor Leeds Sproul, said today—" He regarded it as the duty of Acting Captain Weigand to provide him with appropriate things to say. It was the role of an acting captain.

"It's murder," Weigand told him.

O'Malley hinted that Weigand had better be right. He said that, assuming it was murder, who? This—this Bandelman Tchung?

"Jung," Weigand said. "Not Tchung."

The inspector looked at him aggrieved.

"Call that a name?" he wanted to know.

Weigand shook his head.

"I think he made it up," he agreed.

"He's your man," O'Malley said, with conviction. "Bandelman Tchung. My God!"

You couldn't, Weigand pointed out, arrest a man merely because you didn't believe in his name. O'Malley, red of face, rectified this misconception. You could arrest a man for anything and make him spill it. In the old days— The trouble with you young cops is—

"Baby 'em," O'Malley said. "That's what it is. Baby 'em. When I was your age, Bill—"

Weigand listened with expressions of interest. At proper moments he nodded. When once O'Malley paused for a word, Lieutenant Weigand provided it. "Squeamish." Several times Weigand said, "Right." After a time O'Malley quieted himself.

"Well," he said, "what're you going to do? Sit here all day passing? Get on with it, Lieutenant. Get on with it!"

"Right," Weigand said. "Any special lines?"

Did he, O'Malley wanted to know, have to do everything himself? Did he have to lead Weigand by the hand?

"Right," Weigand said. Arty was in fine form. It cheered Weigand to discover in O'Malley an unchanging verity. Weigand left. O'Malley lighted a cigar, put his feet up, and returned to the sports pages.

Weigand stared at Sproul's lecture notes. He laid them aside and stared at reports, which were incomplete. Unless Loretta Shaw had gone out of a rear window of her apartment in Bank Street and climbed down a fire escape ladder, she had not showed up around 3 o'clock to slug Bill Weigand and Dorian. She was accounted for, the accounting rendered by a detective who had got himself surprisingly wet in the process. It had begun to rain at around 4 o'clock, if Headquarters was interested. Jung was back in his lodging in a rooming house in the West Forties, but it was not quite clear when he had arrived. Somebody had slipped up, there. The others—the Akrons,

Schwartz, Burden, Ralph White and such unlikely sluggers as Mrs. Paul Williams and Dr. Dupont, might have done anything, having been unobserved.

Sproul had died of an overdose of morphine, and had had a moderately bad heart. That made it official. He had been male, white and weighed 210 pounds; in life he had been six feet, one inch tall. He had been—

Weigand grew interested. Sproul had been born in Centerburg, Iowa, in 1896. His father had run a feed store. Sproul had gone to school in Centerburg and to high school and, the feed business apparently proving profitable, to the state university.

He had been—and Weigand lifted eyebrows in amusement—graduated from the School of Agriculture. So Victor Leeds Sproul, the suave taster of the elegant, was a farmer at heart. Apparently it had remained at heart; there was no record that he had farmed. He had been drafted in the other war, but had not got overseas. He had, however, got to New York. The record thereafter was incomplete; men were working on it. It was slow work, his parents being dead and Centerburg being far off. But there were ways, and they were being tried. Even with the most likely avenue—the official records of the French Republic— closed, there were ways. There would be people who had known Sproul when. There were always people who had known everybody when. But it might take time to find them.

This didn't, Weigand thought, looking out the window at the streaming rain, look like being a quick one. There was a good deal, come down to it, to be said for the family murder, with suspects conveniently cooped together. Or, if you were to have murder, for any circumstances similarly restricting. This one looked like being all over the place. However. . . .

He left the other dossiers, most of them incomplete but growing, until later. He spread the dozen sheets of Sproul's lecture notes out in front of him and began a scrutiny. He began it hopefully, sustained by a the-

ory—the theory of the most likely. Assuming Sproul
had been murdered, as and when he was, the most
likely reason was that he had been about to say something in his lecture which somebody did not want said.
If that proved true, it would explain a good deal of the
good deal which needed explanation.

Sproul had planned to begin, it appeared, with in-
nocuous praise of a people and of a nation and of a
nation's way of life. "Centuries look down," he had
evidently planned to quote, and he had capitalized
"Continuity of time." You could reconstruct, Weigand
found—in Paris, as you went about your foolish business in her streets, history looked down on you from
ancient buildings and echoed in famous streets; along
this road Villon had walked and great kings ridden;
down this crooked lane you might have heard an-
guished cries on the eve of St. Bartholomew's Day and
here tumbrils jounced on cobbles. You drew from
these things, Sproul might have been going to say, a
renewed sense of the continuity of life and of civilization, and perhaps he might have meant to add that
barbarians had been this way before, and vanished
finally, leaving no trace.

There was nothing in this, as it appeared, to prompt
murder. It might have been eloquent, if Sproul was
eloquent, and probably he was. It might also, like most
eloquent things, have been a little obvious at the core.
But audiences had grown exigent if they murdered to
deflect the obvious. Weigand turned to the next page.
Sproul had, about there, planned to come down to the
present. History lived in these streets and buildings;
so did the contemporary. "Heard of the Left Bank—
maybe too much," one note ran. "Apologize—but
lived there many years—it, too, part of way of life
gone" . . . "Variety of people . . . all over world.
Spoon River. . . ."

That was not so obvious. Spoon River? Weigand
looked at it. Spoon River?

The Spoon River Anthology, of course; the only Spoon River of which Weigand had ever heard. Edgar Lee Masters. But Masters, about then, had been living, Weigand dimly recalled—having known a man who knew a man—in New York. At a rather odd place in Sixteenth Street, the man who knew a man had said. And—but of course it was obvious. Sproul had intended, almost certainly, to do his own *Spoon River Anthology* on the people he had known in the Paris days. He would say—or would that be too obvious? Weigand's eyes traveled on. It had not been too obvious. Seine River Anthology. Weigand's interest quickened.

Brief, probably acid, summaries of lives. That would be the idea. Not in free verse, one could assume; prose vignettes, quite possibly intended to take the skin off and hang it to the barn door. A project to which skin owners might be expected to object. Names? Weigand's eyes went on. Not names. Letters. The inevitable Mr. A., the infinitely to be expected Miss B. Here—and then Weigand's eyes stopped abruptly and he made a pessimistic remark about his ultimate future. He made it in a tone of honest surprise.

Somebody had been ahead of him, and that he had known. But he had not supposed that his predecessor through the pages of Mr. Sproul's notes would leave markers, as if Weigand were following a paper chase. But that was what his predecessor had done. He had drawn, of all things, a little arrow pointing toward "Mr. A." and he had gone to the further trouble of underlining the notes which apparently referred to Mr. A. Faint pencil marks called Lieutenant Weigand's attention.

Somebody, and evidently somebody who held Weigand's intelligence in notably low esteem, wanted to make matters very clear. Somebody wanted to be helpful. The police department had enlisted, quite without volition, an anonymous assistant. Weigand, after again remarking that he would be damned, followed the penciled lines. The notes here read:

"Odd people among—give some examples—all like a bit of gossip. . . . Mr. A., example—farm boy from Iowa—educated crop rotation—by wits" (Lived by wits?)—"authority on sophistication—but used to sneak off—"

"Hell," Weigand said. There was nothing there; nothing but a joke on the audience. Mr. Sproul had started his anthology with a vignette of Mr. Sproul. Very comical; very—ingrained was the word. A man for the secret joke, the no longer joking Mr. Sproul. Why had the anonymous adviser thought it worth while to draw Weigand's attention to Mr. A.? Unless— Weigand paused to consider the "unless." Unless the adviser, who presumably was the same person who had used a blackjack on the Weigands, wanted to indicate that Mr. Sproul was Mr. Sproul's own murderer. Or unless Mr. A. only appeared to be Mr. Sproul, so that references to him constituted a joke within a joke. The idea intensified Weigand's headache and he stared broodingly at the typed notes. He shrugged and returned to them.

Where Mr. A. had sneaked was to one of the American style restaurants which used to dot Paris in the tourist days, where the homesick might get ham and eggs and, if fortune favored acutely, corn on the cob. That was the secret about Mr. A., apparently—the yearning of the Iowa farm boy for the products of the Iowa farm. Not a vital secret, on the surface. No more revealing, in essence, than would be the yearning of a boy from Marseilles for bouillabaisse. Although Americans of a certain habit of thought might think it revealed more. Mr. A. was, he would take it, Mr. Sproul himself and Mr. Sproul had not murdered Mr. Sproul to keep him from giving Mr. Sproul away. Weigand reached in his pocket, took out a flat box of aspirins, and swallowed a few. He went on to Miss B.

Miss B. was also underlined. Weigand let his eyes
hurry along; they were all underlined; all these alpha-
betical anonymities. The adviser had played no favor-
ites. He went back to Miss B. The notes were cryptic,
which was understandable. Too cryptic? There was
that discouraging possibility. However—

"Miss B. L. Bounti. Tourist came to stay . . . artists
and writers—WRITERS—circumspect. Br. Lovely
lady—curious tastes—surprising under braids . . .
CUT LOOSE."

What, on this framework, had Sproul planned to
build? It was less than a framework; less than a blueprint. It was a penciled rough, such as an architect
might sketch to remind himself of plans he might some
day make . . . Miss B.? Weigand read it again. Braids?
A little girl with braids, who had cut loose in Paris and
revealed curious tastes? Paris was, or had been, a
place for those with curious tastes—for circumspect
young women who had a surprising "b" under braids.
Brain? Or "bees" as in "bees in her bonnet?" But it
would come to the same thing. And was "br" again
"brains" or was it—any one of a hundred other words.
"Bright," perhaps—perhaps she was a bright young
lady. Or perhaps she merely had a brother. Or was
brillig. 'Twas brillig and the jabberwock . . . To hell
with it!

A circumspect young woman who wore her hair in
braids— Then Weigand remembered. Jean Akron's
blond hair was coiled in braids around her head,
unfashionably but with effectiveness. And she had a
brother—she certainly had a brother. And you would
call her circumspect; it was possible to conclude that,
to Sproul, she would have seemed in Paris a "tourist
(who) came to stay." And was an artist or a writer?
No—who was interested in artists and writers. Particularly writers? And was there a kind of leer in the
planned reiteration of one of the varieties of mankind
in which Miss B. was interested? Was there a kind of
leer in the whole passage devoted to her; a kind of

122   *Frances & Richard Lockridge*

slyness, that hinted of hints to come? Hints, could it remotely be, about Miss B. and her brother?

What had Sproul planned to say about Jean Akron, assuming, as it seemed reasonable to assume, that Jean Akron was Miss B.? Something Jean or her brother might have gone to considerable lengths—even to great and final lengths—to prevent his saying? The notes, Weigand decided, left the matter open. They left room for speculation. It would be his duty to speculate. This much he decided: The notes on Miss B. did not, at the worst, discount his theory that Sproul might have been killed to close his mouth; to prevent his repeating, from coast to coast, something which some person would be much inconvenienced by his saying anywhere.

Weigand lighted a new cigarette and continued to Mr. C. He read:

"Mr. C. Artist all know—monkeys."

That was all it said about Mr. C. He was an artist and there was something about monkeys. Weigand stared at it and said "Damn." Mr. C. and his monkeys seemed to be new characters, making belated entrances. If Mr. C. was important, all that Weigand had so far done in listening to people, watching their faces, speculating over their inflections and the words they chose, was valueless. Which meant he would have to start over. On the other hand, he could defer Mr. C. He decided to defer Mr. C.

"Mr. D. . . . excellent nws. Boon c—very boon . . . long in P. very few knew . . . little matter of pad. ex.ac. c.e. Wd. badly in Cin."

To hell with abbreviations. "Excellent nws" indeed. Weigand stared at it. "Excellent news?" Why was Mr. D. excellent news? Mr. D. was not excellent news to Weigand; he was not news at all. "Excellent news—" "newspaperman?" That was evidently possible. And "boon c" would be, obviously boon companion, presumably of Sproul . . . "very boon" might be Sproul's way of saying that Mr. D. let himself go on occasion;

that, like Miss B., he "cut loose." He had been "long in P(aris)" and very few knew—"him?" Or "why" he had been so long in Paris? Had he remained in Paris because of a little matter of a pad. ex.ac.c.e., which, Weigand had to admit, meant nothing whatever to him at the moment. Nor did the information that Mr. D. had "wd," which presumably was "weighed" or "wanted" badly in "Cin." seem to mean much. Unless Sproul was a bad speller and had intended to say that Mr. D. had waited in sin, somewhere. Badly. That made no apparent sense.

But Weigand did have a newspaperman on his list— George Schwartz. The lanky, pleasant copy-reader who was formerly the husband of Loretta Shaw, who was to have married Sproul. And who apparently was still in love with Loretta Shaw. Or, at any rate, wanted to get his arms around her, which might be the same thing. Weigand found himself speculating absently on the nature of love and drew himself harshly back. That was no way for the mind of a detective to behave.

The door opened, and Mullins came in. Weigand looked at him absently.

"Do you ever speculate about the nature of love, Sergeant?" he inquired, in a formal voice.

Mullins stared at him and said "huh?" But he did not seem particularly surprised.

"Skip it," Weigand told him.

"Sure I do," Mullins said. "What'ja think I am, Loot? Other day, I ran into as neat a little—"

"Right," Weigand said. "You'll have to tell me about her, Sergeant. Say in about a month. Right?"

"In a month," Mullins said, "I maybe won't remember. But what the hell? Here's some more reports, Loot."

Weigand waved at the desk. He scrawled on a pad in front of him.

"Pad. ex.ac.c.e." he wrote and tossed it to Mullins.

"What does that mean, Mullins?" he inquired. "Without thinking?"

124   *Frances & Richard Lockridge*

"Padded expense accounts," Mullins said. He stared at it. "Or maybe not," he said. "I don't get the 'c.e.' part."

Weigand stared at him wonderingly.

"Mullins," he said, "you're wonderful. As Mrs. North says."

Mullins looked pleased.

"Did she, Loot?" he asked, hopefully.

"Hundreds of times," Weigand assured him. "She says, 'Mullins is wonderful.' Dorian, on the other hand—"

"O.K., Loot," Mullins said. "O.K. I bit. O.K. But it could mean that. All except the 'c.e.' "

"Exactly," Weigand told him. "You *are* wonderful. Probably it does mean that. And probably 'c.e.' means city editor. Probably it all means that Mr. D., who may be Mr. Schwartz, padded expense accounts when he was city editor of some paper in—probably in Cincinnati, where he is now badly wanted."

Weigand was pleased. Here, at any rate, was something they could check on. The Cincinnati police would cooperate; it was specific. Would Schwartz have killed Sproul because Sproul was about to reveal the peculations of Schwartz's past?

Weigand paused and thought it over, his feeling of accomplishment dwindling. It was unlikely that Schwartz would kill Sproul because Sproul knew so relatively unimportant a secret. If Schwartz was going to do any killing of Sproul, it would much more probably be over Loretta Shaw. If Schwartz killed, he might be expected to kill violently, in response to violent stimuli.

Mullins was looking down at the desk. He said, "Ain't those Sproul's notes?" and Weigand looked at him absently and nodded.

"Look," Mullins said, "I thought you lost them. I thought somebody took them."

"Somebody brought them back," Weigand told him. Mullins waited for him to go on, and he did not go on.

"Just like that?" Mullins said. "Who?"

"I don't know," Weigand said. "Somebody—sent them to me."

Mullins said that was funny. Then, after a moment, he made an addition.

"So they don't tell us anything," he said. "Or the guy wouldn't have sent them back."

Weigand held the sheets out to Mullins and showed him the marks. Mullins said it was sure funny. Weigand agreed.

Presumably, Weigand explained, it wasn't the murderer who had stolen the notes. On the contrary, they seemed to have been stolen by somebody who had, after looking them over, decided to turn assistant detective. Mullins nodded slowly.

"Only," he said, "there's always a double bluff, ain't there, Loot."

Weigand smiled at him encouragingly and nodded.

"Right, Sergeant," he said. "As you say. There's always the double bluff."

Mullins looked down at him.

"Hell," he said. "*Another* screwy one. It's those Norths again."

8

Friday, 12:15 P.M. to 2:10 P.M.

Mrs. North dialed and waited. The telephone buzzed properly and then clicked and spluttered. Absently, Mrs. North reached out and removed Ruffy's right forepaw from the telephone cradle, which Ruffy had been investigating. Mrs. North dialed again and a markedly wheedling voice said: "United States Weather Bureau forecast for New York City and vicinity: Twelve noon temperature fifty-six degrees, humidity ninety-five per cent. This afternoon and early tonight, showers. Not much change in temperature. Drive carefully and save rubber."

Mrs. North said "thank you" and remembered that Jerry told her she shouldn't, because the dulcet voice was really a recording and had no ears. But Mrs. North, although she believed this with her mind, did not really believe it, and it seemed rude to her not to say anything at all, particularly about driving carefully. Mrs. North removed Ruffy's left forepaw, which was partly wedged under the depressible bar in the telephone cradle, parked the telephone and looked out the window. A gust of wind threw rain blindingly against the window, and the window rattled.

"Showers," said Mrs. North. "Probably intended to fool the Germans."

Because this wasn't a shower. This was a deluge.

Mrs. North rephrased the weather forecast, to make it conform with the fact. "This afternoon and early tonight, deluges." Or maybe: "Occasional deluges." It would have to end: "Swim carefully; conserve life belts."

It was, Mrs. North realized, being very boring for the nieces. Here was a Saturday and their first in New York, and on Saturdays sailors came in clusters. Not, Mrs. North thought a little anxiously, that the sailors must be allowed to do Beth and Margie any good. But on a sunny day, girls could look at sailors and know that sailors were looking at them, and that probably was enough.

"It had better be," Mrs. North thought, looking out the window and thinking of the now very disturbing trust put in her by her sister. But they're really such nice little girls.

"Aunt Pam," Beth said from behind her and Mrs. North turned. Beth looked out of the window. "It rains a lot in New York, doesn't it?" she said, conversationally.

"Sometimes," Mrs. North said. "I'm sorry."

"Oh," Beth said, encouragingly, "it isn't your fault, Aunt Pam." But the exoneration sounded rather formal. "You can't help it, really. I expect it's just New York. Or the equinox."

"It's too late for the equinox," Mrs. North said. "At least I think it is. And I don't really know if there is any, Beth. To make it rain, I mean. I think it just happened to rain."

Beth looked out at the window, which streamed.

"It certainly is," she said. "I don't suppose we'll be going out, Aunt Pam. I mean, out anywhere. Like a movie."

It didn't, Pam thought, looking out the window in her turn, look much like it. But the alternative was Beth and Margie and herself and Martha, in a rather small apartment. Especially, she added to herself, Beth.

"Oh," Pam North said, "in New York people don't let it stop them. Because of the subways."

"Can we ride in the subways?" Beth said. "We never have, Aunt Pamela."

Pam said of course they could.

"But some day when it isn't raining," she said. "Today, because it's raining, we'd better take a taxi-cab."

"To a *movie?*" Beth sounded surprised. "Don't you drive your own car at all, Aunt Pam?"

"Not when it's raining, dear," Pam said. "Hardly ever in town, because you can never stop anywhere. It's really cheaper to take taxis."

Beth thought this over and looked at Pamela North with doubt. She compromised, it was evident, by saying she liked taxicabs.

"But papa says they're an extravagance," she added. "He says street cars are good enough."

"Does he, dear?" Pam said. "I expect he's right, at home. Only in New York nobody rides street cars." She thought this over. "Even when there were any," she said. "Except people who just sat in them."

Beth clearly didn't get this. Neither, Pamela North thought, do I. Exactly. But that's just what they did.

"If we're going to a movie," Beth said, after a brief, puzzled pause, "I ought to change my dress. And tell Margie to change hers. Oughtn't I, Aunt Pam?"

Pam said she thought that would be very nice. Between the beating of the rain on the window, and Beth, she felt somehow hypnotized. She rallied.

"I'll tell you what we'll do," she said. "We'll go out to lunch some place. And then a movie, if we find one. Would you like that, Beth?" She looked at Beth. "I'm sorry about the rain," Pam said.

"Oh," Beth said, "I think that will be lovely, Aunt Pam. Could we go to an Automat?"

"Well," Pam said. "Wouldn't you rather go some place else, dear. Where we can sit down?"

"Oh," Beth said, "do you have to stand up in the Automat?"

"You have to walk around," Pam told her. "And it's hard with an umbrella. I think today we won't go to the Automat. Although we will, while you're here." She smiled at Beth, feeling an unexpected kinship. "I used to like them too," she said. "Jerry and I used to eat in them a lot." She smiled, in reminiscence. "I was always thinking the cup would come out too," she said. "And so the coffee went down the drain, of course."

It was a funny remembrance, and the remembrance of Jerry's face when he saw her face as the coffee flowed uninterrupted from the spigot made it even funnier. She looked at Beth and saw the effortful smile on Beth's face and remembered.

"Of course," she said, "you don't know how they work. It wouldn't be funny to you. But it was funny to us."

"Oh," Beth said, "I'm sure it was, Aunt Pamela. It must have been very funny."

This conversation, Pam told herself, is unbelievable. It must be the rain. She turned briskly from the window.

"You and Margie get dressed," she directed. "We'll go out to lunch, to some nice place, and then to a movie. I'll tell you—we'll go to the Roundabout."

"Oh," Beth said. It occurred to Pam that Beth said "Oh" so often because it made her lips look as if they were prepared for a kiss. Pam rejected this speculation, but without finality; she deferred the speculation. "Oh," Beth said, "that will be lovely, Aunt Pam. Is the Roundabout a nice place?"

That, Pam thought, was certainly a question. Since she was taking the girls to the Roundabout primarily because she had once seen a woman who might be a murderer languishing publicly over a man who might be anything, and was certainly not the kind of man little girls should know, it was hard to tell even herself that the Roundabout was "nice." The Roundabout was, in a sense, all things to all people, but more to them in the evening than at luncheon time. But that would be hard to explain to Beth.

Really, Pam thought, the Roundabout was at least two places. At luncheon it was just a pretty good place for luncheon, with a trio including a xylophone. At night it was a place with a floor show, and not really a good place. She and Jerry had gone to see what it was like; it was a place you went to to see what it was like. But that, also, would be complicated to explain to Beth. To Beth, Pam noted, and also now to Margie, who had appeared behind her sister.

"Very nice," Pam said. "It's really very nice, Beth."

Why was it, Pam wondered, that when you praised anything twice in the same words, you inferentially condemned it? She would have to ask Jerry. He would have a theory. He always had theories.

"Very nice," Pam repeated, more firmly than ever. "Change your things, children."

After the simplicity of rain, the Roundabout was surprising. It was too bright and too big, and there were too many mirrors; there were too many tables too pointedly secluded by too many mirrored pillars; there was too much bar with things too shining upon it. Pam wondered what Beth and Margie would tell their mother about it when they got home, and what their mother would afterward write to Pam.

The captain was too welcoming, and his accent was too quaint. But he had them, now, and there was no escape, except to shake a head when he led them toward a table practically under the bar, to continue shaking it in spite of the expression of puzzled surprise in his face, indicating that they were rejecting the very best table in quite the best restaurant in the world, and to nod only when he shrugged toward a table in a corner, where they could all sit with their backs to the wall.

Pam had to shake her head again when the waiter suggested cocktails, shaking it in an undertone to match the tone of the suggestion. Pam had a mental picture of a martini, very cold with beads on the glass—because the glass had first been iced—and a lemon peel twisted over it but not dropped in. No olive, Pam told her mental picture.

"I think the tomato juice cocktail would be nice, to start with, don't you, girls?" Pamela North said, a heroine in her own right. And then, proving that virtue has sometimes rewards beyond itself, Mrs. North looked across the restaurant and saw what she had come to see. She saw Mrs. Paul Williams.

Mrs. Williams was wearing a black silk suit over her corsets, and had let a fur jacket fall over the back of the bar chair. There was nothing languishing about her, although she was sitting between two men, and Pam was disappointed. Mrs. Williams was a busy woman, having a cocktail at a bar before lunch and this was not a discrepancy. Or, at the most, not a discrepancy you could build on. She was not making eyes at anybody. At first, Mrs. North thought she was not with anybody, and then she began to wonder.

Because, without appearing to—without turning to each other, or making any of the physical movements of conversation—Mrs. Williams and the man on her left were talking. He was, from the rear, a not very tall man with dark hair, and he seemed to be looking at his drink while he talked. And Mrs. Williams was looking at her drink as she answered.

It would be absurd, Pam realized, to call their conversation furtive. In the mirrored glare of the Roundabout it was impossible to be furtive, unless you chose to be, in a sense, publicly furtive. Mrs. Williams and the man were not concealing, or trying to conceal, the fact of their conversation. But neither were they advertising it. It occurred to Mrs. North that they were furtive with each other, rather than with the world outside; as if the concealment lay between them, rather than between them and others. But that, Pam North thought, ordering abstractly and keeping her eyes on the two at the bar, was speculation. Of the worst kind. Because they might be, and probably were, merely abstracted; the effect of furtiveness grew out of her imagination, and out of the intentness with which Mrs. Williams and the man—a client?—were weighing what they said to one another.

So the choice of the Roundabout had, and continuing to watch them Pam grew surer of it, resulted in nothing, except the sharing of the noise of a great many other people and indifferent food served with flourishing elaborateness. The tomato juice came, canned and tepid in elaborate ice bowls.

"Oh," Beth said. "What lovely tomato juice. What a *nice* place, Aunt Pam."

Pam was surprised and almost showed it, and decided there was no occasion to show surprise.

"Isn't it?" she said. "So gay."

The man sitting on Mrs. Williams' left half-turned his chair on its swivel, as if he were about to get down. He turned it away from Mrs. Williams, but he seemed still to be speaking to her. She shook her head, and then turned away so that Mrs. North could see her profile clearly.

A girl who looked like a secretary during working hours was standing beside Mrs. Williams and holding out something, and by the color Mrs. North could see it was a telegram. Mrs. North's mind sought an explanation—a story which would match the fact—and decided that the girl was Mrs. Williams' secretary and that she had been told to bring to the restaurant any telegrams which came while Mrs. Williams was at lunch—and that was odd, unless Mrs. Williams had been expecting a telegram of considerable importance—and that the secretary had dutifully brought it.

Still sitting with her profile toward Mrs. North, Mrs.

Williams opened the telegram. It was short, evidently, because her eyes remained on it only for a moment. And it was important, evidently, because for an instant after she had read it, Mrs. Williams seemed to stare beyond it. Then she read it again.

And then, and for an instant Mrs. North thought she must be imagining again, Mrs. Williams seemed to sway on her chair. While Mrs. North stared, and half started up to see better, Mrs. Williams swayed on her chair still more, until it was quite evidently not Mrs. North's imagination. Mrs. Williams swayed to her left, and so toward the bar, and the man on her right, feeling the movement beside him, half turned and as Mrs. Williams sagged toward him, took her in his arms. It was clear and strange, and in slow motion.

Mrs. North started up, pushing back the table, and the nieces looked at her, and then where she was looking.

"Oh," Beth said, "she's sick. How awful."

Mrs. North, without thinking why she was doing it, went rapidly toward the bar, and Mrs. Williams. But you could not go very rapidly, because of the tables intervening, and of the mirror pillars between. She came around the last pillar and Mrs. Williams was still being held by the man on her right, who was looking at her in a surprised way and then at a captain who was hurrying toward them. And then Mrs. North stumbled.

She tried to catch herself and failed quite to do so, and, falling, wondered how she could have been so stupid. She caught herself with her hands, but her head struck the floor too, and for a moment she stayed on the floor, dazed. But she was not hurt, and was getting up already when a waiter reached her.

She shook her head, and said she was all right, and looked toward Mrs. Williams. Now Mrs. Williams was sitting up again, and the man who had been holding her had a relieved expression and she was shaking her head at the captain. Apparently Mrs. Williams was all right, too.

Mrs. North went on to her and when she was close enough said, "Oh, Mrs. Williams."

Mrs. Williams looked at her a moment as if she did not know who she was and then said, "Oh, Mrs. North, isn't it?" Then she smiled.

"I'm perfectly all right," she said. "A dizzy spell. I sometimes have them." She looked at Mrs. North, taking in the situation. "It was nice of you," she said. "But I'm perfectly all right. And to think that you fell."

That was nothing, Pam said. But now Mrs. Williams was not looking at her. Mrs. Williams was looking down at the floor, and then in her lap, and then she opened her purse and looked into it. She had lost something and wanted to find it, Pam thought. She's looking for the telegram, and it's gone. But it could only be gone if somebody had picked it up, and nobody in the little group around Mrs. Williams said anything about having picked it up. Either the secretary or the man with whom Mrs. Williams had been talking might have picked it up, Pam thought. But the secretary, who was making unnecessary motions of assisting Mrs. Williams out of the bar chair, was not handing her the telegram. And the man with dark hair, who had sat on Mrs. Williams' left, was not there. Pamela North looked around for him, but she could not see him anywhere.

Patently there was nothing she could do, except stand there smiling her vague good will, so she said she was glad that Mrs. Williams was all right and accepted Mrs. Williams' rather vague smile of appreciation, and went back to her table, a waiter going along as if to help.

The girls were sitting where she had left them, and their eyes were round.

"Oh," Beth said. "Aunt Pamela. You fell!"

"Yes," Pam said. "Yes, I fell. It was nothing."

"But," Margie said. "Somebody tripped you. We saw him."

Pamela North stared at the girls and they both nodded.

"Oh, yes," Beth said. "Somebody tripped you. We saw him. A little dark man."

A little after one Weigand straightened his neck to get the kink out, looked at the results of his research—and of research done in his behalf—and decided it was time to go to lunch. He took Mullins with him, and explained matters to Mullins over the table. Matters needed explanation.

For one thing, the Cincinnati business appeared to be a washout. George Schwartz was not wanted there by the police; so far as they had yet determined he was not particularly wanted there by anybody. He had worked on a newspaper there; he had been city editor. The police of Cincinnati were making reasonably discreet enquiries about that, casually asking newspapermen the police department knew unofficially. But certainly there had been no scandal about Schwartz and expense accounts which was general knowledge, or which had officially engaged the attention of the authorities. Schwartz had merely resigned as city editor one day and gone to Paris, carrying out a threat often made by newspapermen.

Schwartz's reputation in New York also was reasonably unblemished. If he drank a good deal, and there were intimations that he did drink a good deal, it did not interfere with his work. On the contrary; it seemed that he was highly thought of by his paper and, after two years on the "rim" was being considered, favorably, for a swing job in the "slot." (Mullins said "huh?" to this. Weigand told him; a man on the rim of the copy desk reads copy; the man in the slot is the boss of the men on the rim. Mullins said, "Oh.")

This was research conducted in behalf of Weigand, which meant in behalf of Deputy Chief Inspector Artemus O'Malley, in charge—which meant the patient, dogged work of many anonymous men, some in

blue uniforms and most without them, but with the
marks of their trade on weather-beaten faces and
mouths which were usually hard and hands which
looked as if they had been, often enough, heavy. Such
men were digging after facts; were talking to waiters at
the restaurant in which Sproul had eaten his last meal;
were finding out just what he had had to drink at the
Today's Topics Club and who had served it to him and
what chance there had been for glasses to be tampered
with; were going doggedly, if in this instance not too
patiently, about the probably hopeless task of finding
out where the morphine came from.

That, Mullins and Weigand agreed, was quite a little
problem. Retailers of morphine were elusive and not
inclined to communicate. Nor were they particularly
interested, one way or the other, in the outcome of
murder investigations in which they were not themselves concerned. The police had lines in. Here and
there, in Harlem and on the West Side and in
Yorkville, nervous, cringing little men found themselves looking fearfully up at phlegmatic, mahogany-
faced men and hearing, with acute unhappiness, the
news that the sergeant wanted to speak to them. This
usually meant trouble for the little men, because, even
if they could give no help in the issue immediately
raised, any contact with the police meant trouble. For
several it meant Welfare Island, and enforced cures for
an ailment which few of them regarded as requiring
cure.

So far this had come to nothing, except to the little
men involved. No line led to a peddler who had sold
morphine to those concerned.

"Who," Mullins said, "do you figure in it, Loot?"

Weigand took a pencil and started to write on the
tablecloth. A waiter came over and said, "Please,
Lieutenant, use this, huh?" and gave him a tablet of
paper. Weigand wrote on the paper:

Sproul, George Schwartz, Jean Akron, Ralph

White, Burden, the Shaw girl, the L.D.M. and, after a moment's pause, Herbert Akron, brother of Jean.

"L.D.M.?" Mullins said. "Little dark—," Weigand answered, before Mullins said, "Oh, sure."

Weigand thought a moment longer and, in deference to Mrs. North, wrote down the name of Mrs. Paul Williams. That, so far as they knew now, was the lot. It was too early to be sure, but if they were lucky the name of the murderer was on the list.

"And," Weigand said, "Sproul was going to say something about most of them in his lecture. If I'm right."

"Sure," Mullins said loyally. "Sure."

You took, Weigand said, taking out a penciled list and running down it, "Mr. A." to represent Sproul himself; "Miss B." as the alias of Miss Akron; "Mr. C." to be nobody they knew, and "Mr. D. " to be Mr. Schwartz, who was after all not wanted in Cincinnati. Then, leaving out others you could not place, as you could not place Mr. C., and guessing a good deal, you came out with this:

"Mr. J. . . . glad-hander; modern Bar. Very dif. those days; by no means everybody's fr . . . girl named Antoin. (ette?) and R. Seine . . . Accident?" Y. Charles Burden (because "modern Bar." might mean "modern Barnum," which would fit, in Sproul's style, a lecture agent).

"I don't get it," Mullins said. "What was he accusing Burden of, assuming it was Burden?"

That, Weigand admitted, was generally the trouble. You were building on very little; you had cryptic hints of a story; here a cryptic hint about something which had happened to a girl named Antoinette, presumably in Paris, and to which Burden was somehow connected. Something which might have been an accident and, because of the question mark, might presumably not have been an accident. Most of the notes were similarly cryptic.

There was, after Mr. J., a Mr. H. and the notes regarding him read: "Lit. bloke . . . patronizing; very helpful to young wr.; think H. James. Not suspect stole only thing ever published from young w. 'helped.' "

Now the literary bloke, who was obviously patronizing and might make you think a little of Henry James, was, if anybody on their list, Ralph White. And, regarding White, Sproul had intended to be merciless and outspoken, and against him to make the one accusation which a writer cannot live down.

Mullins nodded.

"Suppose he did?" he said. "Steal somebody else's stuff?"

Weigand shrugged. It was not the truth of the facts alleged which mattered, for the moment; it was the fact of the allegation.

"Of course," he said, "if one of these people killed Sproul to keep him from spilling something, the chances are the something was true. The chances are it was nothing that could be laughed off."

Mullins nodded, but his expression was doubtful.

"Listen, Loot," he said. "We have a lotta trouble figuring which one he meant. And we got time to work it out. I don't see why anybody would be scared much, because people listening to lectures wouldn't connect these Mr. A.'s and Miss B.'s with anybody. Would they?"

Weigand, listening, nodded. It was a point. However—

"Don't forget," he said, "that Sproul was going to say a lot more than we have here. We don't know how much more, but maybe enough to identify. And don't forget that, even if everybody in an audience didn't get it, there might be somebody, or several somebodies, who would."

Weigand, unconsciously pushing the paper aside, began to drum with his fingers on the table. He suggested, talking as much to himself as to Mullins, that they take the case of the man who might be White, "Mr. J." Here the accusation, the sting in the portrait, was fairly simple. Sproul had intended to charge that White had stolen a manuscript, or at the least a developed idea, from some young writer he had pretended to befriend and published it as his own. Suppose the amplified portrait which Sproul had intended in his lecture had been enough amplified to identify White clearly to people who knew him, or knew of him. Suppose that his own rather pompous picture of himself as an author was all that White had to live on; suppose this fabrication had become all there was to White. And suppose that he became ridiculous and contemptible as a writer who had based all his claims on a theft.

Such a story would eliminate White as a man of dignity; it would eliminate him as such not only in the eyes of others, but in his own eyes. With such a story spread, White might be expected to disappear like a toy balloon touched by a cigarette end. Suppose White was, as he appeared to be on one interview, acutely egocentric, with the ruthlessness of an egocentric. Did they then have a motive for the murder of Sproul, and a potential murderer who fitted?

"The way you put it," Mullins said, "hell, yes."

Weigand said he thought so. And they did not know that, with more knowledge, they might not be able to put as good a case against any of the others Sproul had intended to mention. Against Miss B. (and her brother); against Mr. D. and Mr. J. Or against the Mr. K. who came next:

"Mr. K. . . . smooth little Nazi 'hater'; 'Korean' and 'Dutch' . . . Innocent small-time journalist. But was? Wonder now—"

That would be Bandelman Jung; that would clearly hint that Jung was not the hater of fascism he pretended to be, and that his activities in Paris had not been really those of an innocent small-time newspaper correspondent. There would be a strong suggestion, evidently, that Mr. Jung was in fact an agent for fascism. That would interest a good many people, including the F.B.I., and if it proved true. . . .

"Well," Weigand said. Mullins nodded.

"They don't get babied, this time," he said. He thought. "They sure don't," he added.

So there you had another, with perhaps a motive.

"We'll have to get onto the Feds about it," Weigand said. "Maybe we can help each other."

"O.K., Loot," Weigand said. "I'll give the boys a ring."

There were others on the list, Weigand said, who might be interesting, but whose identity was not certain. There was a young woman, for example, who might be Loretta Shaw, which would make her really Mrs. D. But that was guesswork. And it might be possible to tie Loretta in through Schwartz, if it became advisable to tie her in. Or through her direct relationship with Sproul.

"Maybe," Mullins said gravely, "she decided she didn't want to marry him and didn't like to hurt his feelings by telling him. Thought this way would be kinder, sort of."

Weigand smiled and pointed out that it wasn't, really, preposterous. Things about as unreasonable had happened.

"You're telling me," Mullins told him, finishing his coffee. "How about this Mrs. Williams?"

Weigand shook his head. Unless her identity was peculiarly well concealed, Mrs. Williams did not appear on the list. Weigand stood up and took Mullins back across the street. There was, on the top of several papers, a memorandum awaiting him. It was timed at a few minutes after he had left for lunch. It read:

"Mrs. Gerald North called. She says to tell you she is chasing the little dark man. S. K."

Sam Knight, on being summoned, said that was all Mrs. North had said. He added that she seemed pretty much steamed up about something.

9

Mrs. North had ordered ice cream and hot chocolate sauce because he hadn't eaten any bread and she was just lifting the first spoonful toward her lips when she saw the little dark man. He was by the door, waiting at the check stand for his hat and coat, and he was so calm and unhurried that for a moment Mrs. North could not believe her eyes. But she decided she could believe her eyes, because he was certainly little and dark, and also he was certainly the man who had been sitting next to Mrs. Williams at the bar, and talking to her without seeming to.

Mrs. North put her spoon down and put her hand out quickly to Beth's wrist and, lifting her hand to point, said, "Look."

Beth looked.

"Oh," Beth said. "Oh!"

"Is it?" Mrs. North said.

Beth nodded violently and looked at Margie, who had also followed Mrs. North's directions. Margie nodded violently.

"Oh!" said Beth, with indignation. "It's the one, Aunt Pam."

"*Well!*" Pam North said, watching the man take his hat from the check girl and turn around so that she could boost his coat onto him. He was completely at leisure and full of assurance, and it was evident that he

141

did not believe anyone could object to his stealing a telegram from one woman and tripping another. "Because he must have stolen the telegram," Pam told herself, without logic and with utter conviction. It was infuriating, and Pam North agreed unhesitatingly with herself that something would have to be done.

"Wait here," Mrs. North commanded the nieces, who looked at her with surprise. Pamela North, their eyes said, was being a very peculiar aunt; she was acting out of character for an old person. But they nodded.

"I'm going to chase him," Pam North told them. "I'm going to find out what this is all about."

She started and stopped, remembering. She had promised Jerry that, if she simply could not avoid doing dangerous things, she would at least let somebody know she was about to do them. "That way," Jerry North told her, "we'll know where to lay the wreath." And so now she ought, obviously, to tell somebody what she was up to. But the little dark man had got under his topcoat and was pushing it back to get change out of his pocket, and there was no time.

"Beth," Mrs. North said, slowly but commandingly. "Telephone Police Headquarters and get Lieutenant William Weigand. Weigand. Tell him—tell him I'm chasing the little dark man." Mrs. North put even more command in her voice. "Then," she said, "come back here and wait. No matter how long it is, wait."

Beth nodded. Mrs. North transferred her commanding aunty gaze to Margie, who nodded also. The instructions seemed to have taken. Mrs. North started off, because the little dark man was already moving toward the door. She remembered something, and called it back.

"No sailors!" she called.

The girls looked embarrassed and somebody laughed. Mrs. North, because the little dark man was already going through the door, could not make things clearer, although she felt that she ought to. She moved quickly toward the door, going around tables.

One of the captains looked at her with some doubt for a moment, and then looked back at the table and saw the nieces. That, apparently, made it all right, except that the lady was going the wrong way. He stepped forward to direct her in a better direction, but she smiled at him very brightly and shook her head and kept on going. The captain did not want to make a mistake, and it was not until Mrs. North had passed the check stand without pausing and gone out the door that he became really afraid he had made one. However, hostages had been left. He drifted nearer, so that he could keep his eye on the hostages. If this was a new racket, it would have to be a good one.

Mrs. North, on the sidewalk, looked quickly in both directions and almost at once saw the little dark man, walking unconcernedly eastward toward Fifth Avenue through the rain which had now, fortunately, become a drizzle. His felt hat was green, Mrs. North was surprised to notice. It was not a hat she would have cared to see on Jerry, but at the moment it had its advantages. It stood out. Mrs. North, keeping her eyes on the green hat, went along behind.

The green hat reached Fifth Avenue and turned south. It was easy to follow him, Mrs. North found, partly because he seemed to be in no hurry at all, and partly because there were very few people on the sidewalk. The little dark man paused to look in a window and Mrs. North, not wanting to get too close, paused to look in a window in turn. Her window was filled with cutlery, and she saw a carving set which was precisely what they needed. She must, she decided, bring Jerry up to look at it, and at the martini mixer in the other corner, with what was evidently a trick mixing device of some sort. Jerry wouldn't like that, but he might like the carving set, because the knife would be sharp, and Martha, although in all other respects virtuous, was a loss at sharpening knives.

Mrs. North recalled herself with a guilty start, and looked anxiously down the avenue. The little dark man had satisfied himself about the window and was sauntering on. He didn't, Mrs. North thought, move as if he had a thing on his mind. Where, she asked herself, is his guilty conscience? If I'd tripped somebody, Mrs. North thought—

She followed on. He finished the block and, crossing with the lights, began the next. It was drizzling more persistently, now, and Mrs. North remembered that she had forgotten to retrieve her umbrella from the lockstand in the lobby of the Roundabout. It was certainly going to ruin her hat, and her coat wasn't, either, meant for walking in the rain. It had better come to something, Mrs. North thought rather angrily, to repay me for all this. She looked at the back of the little dark man, now half a block ahead, with real animosity.

The animosity increased rapidly as the little dark man sauntered on, never looking guiltily back over his shoulder, never increasing his pace. His insouciance robbed the chase of excitement; there was little to be said for chasing a man who wasn't running and who did not, evidently, at all fear being chased. The man passed Forty-fourth Street and, when he got to it, Forty-third. The rain, having rested, trickling only enough to hold the franchise, began to hurry. Mrs. North was getting very wet. People huddling in doorways looked at her with surprise and doubt.

"Probably all think I'm crazy," she told herself, and realized that she could hear the words. That would fix it up, that would fix it fine. A youngish woman plodding through the rain along Fifth Avenue, with her hat drooping, and talking to herself. She'd be lucky if somebody didn't pick her up for observation.

The lights stopped the little dark man at Forty-second and Mrs. North gained. The lights released him. He crossed Forty-second, walked the half block, came to the nearer stone bench under the nearer lion, and unconcernedly sat down. Mrs. North stared at him unbelievingly. The little dark man had walked half a dozen blocks down Fifth Avenue, in the rain, so that he could sit on a wet stone bench under one of the ineffably pompous Public Library lions. He had stolen a telegram from one woman, tripped another so that she fell on a restaurant floor, walked down Fifth Avenue in the rain and sat under a lion.

Also, it was clear, he had put Mrs. North in a predicament. She could not very well walk up and sit down beside him. She was wet enough in other places, for one thing. And he would be bound to recognize her and he would want to know, reasonably enough, what brought her there, and she could not think of any answer. What, indeed, had brought her there? Aside, of course, from her singularly wet feet? She could walk by and give the whole thing up; she could go up to him and ask, with such politeness as the situation warranted, why he had tripped her, and why he had stolen Mrs. Williams' telegram. And he could deny both, and, if he felt annoyed about it, probably have her arrested. She could hardly stop and look in a window, because there were no windows. She could hardly—but that was precisely what she could do!

She could stop where she was, or about where she was. She could go over to the curb and look up Fifth Avenue, and be waiting for a bus. It was the simplest thing in the world—believe it or not, she could say, I'm waiting for a Fifth Avenue bus. And when a bus came she could shake her head, sadly, and pretend it was the wrong bus; if it was a Fifth Avenue bus, she wanted to go to the Pennsylvania Station. If it was a Pennsylvania Station bus, she didn't. A bus came along, going to Twenty-fifth Street only, and she shook her head at it. The next one was blocks up the street and she looked up toward it, turning just enough so that she could see the little dark man on the bench.

He was still on the bench. But he was not alone on the bench. A rather large man in a bulky overcoat which was too warm for the weather, had sat down beside him. He had sat down casually, and he was not making any show of the fact that he was talking to the little dark man. But he was talking to the little dark man. The little dark man said something, and the man in the bulky overcoat shook his head. The little dark man showed something to the big, bulking man, and the big man shook his head more severely, even angrily. The little dark man looked at him searchingly, and did not seem convinced. The bulky man stood up, still shaking his head.

And then the big man said something loudly enough for Mrs. North to hear. He said, and his voice was angry and contemptuous:

"Nein! Dumkopf!"

The little dark man sat looking up at him, and Mrs. North thought he looked like a child which has been slapped when it expects better things. She was annoyed with the bulking man, because he had hurt the feelings of the little dark man.

She was annoyed at him before she had time to remember that she was also annoyed at the little dark man, with more cause, and even before she realized that the bulking man had hurt the little man's feelings in German. "No," he had said, and something which meant, most simply, "fool." Or blunderer, or half-wit. The little dark man had walked half a dozen blocks through the rain, and sat on a cold, wet bench, to be called a fool in German by a man from whom, it was evident, he had expected other things. Praise, probably.

Mrs. North half-heartedly pretended she was still waiting for a bus. But she began to be excited. She was learning something, even if she did not, at the moment, understand what it was. There were plenty of people who spoke German in New York, war or no war; so many that nobody paid the slightest attention, accepting the enemy language as if, because for so long it had been, it must always be spoken by friends. But there was something funny about this.

The bulking man, having stood up, turned suddenly and walked away. He walked down toward Forty-second Street, and as he neared the corner lifted a hand to wave down a taxicab. The taxi stopped and engulfed him. The little dark man remained sitting on the bench, looking after him.

And then two men who had been walking, idly enough and not noticeably together, up Fifth Avenue from the direction of Fortieth Street, parted without speaking when they were opposite Mrs. North. One went, unconcernedly, toward the curb and reached it just as a black sedan slowed down. He opened the door of the sedan and stepped in and, without seeming to move hurriedly, the sedan continued down Fifth Avenue in the direction which had been taken by the bulky man's taxicab.

The second of the two men who had been walking up the avenue seemed suddenly to have decided he was tired. He walked over to the bench on which the little dark man sat and sat down beside him. The little dark man looked at him and the man who had just sat down said something, and a look of overwhelming surprise appeared on the face of the little dark man. He started, as if to stand up, and the right hand of the man who had just sat down went out and closed on his wrist. It did not, Mrs. North thought, close gently. And the left hand of the man who had just sat down stayed in his topcoat pocket, in a way which Mrs. North remembered from motion pictures.

Forgetting entirely to appear to be waiting for a bus, Mrs. North stared. As she stared the two men got up, standing close together as if they were very dear friends. They turned North on Fifth Avenue, walking toward Forty-second, and as they did so the new man—he was a tall, solid man in a gray topcoat— moved so that he would be on the outside, nearest the curb. As if the little man were a woman, Pam thought, and the tall man was his escort. But also, Pam realized, the move brought the little dark man on the left side of the taller man, so that the hand in the topcoat pocket, and whatever the hand might hold inside the pocket, were very near the little man. Conveniently near.

Pam knew what it was, and realized she had known since the taller man sat down. The little man was being kidnapped! It was—what did Mullins call it?—it was a snatch.

It was preposterous, but it was true. The little dark man was being snatched, no doubt preparatory to being taken for a ride, from under the very nose of the self-satisfied Public Library lion. He was being marched along Fifth Avenue toward Forty-second Street, and no doubt toward the powerful black sedan, under the self-satisfied noses of all New York, including the traffic policeman at Fifth Avenue and Forty-second. And there was nothing to be done about it.

But wasn't there? Pam could scream, but then the little dark man probably would be shot. And I'd probably be shot next, Pam added, with even more concern. She could go up to the two and denounce the kidnapper, but that seemed unlikely to help, and might also lead to shooting. And she could follow, and watch her chance.

She followed. It was as she expected. A sedan was waiting at the corner, in Forty-second Street, facing east, half blocking the cross walk. It was not a black sedan, to be sure; it was sand-colored. But the two men, walking close together in what anyone who did not know would think a friendly fashion, were obviously going toward the sedan. They were going toward it and now they were getting in it, the little dark man first. And Pam, hurrying, could hear the quicker note of the motor as the driver, who looked very like the tall man with the gun in his pocket, accelerated as he let in his clutch.

And then what looked like a miracle happened. The lights turned red against the car, and the traffic policeman whistled and held up a hand. And then Pam realized what she had to do.

Unhesitatingly, with a recklessness born of vast urgency, Mrs. North dodged through the cars moving down Fifth Avenue, angling diagonally out toward the traffic policeman. And when she was near enough, and ignoring the expression of indignant concern on the policeman's face, she began to explain, talking in a hurried, anxious voice.

"Stop them," she demanded. "Stop them. They're kidnapping a man!"

"Huh?" the traffic policeman said. "Listen, lady, you want to get yourself killed?"

"Listen," Pam commanded. "They're kidnapping a man. They're going to kill him. Over there in that car." She pointed. "You've got to do something!"

"Yeh?" the cop said. He was worse than Mullins; infinitely worse than Mullins. Mullins understood things quickly, or almost quickly. "Who's kidnapping somebody, lady?"

The time of the red light was running out. In seconds, the light would change and the sand-colored sedan would be gone, with the frightened little man and his captors. Pam grabbed the policeman's sleeve and shook it.

"Stop them!" she begged. "Stop them—that car there. They're going to kill a man!"

The policeman looked at her and then, finally, he looked at the sand-colored sedan. You could see, looking frantically up at him, that thought was taking place behind the red and weathered face. The face seemed faintly surprised at this. But now the policeman was moving.

He held up an authoritative hand, stopping the southbound cars. Through the clearing thus achieved, he advanced majestically on the unmoving sedan. Pamela North followed, relief spreading over her in waves. At least, it was out of her hands. She watched the policeman, and relief ebbed somewhat.

It was out of her hands, certainly. But the hands in which it was seemed singularly overconfident. It was clear that the traffic policeman did not really believe that the sedan held desperate men, armed and ready to shoot; held killers, ready for anything. The traffic policeman advanced as if they were only cowering motorists, awaiting an earned reprimand, and perhaps a ticket.

The policeman advanced to the sedan, holding up an authoritative hand. He bent over it, and Mrs. North held her breath. This way was wrong; this way was horribly wrong. He should have gone with his gun out, as ready as they. He should—

He stooped and, through a window which someone inside must have opened, stuck his head into the car. He stuck it well in, so that what remained outside looked very peculiar. It was also very large, so that Mrs. North could not see over or around it. Mrs. North held her breath.

The traffic policeman, however, emerged. He did not look alarmed, or surprised or anything Mrs. North could put a thought to. He stood away from the car and, as he stood away, the car started, since now the lights had changed in its favor. The sedan crossed Fifth Avenue and continued toward the east, and Mrs. North stared after it with open mouth. The New York police department just didn't care! She couldn't believe it.

Mrs. North turned indignantly toward the official culprit, and discovered that he did not look at all like a culprit. He was staring at her, and his stare was measuring and not, she thought, really sympathetic.

"Well, lady," the policeman said. "Friend of yours, huh?"

"Friend?" Mrs. North said. "Friend? Who?"

"The little guy, lady," the policeman said. He said it

with great, rather sarcastic patience. "The little guy. Friend of yours, huh?"

"No," Mrs. North said. "I know him, in a way. But—"

"So you know him in a way," the policeman said, heavily. "Think of that now, lady. So you know him in a way."

"He—" Mrs. North began, but the policeman was shaking a heavy head at her.

"I wouldn't, lady," he said. "Don't waste it on me, lady. We got guys who like to hear stories like that, lady. You tell it to them, huh? Do you want to pay for a taxi, lady?"

"Pay for a taxi?" Pam North repeated. "Why should I pay for a taxi? I don't want a taxi."

"All right, lady," the policeman said. "It's nothing to me. We'll get you the wagon, lady."

"Wagon?" Mrs. North repeated. "You don't mean—you're not going to arrest *me!*"

"Sure not," the policeman said. "Sure not, lady. Just take you over to the station house so you can tell the boys about it. How somebody was kidnapping a friend of yours, and things like that. You wouldn't call it an arrest, lady."

Pamela North found she could only stare at him. She could only stare at the second policeman who, in answer to a signal from the first, came across from the far corner of Fifth Avenue and Forty-second, where he had been standing without, it seemed, a care in the world. It was clear now, however, that he had merely been waiting to arrest Pamela North.

Pam found difficulty in believing that anything of this preposterous kind was really happening. She did, however, rally enough to pay for the taxicab which took her to the West Forty-eighth Street police station. And once there, and after a considerable wait, she had a great deal to say to the sergeant at the desk.

But by that time it was well after three o'clock and

the little dark man, probably, was dead. That thought, as she waited for the half-convinced sergeant to make a telephone call which was oddly received, crowded out almost all other thoughts. He was almost certainly dead, the little dark man, and with him whatever he knew about the murder of Victor Leeds Sproul.

It was only quite late that another thought managed to get through. Mrs. North remembered her nieces, waiting at their table at the Roundabout. And alarmingly exposed to sailors.

10

Bill Weigand looked down at the Norths and smiled and said he had thought he would find them there.

"And where," he added, "are the nieces? The famous nieces?"

"Famous?" Jerry repeated. "Sit down, Bill. At home, with Martha. We're on vacation. Why famous?"

Weigand sat down and said that it was merely a manner of speaking. He looked at Pamela North with amusement.

"All right," she said. "Say it."

Bill told her he hadn't anything to say.

"Well," Pam said, "how could I know? They took him right from under the lion, in broad daylight, except that it was raining, of course. And that one did have a gun."

So, Weigand told her, did the other one. It was a habit they had.

"Well," Pam said, a little hotly. "They didn't look like cops. You can always tell a cop."

Weigand said, "Ouch."

"These just looked like anybody," Pam said. "How could I tell?"

"Right," Bill Weigand said. "And, by the same token, how could Patrolman O'Brien, of Traffic A?"

Pam said, all right, she'd got herself into it. And Bill had got her out. And she supposed it was funny.

"Sort of," Bill Weigand agreed. "The Feds pick up a suspicious character, who consorts with a known agent, and we start to take him off quietly to ask him some questions. And you tie up traffic at Fifth Avenue and Forty-second Street trying to get them arrested. And attract attention generally."

"And," Pam said, "get arrested for my trouble."

Weigand told her she hadn't really been arrested. She had merely been invited to explain.

"By two very large policemen," Pam pointed out. "Don't be technical. What would you call arrested?"

"Booked," Weigand told her. "On a charge. Like conspiracy to commit espionage. Or harboring. Or being a suspicious character, as you certainly were to O'Brien. He must have thought you were a great friend of the little man's to go to all that trouble for him."

Pam said she didn't see it. She didn't like to have people killed. Even if they weren't friends. And she had no way of knowing. Bill Weigand was still looking at her with amusement, and finally she smiled back and said, "All right, I got into it. Again. Was he?"

"Was he what?" Weigand said, and felt that, in the time he had known Mrs. North, he must have said that a hundred times. "Was he what, Pam?"

"A spy," Pam said. "Did he kill Sproul because— because Hitler told him to. Or Hirohito? And did he have the telegram for Mrs. Williams? And is she a spy, too? And why did he trip me?"

"Really, Pam," Jerry said. "Really, baby."

"He doesn't say," Bill Weigand told her. "Or, exactly, he says 'no' in a great many words, all very indignant. He says he is a fugitive from the Nazis, as everybody knows; that he knew Heinrich as another anti-Nazi and that the F.B.I. has made a terrible mistake. He says this at length. The last I heard they hadn't got around to Sproul, although we asked them to bear it in mind. It's not what they're chiefly interested in, of course."

"Heinrich?" Mr. North repeated. "Who's Heinrich?"

Heinrich, Weigand told them, was the bulky man Pam's little man had been talking to under the lion. ("Your little man is Bandelman Jung, Pam," Weigand interjected. "Or says he is.") Heinrich was not an anti-Nazi, whatever Bandelman Jung thought, or wanted others to think he thought. Heinrich was a bona-fide enemy agent, like you read about. About Grade C, but genuine. The F.B.I. followed him around, and snaffled off people he spoke to. Heinrich was being very useful, but not to the Reich. The F.B.I. was enjoying Heinrich very much.

"You'd think," Pamela said, "that Heinrich would begin to suspect, after a while. I mean, never being able to talk to anybody twice. You'd get to feel—sort of puzzled. Lonely, sort of."

Bill and Jerry agreed. But Heinrich was not, so far as was yet revealed, a sensitive man. Heinrich didn't seem to notice.

"Of course," Pam said, "maybe it's been that way all his life. Maybe he doesn't notice any difference. He looked a little like that."

They let the question of Heinrich's possibly thwarted life die gradually among them. Weigand drank a Martini, because it was technically before dinner, but declined food because he had actually had some sandwiches when it looked as if he wouldn't get away. Jerry North happily explored the earthenware pot which had contained pot au feu, a specialty of the house. Mrs. North looked abstractedly at a silver dish which had contained sole marguéry, let remembrance appear momentarily on her face, and said that Bill had wanted to know about the nieces.

"Tell him, Jerry," she directed.

Jerry said it was sort of funny.

"Pam called up," he said, "and went on about the

nieces, which she'd left somewhere. So I had to drop what I was doing and go after them. And whatever led you to the Roundabout, Pam? A loathsome place."

"Isn't it," Pam said. "Mrs. Williams. And she was there, too."

"Well," Jerry said, "the nieces were there, all right. Right where Pam had left them. And were they having a fine time."

"Sailors?" Bill wanted to know. Jerry shook his head.

"Marines," he said. "Very fine Marines, as it turned out. One of them was a Ph.D. and probably Phi Beta Kappa from the way he talked, and the other was Princeton. Very fine Marines. They treated me very nicely, when Beth introduced us. They stood up and called me 'sir' and evidently wanted me to sit down very quickly, because I was old and infirm and they didn't want me collapsing on their hands. Beth and Margie thought so too, I noticed."

"Nonsense," Pam said. "You look fine, Jerry. Not old at all. Really."

Bill and Jerry looked at each other and didn't say anything. Then Jerry went on.

"The boys were very much afraid I'd think they'd picked the girls up," he said. "By that time they'd discovered, probably, that the girls were a little younger than—well, a little younger than they'd thought. They looked a little worried. And they were, in a nice way, rather severe with me. They indicated that we were taking rather a risk, leaving nieces about. One of them was very serious. He said—well, he said:

" 'I don't know whether you know, sir, but there are some men around who wouldn't understand. Sailors, you know.'

"And the other Marine nodded, very gravely, with a kind of worried look. So I thanked them, and brought the girls home. Beth said, on the way, that she thought Marines were much nicer than sailors. And Margie said, 'But Beth, Uncle Jerry was a sailor,' and Beth said, 'Oh, but that was such a long time ago. Things were different, weren't they, Uncle Jerry?' "

"And what did you say?" Pam wanted to know.

Jerry shrugged.

"I said, 'Sure!' " he told her. "What did you expect me to say?"

Pam looked a little worried.

"Do you suppose things are different, Jerry?" she said. "Ought we to do something about it? For the nieces, I mean?"

"No," Jerry said. "I don't think things are very different. I think the nieces will be all right. If we watch them."

Pam thought it over and Fritz looked down at her and said, "Ice cream with hot chocolate sauce, Mrs. North?" Pam looked tempted and shook her head. She ordered coffee and so did Jerry, and Weigand joined them. The coffee came.

"Where are you?" Jerry said. "Do you know yet?"

It hadn't been twenty-four hours yet, Weigand told them. They sounded like Inspector Artemus O'Malley. No, he didn't know.

"How's Bandelman Jung for a choice?" Jerry wanted to know. Bill Weigand shrugged. He said that, obviously, it could be. Certainly Jung had been into things.

"He was the guy you chased," he said. "Or the chances are he was. He left fingerprints in the speakers' room, all right. He was—probably he was the man who stole the lecture notes and—brought them back."

"What?" Pam said.

Weigand told them about it. Or told them as much as he thought they ought to know.

"And sent them back to you by messenger," Pam said. "That was funny. Were there prints on the notes?"

Weigand shook his head. He said, "gloves." Pam said Jung sounded like the murderer to her.

He could be, Weigand agreed. Certainly he had been

doing a good many things, some of them in connection with Sproul's death, which needed explanation. But the trouble was that a good many others could be, too.

"Opportunity?" Jerry said.

"Right," Bill Weigand said. "And motive, in most cases."

The dose of morphine—what Dr. Francis called a "massive dose"—could have been given either during the dinner Sproul had eaten with his friends before he went to the Today's Topics Club, in which case the food he had taken would delay its action, or in the drinks he had had with Mrs. Williams immediately before he went out to speak. The two times represented, approximately, the extreme limits of the probable period. Those at the dinner had been the two Akrons, Schwartz, Loretta Shaw, the pompous Mr. White and Y. Charles Burden. Not Jung, not Mrs. Williams. But Mrs. Williams had had an opportunity later, at the club. There was no evidence that Jung had had an opportunity; as nearly as they could tell by tracing the drinks from the bar to the consumer, he had had no opportunity. Certainly it was hard to see how he could have put morphine in the first drink, partly consumed before Mrs. Williams took Sproul to the speakers' room. He might conceivably have got near enough to the waiter who was carrying the second drink upstairs to have spilled in the poison, but the waiter was sure he hadn't. Mrs. Williams had had an opportunity to poison either drink; Loretta Shaw had had an opportunity to poison the one served upstairs.

"So did I," Jerry interjected.

"So did you," Bill Weigand agreed. "Did you, by any chance?"

"No," Pam said. "Sproul was a best seller. Don't be foolish, Bill."

They came to motives, and Weigand summarized the evidence of the lecture notes. It was, he warned them, cryptic evidence. In no case, for example, was it clear enough to take into court. They were trying to trace down the hints, but that was slow work. The police in Cincinnati were still investigating Schwartz's past, for example. So far they had discovered only that he left a newspaper of which he had been city editor, rather suddenly. They had also discovered a disinclination on the part of the remaining executives to talk very openly about why he had gone.

They had talked to the publishers of White's first and only book, and they were comparing it—a man who was supposed to know about such matters was comparing it—with a manuscript of White's which White's depressed agent had been persuaded to lend for the purpose.

"How—?" Pam began.

"For style tricks," Jerry said. "I suppose, Bill?"

Bill said he gathered that was it. And would it work?

"If he has mannerisms, it might," Jerry said. "If he has the same mannerisms now he had when his first book came out. It was damn near unreadable, by the way. If he stole it, not worth stealing. Of course, maybe he 'improved' on the original idea; made it his own. Maybe it wasn't so bad originally. But I'd hate to guess much on the results your expert gets."

Bill Weigand said he wasn't betting much on it. But he could think of no better way to check on the scandalous hint which Sproul had planned to make in his lecture. Unless, of course, they could find the man from whom Sproul had stolen.

"We'll work on that too, if we have to," Weigand said. "Look for a needle in yesterday's haystack."

No motive was certain. They didn't know enough; it was not a simple, comfortable murder for money or safety or, so far as they could guess, hatred. But it might be any of these. They might be barking—no, whining—up entirely the wrong trees. But they had to use the trees they had, until they got more—Schwartz and Loretta Shaw, the Akrons, Ralph White and Y. Charles Burden.

"And the little dark man, with the funny name, and

Mrs. Williams," Mrs. North insisted. "And German
spies. Or Japanese."

"Mrs. Williams or little Jung," Weigand agreed,
without enthusiasm. "For the record, to keep it
straight, and for Mrs. Pamela North. But why Axis
spies?"

"Because," Pamela told him, "Mr. Sproul was
really a—a British agent. Or a man from G-2. And he
was on their trail."

Weigand shook his head.

"No," he said. "Not a British agent. Nor a man
from G-2. Nor an F.B.I. man in disguise. Give us some
credit, Pam. Sproul was just a man who wrote books,
who had lived in Paris, who was about to lecture to
clubwomen. With the tacit approval of the O.W.I., to
be sure. But he was nothing official."

"Well," Mrs. North said, "he had a list of enemy
agents in this country and he was going to turn it over
to the F.B.I. He found out about it in Paris, because he
knew somebody before the war started and got drunk
and boasted. Or maybe not a list of names; maybe just
some leads we could follow up. And maybe they were
more important than he knew, and they killed him
because of that. Couldn't it be? You don't know it
isn't, do you?"

Weigand agreed they didn't know it wasn't.

"However," he added, "we can think it wasn't. We
can think that Sproul was killed privately."

"Privately?" Mrs. North repeated. "In front of all
those people?"

"For private reasons," Weigand said. "Be yourself,
Pam. Somebody killed Sproul because they didn't like
Sproul, or what he was going to say, or going to do, or
had done or said. For personal reasons, as distinct
from impersonal reasons, if you like it better that
way."

The three sipped coffee. Jerry North held up his left
hand and began bending fingers down on it.

"Schwartz because of something in his past that

Sproul was going to reveal," he said. "White for ditto." That took the first two fingers. "Akron and sister Akron for ditto." He turned down one finger for the two. "Burden for—?" He looked inquiringly at Weigand.

"Ditto, I suppose," Weigand said. "Or—because for some reason he didn't want Sproul to go on with the tour? I'll admit I can't think of any reason. And Schwartz, to go back, because Sproul had alienated Mrs. Schwartz's affections."

"All right," Jerry said, turning down a finger for Burden. "Jung because of something in his past, again; Loretta—" Jerry looked at his hand and discovered that, although he had been forced to utilize his thumb, he had run out of fingers. He moved to the right hand. "Loretta Shaw for what?" he asked.

Weigand shook his head.

"Unless she didn't want to marry Sproul after all, and didn't want to hurt his feelings by saying so," he said. "Really, I wouldn't know. Nor would I have any idea why Mrs. Williams should kill Sproul, unless at the last moment she felt she had made a dreadful mistake in engaging him to lecture at the club and was doing her best to correct it."

"Flippant," Mrs. North said, with disapproval.

"Your flippancy, to start with," Bill Weigand told her. "She's your Mrs. Williams, Pam. All yours. You can also have Dr. Dupont."

"Dupont?" Mrs. North said.

"The president of the Today's Topics Club," Jerry told her. "The old man who fainted."

"No," Mrs. North said, "I don't want him. I'm not sure I even want Mrs. Williams. Did the little dark man have the telegram?"

The two men looked at her and then at each other. Finally Jerry North shook his head.

"She's got me this time," he admitted. "I knew it would come some day." He turned to his wife. "What telegram, dear?" he said. "If it isn't a secret?"

"The one Mrs. Williams got, of course," she said. "The one Mr. Jung took. At the restaurant, I told you."

Bill Weigand looked at Jerry North, and Jerry shook his head.

"You told me you saw Jung and Mrs. Williams talking," he said. "And that Jung tripped you and you decided to chase him. Then you told me all about the chase, block to block, and about being arrested and what you said to the sergeant and what the sergeant said to you, and about telephoning Bill and having him talk to the sergeant. But nothing about a telegram."

"Well," Mrs. North said, "that's funny. Because that was the whole thing. That was what made Mrs. Williams faint. Unless it was too much to drink. A yellow telegram."

She told them about the telegram which had been delivered to Mrs. Williams at the bar. Weigand said it was better late than never, but— He got up.

"I'll find out," he said, and went across the wide, main room at Charles to the telephones behind the desk. After a little while he came back, looking unexpectedly annoyed.

"Cooperation!" he said, with vigor. "A fine lot of cooperation they give us!"

The Norths looked at him and waited.

"The Feds," he said, after a moment of staring with indignation at the wall, "decided they didn't want Mr. Jung. Or, rather, that they didn't want him locked up. They want him loose with a string attached, like their Mr. Heinrich. And so they listen to him, and say 'Yes, Mr. Jung, certainly, Mr. Jung' with a lot of politeness and turn him loose. And they say they don't want to pick him up again unless we have a charge against him which will stick, because they think he may be very useful roaming around and meeting people. And that is known as cooperation."

"Well," Jerry North said reasonably, "do you want him? Have you got a charge?"

Weigand said they could make one; tailor-make it. Long enough to talk to Mr. Jung. But— He shrugged.

"I suppose actually it doesn't matter," he said. "And Jung is more theirs than ours. They caught him, after all. Only I'd like to clear up this little matter of the telegram. Because he didn't have it, Pam."

Pam waited.

"They looked over what he did have," Bill Weigand told her. "Before they got polite. No telegram. Of course, they had no reason to ask him about a telegram, since you hadn't gotten around to mentioning a telegram. However—probably it's nothing. And we can pick him up and ask him. Or ask Mrs. Williams, if it begins to look important. We can also ask Mr. Jung why he tripped you, Pam."

That, Pam said, was easy. He had tripped her because he thought she was going to chase him, the way Jerry had. But then he had discovered that she wasn't going to chase him, so he hadn't run, but had merely gone on and had lunch. And then after lunch, she had chased him. But then he hadn't noticed, or hadn't cared. Because by then he had read the telegram and it wasn't important and—and had probably thrown it away. And he didn't know that Pam knew he had tripped her. Pam said it was very simple.

"Well," Weigand said, in doubt. "Probably we'll have to pick him up and ask him. And ask Mrs. Williams about the telegram."

Meanwhile, Weigand pointed out, it was all very pleasant, but he had to go back to his office and look at reports. You never knew about reports.

You never did indeed, Weigand thought, looking at the one before him. On Friday morning, some hours before Sproul was killed, Loretta Shaw and George Schwartz, duly provided with physicians' certificates, had applied at the marriage license bureau and had received, in routine procedure, a license to marry.

Weigand, digesting that, looked at another report.

Schwartz had been fired, summarily, from a Cincinnati newspaper of which he had been city editor when he was caught permitting the flagrant padding of expense accounts. It was assumed that after authorizing payment of the accounts, he had split proceeds with the two men chiefly involved. Schwartz had admitted initialing accounts he knew to be fraudulent, but denied having profited personally. He had insisted that he passed the accounts only because the men submitting them were underpaid and in emergency need of funds. Apparently there had been some reason to credit this explanation, since the newspaper had not prosecuted and had merely dismissed all concerned.

Jung, on being released by the F.B.I., had gone to his rooming house, and presumably to his room, and perhaps to bed. The F.B.I. was keeping an eye on him, for everybody.

Schwartz and Loretta Shaw had met for dinner and had gone to a musical comedy, where they still were. The detective, watching them, and the show, from standing room, had called during a love duet on stage, explaining that it seemed as good a time as any other to go to the lounge and telephone. Otherwise, the detective said, he was enjoying the show. He said the third dancing girl from the left was a lulu.

Jean Akron and her brother were at home in their apartment on Park Avenue. The detective assigned to them didn't know what they were doing, but thought they were entertaining friends and maybe playing bridge. The doorman, judiciously approached, had said he thought they had guests.

Y. Charles Burden, who lived in Westchester, had gone to Westchester, by train.

And Ralph White, whether intentionally or not, did not appear, had slipped the man who was keeping an eye on him and disappeared. The man, chagrined, was waiting in the vicinity of White's small apartment west of Seventh Avenue for his client to re-appear.

Nobody was following Mrs. Williams, or Dr. Dupont or the other casuals of the affair. Weigand had run out of men.

But it might, he thought, be worth while telephoning Mrs. Williams and asking what Jung had had to say and if he had stolen a telegram from her. He looked up the number and gave it to the police operator. After a few minutes the police operator said that the number did not answer.

Weigand's head ached again. He telephoned his own apartment and Dorian did answer. She said her head ached too, and when was he coming home?

"Now," Weigand said.

Everything was under control, he decided. Under control and, at the moment, static. But there was no evident need for hurry. This time, at any rate, the murderer seemed to be content with one victim.

11

Wilfred Tingle clanged the vestibule door open as the Wall Streeter slowed beside the platform, and attacked the pile of luggage stacked opposite it. He worked fast so as not to hold up his people, already almost half an hour late, and already in bad morning tempers. He beamed at those already standing in the door to Car 620, his charge from Pittsburgh, and said cordially, "Yes, sir, yes, ma'am. Jus' a moment now. Yes, sir." He shoveled the luggage into the waiting hands of red caps and, when the last piece was lined up with the rest, took his stand on the platform just outside the door. His hand was ready to help, or be helped.

He guessed the room cars paid off, after all. You didn't have so many people, usually, but they tipped better. You could figure maybe half a dollar a head in from Pittsburgh, or maybe the average was nearer forty cents, because you had to count women traveling alone, who seemed, some of them, to think the car made up beds automatically, and polished shoes by miracle. Still, you got a good tipping class of people in the room cars, ordinarily.

"Thank you, sir," Wilfred said. "Just pick out your bags please, sir. Thank *you*, sir. There's your big bag right there, sir. Thank you—"

The passengers stood in front of the row of bags and

166

peered at it. Some of them shivered in the air, damp from the rain of the day before. Some of them growled at the red caps, and some were hearty and most of them seemed to be in a hurry. And none of them missed Wilfred's assisting hand.

They stopped coming and Wilfred turned to go back on the car, to strip the beds which had been occupied late, to stow the pillows he had left out so that early risers could rest comfortably while they waited—and some of them had got up as far back as Philadelphia, for reasons which did not appear to Wilfred—and to ride on the Pullman into the Sunnyside yards, and eventually to go home to Harlem. But, turning, Wilfred stopped.

There was still one bag standing on the platform, and a red cap was looking at it doubtfully.

"Somebody miss one," the red cap said. "Somebody jus' forget all about it."

The red cap laughed, shrilly, infectiously, at nothing in particular.

"He sho' did," the red cap repeated. "He jus' forget all about his prop'ty."

Wilfred did not join in the laugh. It was up to him to retrieve the bag, if he could not find the owner. He would have to turn it in and make out a report, and this would delay his return to Harlem, where he had reasons to want to be as soon as possible. Wilfred scowled at the bag and said that some people was the damnedest fools he evuh saw. To the red cap he said, "You keep your eye on it a minute, huh, big boy?" and went back into the car. Maybe somebody had dropped off to sleep again.

There was nobody in Bedroom A and there was nobody in Bedroom B, but the door of Bedroom C was closed, which was odd, and Wilfred knocked. There was no answer and he pushed it open.

Sure enough, he thought, somebody dropped off to sleep again. That sort of thin man who didn't look so good when he got on at Pittsburgh almost as soon as the car was opened, waiting on a dead track to be picked up by the St. Louis train. He was lying now stretched out, except that one leg dangled from the knee, on the long seat across the room. He was using one of the pillows Wilfred had left out.

But there was something sort of funny about that. He wasn't using the pillow under his head, the way pillows were meant to be used. He had the pillow on top of his head. That was mighty funny.

Wilfred was worried already, but he went on in. He touched the man's shoulder, gently and uneasily.

"We's there, suh," he said, his accent broadening as it did when Wilfred was worried. "We's in New Yo'k, suh. We's—"

Wilfred stopped, because the man was not listening. And Wilfred stretched out one shaking dark hand and pushed against the pillow, so that it fell away from the man's head. Wilfred stared down at the suffused face.

"Man," Wilfred said. "You is suah enough there. You is whe'evuh you is going."

And then Wilfred pushed the pillow back convulsively over the face and started running. He also started yelling. At the door of the next car he found the Pullman conductor and, growing more excited as he thought about it—until it was hardly possible to understand what he was saying—tossed murder in the conductor's lap.

"It look to me like he was smothered," Wilfred told the Pullman conductor, and led him back to Bedroom C. The conductor, who had been twenty-five years in Pullman service without encountering anything similar, pushed away the pillow. It looked to the Pullman conductor, also, as if the occupant of Bedroom C, Car 620, had been smothered. It looked as if somebody had put one of the convenient pillows over his face and pressed down hard, and kept on pressing.

It looked the same way to the railroad police, and to the precinct homicide men who answered their call.

And the assistant medical examiner who responded, assured them that they were right. By that time, by the time a headquarters squad under Detective Lieutenant Fahey took over, Car 620, detached and ostracized, was on a siding in the Sunnyside yards.

It took only the briefest of observations to determine that the thin, gray-haired man in Bedroom C had been murdered. Someone had used one of the pillows Wilfred Tingle had left out for his passengers' comfort, and used it to smother the passenger. After photographs and fingerprinting, and formal assurance of death by an assistant medical examiner, it took hardly more time to make identification (tentative) of the murdered man as Robert J. Demming, resident of Pittsburgh. From then on, things went more slowly.

It became evident, almost at once, that an issue of jurisdiction was involved. Was Robert J. Demming alive when Bedroom C of Car 620, rolling through the Pennsylvania Railroad's tunnel under the Hudson, passed the judicially important line separating New Jersey from New York? Lieutenant Fahey did not know; the assistant medical examiner did not know. Mr. Demming had been dead only a short time when the shaking hand of Wilfred Tingle brushed the pillow from his face. But that time could not be measured in seconds.

But possession of the body seemed to be nine-tenths of the law, or at least enough of the law to go ahead on. New Jersey, Lieutenant Fahey rather unhappily supposed, would not contest; New Jersey would, almost certainly, be pleased to waive Mr. Demming to the State of New York, and let the State of New York worry. Lieutenant Fahey, representing the State of New York, began to worry.

Part of it was easy. Mr. Demming (tentative) had boarded Car 620 in Pittsburgh at about 10:30, when it was on a siding waiting for the express from St. Louis which was to pick it up. The express from St. Louis duly picked it up forty-five minutes later. Presumably Mr. Demming slept during the night, and certainly he was alive the next morning. He was one of the early awakeners, Wilfred Tingle could testify. The train had not yet reached Philadelphia when Mr. Demming, fully dressed, rang for Tingle and asked for a 110-volt converter so that he could use a standard electric shaver. Tingle had brought the converter. About fifteen minutes later, as the train was by-passing the Thirtieth Street station in Philadelphia, Mr. Demming had come out of his room and gone back to the diner. Half an hour later, after the train had stopped at North Philadelphia and was running on toward Trenton, Mr. Demming came back to Bedroom C. By that time, Tingle had bundled up used sheets from the lower berth, put the spare mattress back in the upper berth, removed dirty towels and left two pillows on the long seat for Mr. Demming's greater comfort.

Tingle had not seen Mr. Demming again until he found him dead. He had a vague, unreliable, belief that the door of Bedroom C had been closed by Mr. Demming after he had returned to the room. He was certain it had been closed as the train passed New Brunswick, when he began to attend to the passengers who wanted to get off at Newark for transfer to the Hudson & Manhattan lines, and downtown New York. He had knocked at the door then, to find out whether Mr. Demming was going through to the Pennsylvania Station, and had received no answer. He had assumed Mr. Demming was, and had gone on.

After Newark, he had attended to passengers leaving at New York, picking up their bags and piling them in the vestibule. And when he reached this point, Tingle remembered something and his eyes rolled.

"He'd done put his bag outside," Tingle said. "Mostly the passengers leave them under the seat for me to haul out, but this gentleman had got it out and put it outside his door. I figured—"

Tingle, it turned out, assumed the gentleman did not wish to be disturbed, and so had not offered to brush his clothes. Tingle thought, it became apparent, that the gentleman was using the individual toilet facilities which were an advertised, and actual, feature of the new-style bedrooms. Tingle had therefore taken the bag and piled it with the others in the car vestibule. When the train stopped he had put it out on the platform. That was all Tingle knew.

Lieutenant Fahey said, "All right, boy," and interviewed the Pullman conductor, who could add little. He had not seen Mr. Demming, whose tickets had been collected in the station at Pittsburgh. All Mr. Demming was to the conductor was a mark on a chart, showing single occupancy, Pittsburgh to New York, of Bedroom C, Car 620.

Between New York and Pittsburgh, the train had stopped at Altoona, Harrisburg, Paoli and at North Philadelphia. Thereafter it had stopped only at Newark. The Pullman conductor suggested that the person who murdered Mr. Demming had either ridden with him all the way from Pittsburgh or got on at one of the intermediate stations, ending with North Philadelphia.

"How about Newark?" Lieutenant Fahey wanted to know. The conductor shook his head decisively.

"We are not allowed to take on passengers at Newark," he said. "Stop only to discharge."

"Would you have seen anybody who tried to get on at Newark?" Fahey insisted.

"Somebody would," the conductor insisted. "Nobody gets on there."

He was positive about it. But it had to be checked. Fahey's men rounded up the crew of the train, from porters up, and questioned. Nobody had seen anybody get on the train at Newark. Each man questioned looked startled, and said that nobody was allowed to get on at Newark. It was against the rules.

"Somebody who was going to kill a guy might take a

chance on a company rule," Fahey suggested to the train conductor. The train conductor looked startled and a little shocked. This, his expression said, was a remark which made light of the company rules, of which light was not to be made. After that, he said flatly that it was impossible for anyone to get on at Newark without being seen.

It began to look to Lieutenant Fahey as if the weight of the investigation was going to fall on the authorities of neither New Jersey nor New York, but on those of Pennsylvania. New York was left holding the body; Pennsylvania presumably held the facts, and the background. Unless—unless, of course, somebody had gone to the trouble of going at least as far from New York as North Philadelphia in order to ride back on the same train with Mr. Demming and kill him. This seemed, to Lieutenant Fahey, to be going a long way around. In any event, Lieutenant Fahey decided, Pennsylvania was the place to start.

He left the boys at it and drove back to Headquarters. He got in touch with Pittsburgh and told Pittsburgh that its Mr. Robert J. Demming (tentative) was dead in New York of smothering, and it looked like their baby. He reported direct to Deputy Chief Inspector Artemus O'Malley, Lieutenant Weigand, acting captain and Fahey's immediate superior, being elsewhere. O'Malley agreed it was Pittsburgh's baby, for the moment. He said, sadly, that it looked as if Lieutenant Fahey was going to have to make a trip to Pittsburgh, eventually. Lieutenant Fahey, who disapproved of travel, sighed and said there wasn't any hurry, was there? Pittsburgh had better look around first, hadn't it? O'Malley nodded absently and went on reading his mail.

Lieutenant Fahey had been gone several minutes when Inspector O'Malley sat up as straight as he could, considering his structure, and said he'd be damned. He snorted, glared around the room, and commanded his secretary.

"Get Weigand!" he commanded. "Get Fahey."

Fahey was easy to get. He came back and looked at the letter and said he'd be damned. Lieutenant Weigand was not easy to get. Lieutenant Weigand had been in and had gone out. He had left telephone numbers at which he might be reached.

12

Mrs. Paul Williams, seated behind her desk in her law offices in Forty-fourth Street, was more corseted than ever. She had sent word that she was engaged. Weigand had promised to take only a few minutes. She had, testily, agreed to allow him a very few. When Weigand sat across from her in an uncomfortable chair, dedicated to clients, she sat in her own chair as if Weigand were about to leave at any instant. She said, "Well, Lieutenant?"

Weigand wasted no time.

"You lunched at a place called the Roundabout yesterday," he told her. "You met a man named Jung—Bandelman Jung—at the bar. He stole a telegram from you. What's it all about?"

The way to find things out was to ask, Weigand believed. If that failed, of course, you had to use other means.

"Jung?" Mrs. Williams repeated. "Oh, the funny little man. Is he one of your men, Lieutenant?"

"No," Weigand said. "He's not one of us. What did he want?"

"He was ridiculous," Mrs. Williams said. "He wanted to know if I killed Mr. Sproul."

Weigand looked at her.

"Just like that?" he said.

"Just like that," Mrs. Williams assured him. "He

sat down beside me at the bar and said, 'Mrs. Williams, please. Did you kill Mr. Sproul?' "

That was remarkable. Weigand said it was remarkable.

"It was preposterous," Mrs. Williams corrected. "Such things shouldn't be allowed." She stared at him. "Such things aren't allowed," she said. "He could have been arrested."

"Yes," Weigand agreed. "Was that all he said? I take it you told him you didn't kill Mr. Sproul, by the way?"

Mrs. Williams looked at him hard and decided to skip it.

"No," she said. "He kept insisting. Was I sure I hadn't killed Mr. Sproul? I ordered him to quit bothering me."

"And—" Weigand prompted.

"He said that he was asking everybody," she said. "Everybody who was there—at the club. He said they all denied it. He was entirely ridiculous; he was—plaintive about it. As if everybody was in a conspiracy against him." She shook her head. "Obviously," she said, "he should be committed for observation."

It did, Weigand thought, sound as if Mr. Jung's mind would bear looking into.

"Your secretary brought you a telegram while you were there," he said, guessing a little. "We have reason for thinking Mr. Jung stole it. Did he? And why?"

"You mean," Mrs. Williams said, "that that Mrs. North thought somebody stole it. Don't you? She's irresponsible."

Weigand, unruffled, agreed that Mrs. North thought Mrs. Williams had received a telegram, and that Jung had stolen it. He saw no reason for correcting Mrs. Williams' impression of Mrs. North's responsibility. The point, he repeated, was whether she had received a telegram, and whether Jung had stolen it.

"I got a telegram," Mrs. Williams agreed, coldly.

"From an out-of-town client, making an appointment with me for this morning." She looked at her watch. "For ten-fifteen," she said. "Which is five minutes from now, Lieutenant. And I fail to see that it concerns you in any way whatever."

She half rose, to end the interview. Weigand obediently stood up.

"I gather," he said, "that Mr. Jung didn't steal the telegram?"

Mrs. Williams entirely rose.

"Certainly not," she said. "Why should he? Nobody stole it. I brought it back here, had my secretary make a note of the appointment, and threw the telegram in the waste basket. And you're wasting the time of both of us, Lieutenant."

Weigand said, in a voice without particular expression, that he was sorry. He added that it was something detectives often did, always with regret. But it was sometimes necessary. He moved toward the door and then turned, remembering something.

"By the way," he said, "Mrs. North said you fainted, or almost fainted, after you got the telegram. But obviously the message couldn't—"

"Certainly not," Mrs. Williams said. "It was—it is a physical peculiarity, Lieutenant. Sometimes when I eat or drink hurriedly, or when I'm nervous, a—a pressure results which seems to affect nerve ganglia, so that I momentarily feel faint. That happened yesterday. It had nothing to do with the message, of course."

Weigand said he saw, and that she was very kind. He left the office and closed the door behind him. There was no one in the stiff chairs in the outer office, where visitors presumably would wait. Mrs. Williams' out-of-town client had evidently not arrived. Weigand looked at his watch, found it still lacked a minute or two of ten-fifteen and went on.

He stepped into the elevator and started down. Mrs. Williams' secretary reached the elevator corridor just in time to see the top of the elevator disappear. She returned to the office and picked up the telephone and said that she was sorry, she had been unable to catch Lieutenant Weigand. She looked up in time to smile at a rotund gentleman from New Darien, Connecticut, who was coming in, and to tell him that Mrs. Williams was free to see him now.

It was almost ten-thirty when Weigand pushed a button beside the name of Loretta Shaw in the vestibule of a walk-up apartment behind Altman's in the Murray Hill area. It rang a bell; Weigand could hear the bell. Nothing else happened, so Weigand pressed the button again, and the bell rang again. Still nothing happened. Then a telephone began ringing, and it sounded as if the telephone bell was in the same apartment with the doorbell. The telephone bell kept on ringing. Then Loretta Shaw opened the outside door of the vestibule and came in from the street and said, without pleasure, "Oh. You."

"Were you coming to see me, Lieutenant?" she said and Weigand, because it was obvious to both of them, merely nodded. The telephone bell kept on ringing and Loretta Shaw listened to it.

"It sounds like mine," she said, and began groping in her bag for keys. It took her a woman's time to find her keys. Weigand, for reasons not entirely clear, but probably having to do with Dorian's similar gropings, was somewhat disarmed. But Loretta Shaw found her keys and opened the door and ran ahead up the stairs to the second floor apartment in front. Weigand came after her. She unlocked a second door, ran across a wide, comfortable room to a telephone and reached it just as it stopped ringing. She took the telephone from its cradle and listened and said, "Damn."

"Why is it—" she began and then, evidently remembering who Weigand was, stopped.

"I don't know," Weigand told her. "It always does."

She did not respond. She threw hat and light, fuzzy coat on a chair and faced Weigand and said, "Well, Lieutenant?" She did not welcome him.

"You've been having me followed," she charged, when Weigand said nothing, waiting.

Weigand said, "Right."

"Yesterday," he said. "Up to last night. A man saw you home. Then I called the man off."

He had not wanted to call the man off, or any of the other men off. But Inspector O'Malley had had other notions; he had wanted to know how many men Weigand thought he was entitled to, and where he thought the men he was using were getting him. So the men had been called off.

"Why follow me?" Loretta Shaw wanted to know. "Do you think I killed Lee?"

"I don't know," Weigand said. "Did you?"

"I was going to marry him," the girl said. "Why should I?"

Weigand said they might as well sit down. This was evidently going to take time.

"You're making it hard for everybody, Miss Shaw," he told her. "Including yourself. You weren't going to marry Sproul. You were—are—going to marry Mr. Schwartz."

The girl looked at him and sat down. Weigand sat down where he could see her face, and nodded at the expression on it. "Yes," he said.

Loretta Shaw said he was crazy. He had things mixed up. She had been married to George Schwartz. A long time ago, in Paris. She had divorced him.

"I know," Weigand said. "And Thursday you and he got a license to marry again. While you were still pretending to be engaged to Sproul. And before Sproul was killed."

The girl said there must be some mistake, but she did not say it with conviction. Weigand merely smiled and shook his head and waited. He was good at waiting.

"Suppose we did," she said, when he had waited her out. "What then?"

"Then you'd get married to Schwartz," Bill Weigand explained. "Instead of to Sproul. The inference is that you knew Sproul wouldn't be marrying anybody, because Sproul would be dead."

The girl looked at Weigand with contempt. She said that, if she understood what he was saying, he was assuming that she and George were fools. "Utter damn fools," she said.

Weigand nodded, rather affably.

"We're not," she said. "If we had known what was—what was going to happen, that's the last thing we would have done. Obviously."

"People do foolish things," Weigand told her. "We often find the things they do helpful. If you and Schwartz weren't fools, what were you? If you didn't know Sproul was going to die, what did you plan to do about him?"

The girl looked at him; he could feel her trying to get under the surface and find out about him. You could only guess at her purpose. Perhaps she was trying to discover what she could get away with; perhaps she was trying to decide if he would recognize the truth if he heard it. She would, whatever her purpose, pretend it was the latter.

"You wouldn't understand," she told him. It was the inevitable opening. Weigand made the inevitable answer to it. "Try to make me."

"No," she said. "It isn't clear enough. It—it isn't one way or the other. It was the way I felt at the time, after George and I—after we talked. It seemed simple and we were just going to tell Sproul. It was—" She broke off and stared at him. "People feel one way at one time and another way right afterward," she said. "Or I do. Do you understand that?"

Weigand was tired of being led carefully by the hand through the kindergarten of psychology.

"Look," he said. "The only way to talk to people,

Miss Shaw, is to assume they can follow what you say—that they have enough experience to understand simple things. Maybe you find out they haven't. That's just too bad. But if you want to tell them anything, you have to try to get across. Suppose you just assume I can understand. You felt Thursday afternoon some time that you would rather marry George Schwartz than Mr. Sproul. You agreed to apply for a marriage license with him. Then afterward you weren't so sure. Right?"

"It's more complicated than that," she said. "It's like being different people. Or going around and looking at things from another direction. And finding they look different."

Weigand felt himself being sucked into it.

"Everything," he told her, "is more complicated than the simplest words for it. Tritely, we feel more than we can say. And so the person we're talking to has to help. You say, 'I thought Thursday afternoon I wanted to marry Schwartz. Later I changed my mind, or almost changed my mind.' All right—that isn't all of it. I know that isn't all of it. But we can't spend the day on it."

"I know," she said. She smiled for the first time. "Isn't it awful?" she said.

Weigand did not intend to smile in response, but he almost did. He said, "Right."

She said she would try to explain, then. She and Schwartz had been married. In Paris. Weigand knew that? All right, then. Something had happened and they thought they didn't want to be married any longer. Perhaps they didn't; perhaps they were right then. Perhaps they shouldn't be married. "Lee said we were wrong for each other," she said. They—she and Schwartz—came back to the United States at different times, and met again only a few months ago. And then she was engaged to marry Sproul. And then she discovered that she was not really sure.

"And Schwartz?" Weigand said.

"He was sure," she said. "Or thought he was sure. He wanted us to get married again. He said it was all Lee Sproul. All our trouble. He had—he had a theory."

She looked at Weigand a little helplessly. "I don't know," she said. "It sounds crazy. Like something in a—in a psychological novel. Maybe it is something George just—made up. Without knowing he made it up."

Weigand shrugged. They were going back into it.

"Just tell me," he said.

She looked at him doubtfully. She didn't, she said, quite see why she was telling him what she was. Weigand simplified that for her. She was telling him because she had to explain an action that looked, from a police point of view, very strange. She was telling him so much because the explanation was, from her point of view, complex. She nodded.

Schwartz's theory, as nearly as she could understand it—"and express it"—was that Sproul had deliberately broken up their marriage. He had worked on both of them, persuading each separately that their marriage was wrong. He had done it, not primarily to get her—"although he wanted me, in his way"—but to prove a point.

"We were living—oh, call it simply," she said. "With emotional simplicity. We were contented. Sproul didn't believe in that; didn't believe people could live simply and contentedly. He thought—oh, that the emotions were a turmoil. Like Freud. And we violated a theory; maybe a theory he'd built his whole life on. But if we stopped living simply, his theory would be all right again. So he—he tried to unsimplify us. And apparently he was right, because it worked." She listened to herself doubtfully, and looked at Weigand with the doubt in her eyes. "There was more to it than that, the way George said it," she said. "He talked for hours. He said there was malice in it too, and jealousy—not jealousy of him, but of the fact that we were happy with each other." She broke off. "That makes us sound like children on a honeymoon," she said. "We weren't. Things went wrong, and we had doubts, and we did and said things and—but under-neath we were happy to be together, and didn't want it changed. And Sproul changed it. Anyway, that's what George thought." She paused again. "I guess that's what I think too," she said. "The way I felt Thursday. I'm talked into it again."

She examined Weigand's expression.

"I'm a fool," she said. "I get to talking. All this hasn't anything to do with what you want to know."

It had, Weigand thought. More than she realized at the moment. He was sorry about that.

"How did Schwartz feel about all this? About what he believed Sproul had done?" he wanted to know.

"He hated Sproul," she said. "He said he was—oh, a lot of things. A vivisectionist. That—that people like him shouldn't—"

She understood then, and broke off. And this time her eyes were frightened, and she tried to hide it.

"Shouldn't be allowed to what?" Weigand said. "Live?"

"Oh, no!" she said. "You don't understand."

But she was too hurried. Too emphatic. Schwartz had said something like that. He would have to get it out of her, which wasn't going to be pleasant. Or easy. And then the doorbell rang.

The girl didn't move. She did not seem to hear it. But she heard it all right. Weigand guessed, not think-ing it was a hard guess.

"Let him in, Miss Shaw," he said. "Get it over with."

She seemed about to rebel, but she went across the room and pressed a button behind a door. They could hear the downstairs door open when the catch was released, and hear it close again with a small, heavy bang. They could hear feet on the stairs. Weigand stood behind the girl when she opened the door. She said, "George!" in a tone of warning and Schwartz looked over her head at Bill Weigand.

"Hello, copper," Schwartz said. "Bullying women?"

Weigand looked at him.

"Just until you got here, Schwartz," he said. "Just until you got here."

Schwartz stood for a moment with an arm around the girl's shoulder. He said, "I'm sorry, honey." He led her across the room to a chair, and put her in it and turned to face Weigand.

"Well, copper?" he said.

"Well," Weigand said, "I hear you threatened to kill Sproul." Weigand's tone was conversational.

"No!" the girl said. "No, George. I didn't—you know I didn't!"

"It's all right, honey," Schwartz said. "These cops! Smart boys, these cops. Aren't you, copper?"

"Enough," Weigand said. He waited. "So Miss Shaw was lying?" he said. "Maybe she threatened him?"

Loretta Shaw looked at Weigand and hated him. Weigand was not, for the moment, particularly fond of himself. However—

"So I said I'd like to kill him," Schwartz said. "So you arrest me and knock a confession out of me. It must be swell to be a cop. All right. I said I'd enjoy killing Sproul. I would have enjoyed killing Sproul. Intensely."

"But of course you didn't," Weigand said. His tone was intentionally weary.

"I didn't," Schwartz said. "There's no of course about it. It just happened that I didn't. Maybe I would have, some day. If he got in my way again. I hated the bastard." He said the last without emphasis, but in a way which made it sound as if he had hated Sproul a lot. It was rather startling, the way he must have hated Sproul.

"I'll work it out for you," Schwartz said. His tone

had contempt in it. "I was violently jealous of Sproul because he had taken my wife. I hated him and wouldn't have minded killing him. I found out that my wife—my former wife—was really going through with marrying him, although I felt that she still loved me. I—I threatened to kill Sproul if she didn't remarry me and to keep me from doing that she went so far as to get a license to marry me. But I got to thinking it over, and I thought I'd better kill Sproul anyway, to be on the safe side, and so I gave him a dose of morphine. Is that enough for a jury, copper?"

"Plenty," Weigand assured him. "Do you want to say that was the way it was?"

"It wasn't that way!" the girl said. "You know it wasn't that way! Tell him it wasn't!" The last was to George Schwartz.

Schwartz looked down at her and smiled a little.

"What's the use?" he said. "That's the way the copper wants it to be. That's a nice, easy way for it to be. Isn't that right, copper?"

Weigand looked at him and felt tired. All melodrama and complexity, these people were. But easy to see through. Childishly easy. He was supposed to reject this theory because it came from Schwartz, who would not advance it if it were true; who advanced it as if it were an absurd theory, gauged to the immature mind of a policeman. Weigand was supposed to be stung by the reflection on his mind, and to reject the theory with annoyance. Whereas the theory might be true, and all this an intellectual's obvious game. Weigand's temper frayed at the edges; he knitted it up again before he spoke.

"I'd like an easy solution," he said. "Obviously, Mr. Schwartz. Would you like me to accept yours?"

Weigand did not sound angry. He did sound a little as if he were speaking to a small boy. Schwartz did not seem to notice it, but the girl did and she looked at Weigand with eyes which held speculation.

Schwartz's mind had room only for its own emotional subtleties. He told Weigand what it was he didn't give what Weigand thought.

"You ought to," Weigand advised him. "You really ought to, Mr. Schwartz. Do you want me to accept this as a confession that you killed Sproul?" He was patient, now. Schwartz was listening, now; he heard tired patience in Weigand's voice. He looked a little embarrassed, suddenly; Weigand suspected that he was looking at himself, and being a little surprised by what he saw.

"Am I to take it that you really want to find out?" Schwartz said. It was an effort to get his feet under him, and sounded like it. "Or are you just asking?"

Weigand said, "Oh, for God's sake."

"All right," Schwartz said. "Maybe I was wrong. No, I didn't kill Sproul, Lieutenant. And Retta didn't. But I worked out some very fancy ways to kill him, from time to time. In my mind. In day dreams."

"George!" Loretta Shaw said. "You mustn't—"

"Very fancy plans," Schwartz insisted, but his tone was light and amused. "Sealed rooms and everything. One of them was new."

Weigand went along.

"I doubt it," he said. "I doubt it, Mr. Schwartz."

"So," Schwartz said, "you read them too. Carter Dickson?"

"Sometimes," Weigand said. "Only it's John Dickson Carr for sealed rooms."

Schwartz shook his head.

"I don't see that it makes any difference," Loretta Shaw said. "I really don't."

Atmospheres changed rapidly with these people, Weigand thought. Now they were both very amiable. Which proved nothing; murderers could be amiable when not a-murdering. None of this proved anything, one way or the other. But while the atmosphere lasted it was worth utilizing. Weigand relaxed and lighted a cigarette and gave the impression of a man who had concluded his business and was about to go, but was in no hurry to go.

"Right," he said, and then after a pause, during which Schwartz and the girl looked at him with mild interest, he went on.

"Frankly," he said, "and without prejudice—you people puzzle me a little. All of you—you two, Sproul as was, Mr. White and the Akrons. Particularly Mr. White."

"Do we?" Loretta said. "Why? And why Mr. White particularly?" She paused, smiled and said: "Not that I can't see how he might."

The three of them shared appreciation of Mr. White, needing no words.

"Right," Weigand said, after a moment. "That's precisely it. Here is Mr. White and he is—well, what he is. Apparently he strikes the two of you much as he strikes me. One of you didn't like Sproul, the other was going to marry him. There was tension between the two of you about him. Akron doesn't seem to like anybody—except his sister. Little Mr. Jung—" He broke off and started over. "What I'm trying to say," he said, "is that you formed a group which wasn't—well, well assorted. And yet you formed a group. You all, even you, Schwartz, went to a dinner celebrating Sproul's lecture tour. And all the time I've felt that you were—well, sticking together. However you felt about one another. It makes a kind of disunited united front."

Weigand invited confidence; I am, he thought, being very lulling. Without prejudice.

"Not Jung," Schwartz said. "Definitely not Jung. As for the rest—well, I know what you mean. I'd never thought about it, particularly, but I know what you mean. It's a hangover from Paris, I suppose."

"Yes?" Bill Weigand said, and waited.

"It's merely," Loretta Shaw said, "that we were a little group of roughly one kind of people in a much larger group of another kind of people. Isn't that it, George? We went around in little circles."

"Concentric," Schwartz said. "Yes, Retta, I suppose so. And when we came back we—well, brought our difference with us. Along with our differences. Our difference from other people, I mean. Although it was imaginary here. I suppose that it is merely that we had shared certain experiences and felt that we knew one another better than we knew other people." He paused and looked abstractedly past Weigand. "Sometimes it seemed as if only that was real," he said. "As if afterward we had been only playing out the string. Or it felt that way at first. Now it's wearing off; we haven't been as united lately as we used to be. After this I suppose we won't be united at all. But I can imagine how we would seem to an outsider." He smiled, and looked at Weigand. "My use of that word explains the whole business," he said. "Doesn't it? It even includes Mr. White, who's certainly a funny guy if there ever was one."

"Very funny," Weigand agreed. "Do you suppose he would steal somebody else's work and pass it off as his own?"

There was a pause. You can hear the brick drop, Weigand thought. Schwartz and Loretta Shaw looked at each other and then at Weigand. She left it to Schwartz, who said he wouldn't know.

"But there was a story to that effect?" Weigand said. It was not really a question.

"There were a lot of stories," Schwartz said. "About everybody. Our friend Mr. Sproul was a great spreader of stories. I may have heard one about White. I wouldn't know whether it was true. He may have heard stories about me. He wouldn't know whether they were true, or what the truth about them was."

He stared at Weigand. The atmosphere was changing again. But the interlude had been useful; maybe it had been useful. Weigand twisted out his cigarette.

"I got the story from Sproul's notes," Weigand told

them. "I got several stories." He let it lie, for what they wanted to make of it. He took up another tack.

"How long were you planning to marry Sproul, Miss Shaw?" he wanted to know. "How long were you engaged to him?"

The girl thought a moment and said about a year, more or less. Weigand registered surprise.

"Wasn't that a good while?" he asked. "I mean—I should have expected you to marry as soon as you thought it would be a good idea. Being sensible people."

And, he did not add, informal people. He thought of Mullins' description of the group and did not let his face show what he had thought.

"She really knew better," Schwartz said. "When it looked like coming to the point, she had more sense."

His tone was resolute; more resolute than convincing. Loretta Shaw shook her head slowly.

"No," she said. "Not honestly. In the last few months, yes. But there was a while before that when I would have married him any time. Only he wasn't in any hurry." She looked at Schwartz. "That's how it was, George," she said. "I'm glad now, but that's how it was. He kept putting it off. I didn't."

"Right," Weigand said. "I have to be personal, you know. I may as well go on. Did Jean Akron have anything to do with it? His hesitancy, I mean?"

The girl flushed. But she looked at Weigand, and her voice was calm.

"Perhaps," she said. "I think so now, anyway. I didn't then. I thought—oh, that there were some arrangements he had to make first. But perhaps it was Jean."

Weigand nodded. He said Jean's brother seemed to think so. He added that they were devoted, for brother and sister.

"He is," Schwartz said. "I don't know about Jean. Lately. I think she's—well, been noticing Y. Charley a good deal."

"This devotion—?" Weigand said.

Schwartz shook his head.

"She keeps house for him," he said. "She's useful to Herbert Akron, and Herbert Akron is very devoted to people who make him comfortable. He doesn't want things upset. He can be pretty violent about it, because he's a pretty violent guy, apparently. We never knew him very well; he dropped in and out, seeing his sister, coming on business mostly. He wasn't one of the group. Neither was Y. Charley, for that matter. But a lot of people you haven't heard of were."

Loretta Shaw picked it up. She said there was no reason why it should be somebody from the group, or that part of the group Weigand knew.

"A lot of other people didn't like Lee," she said. "A lot of them may be in New York."

Weigand nodded and said, "Right." He added that they would broaden it out later, if they had to; that it was early days yet.

"We merely take people up as they come along," he said. "Without prejudice."

He stood up.

"We're still suspects, I suppose?" Loretta Shaw said, her voice carefully light.

"Oh, yes," Weigand said. "Maybe one of you did it. Maybe you, so you wouldn't have to marry Sproul. Or for some other reason. Maybe you, Schwartz. So she couldn't marry him. Or for some other reason."

"Naturally," Schwartz said, and his tone matched Weigand's. "Naturally we deny it."

"Naturally," Weigand said. "Why not?"

He started toward the door and the telephone bell rang. He hesitated and Loretta Shaw answered it. She said, "Why, yes, he is," and turned to Weigand. "It's for you," she said. Weigand took the telephone and listened and said, "Right." He looked at the two a moment, speculatively.

"I'll probably be back," he said, in a different voice.

He went out and down the stairs and into the Buick.
He went downtown fast.

Weigand read the letter again. It was written on the
stationery of a Pittsburgh hotel, in long hand, and the
signature was legible enough. It was addressed to
"Officer in Charge, Homicide Bureau, Police Headquarters, New York City." It read:

Dear Sir:

   I believe I have information which may help you
   solve the murder of Mr. Victor Leeds Sproul. Since
   before giving you that information, I must conduct
   certain investigations of my own, I am leaving for New
   York tonight on the 11:15 train. I will come to your
   office some time during the morning and I would appreciate an interview with the officer in charge of the
   Sproul investigation."

The writer was "sincerely yours." He was Robert J.
Demming. And he was dead, per the report of Detective Lieutenant Fahey. Weigand looked at the enve-
lope, clipped to the letter. He was dead because it had
rained heavily the day before; so heavily that airplanes
between Pittsburgh and New York were grounded; so
heavily that a letter marked for air-mail had come
through by train. And as a result neither air-mail
postage nor special delivery stamp had got the letter to
men who would have known what to do about it until
Mr. Demming was dead.

If the letter had come by air-mail it would have
reached him the evening before, Weigand thought.
And if it had reached him the evening before, Mr.
Demming would not have been left to his own re-
sources. They might have thought that Mr. Demming
was probably a crank; they would have thought that
Mr. Demming was probably a crank. But a crank who
brings his crankiness personally from Pittsburgh to
New York is not a crank to be ignored by policemen

very anxious for information. As God knows we are, Weigand thought, with annoyance. So Mr. Demming would have been met and safeguarded.

And that, Weigand thought immediately, would have done them no particular good, because Mr. Demming would have been dead by the time they had met him. Unless they had gone to North Philadelphia, where they would not have gone. Or—wait a moment—to Newark. They would not have gone there either. But—

"Yeh," Lieutenant Fahey said, as Weigand looked up at him. "A hell of a note, ain't it?"

Weigand agreed. He asked Fahey a question. Fahey shrugged.

"That's what they say," he told Weigand. "They're pretty positive. Whoever killed him must have ridden with him from at least North Philadelphia. Sure the train stops at Newark. And sure nobody could have got on there. That's what they say."

He shrugged slightly.

Weigand tossed him a sheaf of reports and shrugged in turn. Fahey leafed through them and said it was sure a hell of a note.

The reports were from watching men who had had eyes on certain people until six o'clock that morning, when their tours of duty ended. They had not been replaced, because Inspector O'Malley had decided it wasn't necessary; because, Weigand admitted honestly, he had himself been fairly sure it wasn't necessary, and had made no argument. The reports showed that at six o'clock that morning, barring devious exits from their apartments and furnished rooms, and homes in Westchester, the people being watched had been under observation in New York City. They had not been in North Philadelphia. At 6:40 the train on which Robert J. Demming was riding, bringing information to the police, left North Philadelphia for New York. At that time Mr. Demming was alive.

If the murderer of Mr. Demming got on the train at

North Philadelphia, he was not George Schwartz, at home in his hotel in the Forties, or Loretta Shaw, at home in Murray Hill; it was not either of the Akrons, nor Mr. White nor Y. Charles Burden. It was not Mrs. Paul Williams nor, on the basis of another report, this time from an F.B.I. man, the little dark Mr. Jung. It was, in short, not anybody who had so far entered the sprawling, unsatisfactory picture of the Sproul investigation. And if that was true, Weigand had so far got precisely nowhere, which was discouraging.

But if it were Newark, now—there had been time enough to get to Newark by tube train and to meet the train which was bringing Mr. Demming. A murderer would have had to move briskly, but murderers must expect to make some sacrifices.

Weigand called Mullins and gave Mullins instructions. Mullins looked grieved and said, "Newark?" in a certain tone. When Weigand nodded, Mullins said, "O.K., Loot, but how about using a department car?"

"So long as it isn't connected with you, O.K.," Weigand said. "But remember, you're not a cop. You don't show any badge. Remember, you may have to testify, eventually."

"Yeah," Mullins said. "If you can get it in. Which you can't."

That, Weigand told him, they would let the D.A.'s office worry about. When and if. The D.A.'s office could tell it to the judge. At the least, they would have the information.

"O.K., Loot," Mullins said. Mullins departed.

Mullins consulted time-tables and ordered a car from the police garage. He drove discreetly through the Holland Tunnel and followed signs to the Pulaski Skyway. He followed a sign which said "Newark Business District" and dropped down an incline from the elevated highway into the turmoil of New Jersey traffic. In Newark he had time to find a parking lot and deposit the car, and afterward to walk a block to the

Pennsylvania Station. Mullins bought a Hudson and Manhattan ticket to New York and noted the cost down in the notebook which was sacred to the expense account.

Mullins climbed stairs to the platform. A multiple-unit train waited, with doors open and a few passengers sitting disconsolately inside, to the right of the platform as he faced in what was, he decided, the direction of New York. Mullins sauntered along the platform, lighting a cigarette; looking, he trusted, like a passenger stretching his legs until the last minute. He paused by the open door of one of the cars and gazed in abstractedly. (And a small, furtive man, who knew the build of the Mullinses through long, and rather unsatisfactory, experience, arose with an air of great preoccupation, kept his face averted, and sauntered back through two cars. Reaching the third, he sauntered out, stood for a moment abstractedly on the platform and, being sure Mullins was looking the other way, darted down a flight of exit stairs. The small furtive man didn't know whether they were after him again, but usually they were. Mullins, pleasantly assuring himself that nobody would take him for a policeman, continued his ambling patrol of the platform.)

Red caps appeared on the platform and began to look up the line. The head end of an electric locomotive appeared, and pulled a string of cars slowly along the platform, on the left as Mullins faced New York. Doors began to open and porters in white coats peered out. Red caps ran with the train along the platform, having picked their doors. The train stopped and porters began shoveling bags to the platform. Mullins loitered near one of the doors, well back in the train and in the Pullman section.

There was only a little luggage to come out of the car he had picked, and red caps clustered around it hopefully. Several people came out, pointed at bags and went off with porters following them. At the doors of the Hudson and Manhattan cars, trainmen began to call, "This train for downtown New York. This train for downtown New York." Mullins moved up half the length of a car, toward the locomotive, and then walked down briskly toward a door. He reached it just as the porter was stepping back inside. Without hesitation, Mullins followed the porter inside. The porter looked at him.

"So this is Newark, huh?" Mullins said, with heartiness. "Doesn't look like much, George."

"No, suh," the porter said, continuing to look at him. Mullins remained bland.

"You don't stop long," Mullins said. "Didn't have time to get back to my own car."

The porter looked at him and quit looking at him.

"No, suh," he said. "Jes' for people to get off. You goin' to the Pennsylvania Station, suh?"

"That's right," Mullins said. He walked past the Negro, now moving rapidly. He moved forward in the car and was half way along it when the train started. He reached the door ahead and found a porter closing it.

"Hold it, boy," Mullins said. "I want to get off!"

The porter shook his head and said, "Sorry, suh."

"Can't open it now," the porter said. "We's started, boss. Guess you'll jes' have to go on to New York, boss."

Mullins guessed so too. He remembered the police car parked in Newark, realized he would have to go back to Newark and get it, and said, "Damn."

"Yes, *suh!*" the porter said. Mullins, thinking with exasperation about the return trip to Newark, went to the men's lounge at the end of the car and sat down and lighted a cigarette. Anyhow, it had worked. He wouldn't, he decided, have to tell the Loot about getting caught on the train and having to go back to Newark for the car. It had worked without too much difficulty, but probably with the maximum difficulty to be expected. With more luck, he might have avoided conversation with the first porter, who might be expected to remember him. But he did not see how, without hopeless bungling, he could have had worse luck, and he was on the train.

So anybody could have boarded Car 620 in Newark by going to the trouble of pretending that he was a passenger on the train, and got off when the train stopped to stretch his legs, and had boarded it again before it left, entering through any car and pretending that his assigned accommodations were on another car. Anybody could then go to Bedroom C, assuming he knew Mr. Demming to be in Bedroom C, walk in, smother Mr. Demming, walk into the lounge—either lounge, depending on sex—or walk through to another car, get off at New York and go about his business.

But how would you know the room in which your victim was waiting? Mullins puzzled over that. Then he remembered that, while he stood on the platform, the Pullmans had crept by slowly, and that he had had time to look in the windows. If he were looking for someone, and watched carefully, and took his position far enough back along the platform so that most, at least, of the Pullmans would pass him before the train stopped, he would have a fair chance of spotting his man. But only, Mullins thought, a fifty-fifty chance, since the person you wanted might be sitting on the opposite side of the car.

Mullins shook his head at that. A fifty-fifty chance wasn't, he thought, as good a chance as a murderer would want to have. That wasn't good enough. Mullins, utilizing the fifteen minutes from Newark to New York with furious intensity, tried to think what was good enough. His mind stuck. He tossed the cigarette into an ash receiver as the train began to come up out of the tunnel and walked forward through the next car. Then it came to him.

The next car, unlike the one through which he had passed previously, was a room car and the corridor ran down one side. All the passengers, therefore, were on the other side and, if the windows went by slowly enough, you could look into their rooms. And Mr. Demming had been killed in such a car; it was only possible to kill him, as he had been killed, in such a car. So—

At the Pennsylvania Station, Mullins left the train, unchallenged. He pursued a new thought to the information booth in the center of the station, and got a folder of Pennsylvania trains. He followed hieroglyphics to trains between New York and Pittsburgh, eastbound, found the 11:15 and, in another column, found the paragraph concerning its "Equipment." He read:

> Pittsburgh to New York:
>   Fourteen sections, one drawing room
>   Ten double bedrooms.

He also found a note:

> "Cars ready for occupancy, 10:30 P.M."

Mullins, leaning against a convenient section of the wall, continued his researches gladly, if a little laboriously. He discovered that, as nearly as he could tell, the train on which Mr. Demming had arrived, dead, had come through from St. Louis, although Mr. Demming had not. Mr. Demming had got on a made-up car in Pittsburgh—one of two cars ready for occupancy at 10:30 P.M.—gone to sleep, been picked up in his car by the train from St. Louis and ridden on to death. So the person who wanted to spot Mr. Demming, and was willing to go to a little trouble, would have only to look in the windows of two cars. If he knew Mr. Demming well enough to know his habits, he probably would be able to decide whether to seek him in the room car, or in the open-section car. And if he wanted to go to still more trouble, he probably could find out, by asking, where in the train the two cars picked up at Pittsburgh would be. Probably, Mullins thought, at the end of the train.

Mullins, impressed with his rapid progress, found
the station-master's office, identified himself, and
asked questions. It would be possible for a person with
a plausible story—the desire to meet an invalid rela-
tive, for example—to find out through the information
service in New York where the cars from Pittsburgh
would be in the train from St. Louis. It probably, a
clerk told Mullins, would be possible to find out
whether anyone had sought that information by inter-
viewing the men on the telephone information service.

Mullins thought of pressing his quest, thought better
of it, decided the car would be safe for a while longer
in Newark, and went down to Headquarters by subway. He felt that the Loot would be pleased with him.

Weigand had watched Mullins set out for Newark
and, for the first time he could remember, felt a little
envious of the sergeant. Mullins was, at any rate, up
and about things. He, Weigand, had only to sit, and
look at papers, and think. He found the prospect
uninviting. Now, he decided, would be a fine time for a
hunch. He made himself receptive to hunches and
waited. No hunch came. He lighted a cigarette,
drummed his desk with tired fingers, and decided that
logic would have to serve. He looked for a crevice in
the case through which logic might creep. He saw
none.

He went back to reports, checking the dossiers of
those involved. He read again that Schwartz was not
really wanted by the police in Cincinnati; he noted
once more that Sproul had lived, and presumably
flourished, during his youth in Iowa. He noted that
Mrs. Paul Williams had been born in a Boston suburb
and was a widow with two children; he observed that
Burden lived in Westchester and had offices on Madison Avenue and was highly thought of in the lecture
business—was generally, indeed, considered the man
at the top of the heap; he saw that—

Then he stopped and turned back to the report on
Burden, and a statement that his eyes had slid over

first now caught and held them. Mr. Y. Charles Burden had, some weeks earlier, insured the life of Victor Leeds Sproul for $50,000, showing his contract with Sproul to prove an insurable interest.

The detective investigating—Stein, Weigand noted; good man, Stein—had continued his inquiry further on this point, had dug up the agent who had written the policy, and had made a separate report on the facts elicited. Weigand looked up the second report.

Burden had applied for the insurance on Sproul three months previously, a few days after he and Sproul had signed their contract. He had submitted that he had made at that date considerable expenditure preparing for the tour, and was preparing to make further expenditure; he had submitted that $50,000 would be only adequate recompense, in the event of Sproul's unanticipated death, for moneys already expended and to be expended, profits presumably to be derived and loss of prestige and confidence involved should Sproul be unable to complete the tour. The insurance agent had doubted whether it would go through and had suggested certain changes in the Sproul-Burden contract.

These had been made. The revised contract set up a partnership, limited in scope to the tour in question, between Sproul and Burden. Under this contract, reciprocal policies had become possible and had, in fact, been written. But, in view of the permanence of Burden's organization, and the evident fact that it would continue, even after his death, to direct the tour on which Sproul would then have embarked, the insurance taken by Sproul on Burden had been in the comparatively nominal sum of $5,000.

That covered the ground, Weigand decided. It also opened the view. It gave Burden the simplest and most obvious of motives, assuming he wanted $50,000 badly enough; assuming he needed $50,000. Weigand looked at the other report and sighed. There was no evidence that Burden did need $50,000.

But the evidence that he did not need $50,000 was, when you came down to it, hearsay evidence. Everybody thought that the Y. Charles Burden Lecture Bureau was in fine shape, hitting vigorously on a multitude of cylinders. But that was merely what everybody thought; they might be thinking what they were supposed to think. The Y. Charles Burden Bureau might be going fast on the rocks. And the Sproul tour, which promised to pay off, might be running into trouble.

After all, Weigand thought, Paris in the old days was getting a little old days itself. And Mr. Sproul was not, after all, quite an Elliot Paul. Perhaps since the tour was planned, and contracts for appearances signed, clubwomen had found a new interest in newer and more immediate things. Perhaps they were all listening to returned war correspondents, and being urged to shake off a lethargy which they, and not the correspondents, were assumed to feel. In that case, they might be canceling Mr. Sproul—assuming that they could, legally. That would have to be looked into.

By assuming enough, it appeared, you could assume a motive for Mr. Burden; a motive with a dollar sign in front of it, which was after all the most conventional juxtaposition. Weigand found himself brightening somewhat. He filed this new information in his mind and continued. He read that Herbert Akron had knocked down a man at a party because the man was, in the opinion of Herbert Akron, paying insulting attention to Jean Akron; he read that Jean was generally reported to have been much in Sproul's company some months earlier, but less in recent weeks, and that people had wondered what was between them; he learned that, four nights before he died, Loretta Shaw had suddenly slapped Sproul's face when they were dining together at a rather prominent table in a rather prominent restaurant, and then had burst into tears and gone out of the place almost at a run.

"Well, well," Weigand said. "Well, well, well!"

The telephone bell rang and Weigand said, "Yes?" into the transmitter. He said, "Who?" and jotted down a name. "Emmanuel Burkholdt." He said, "Yes?" again, listened, said "Thanks, Mr. Burkholdt" and cradled the telephone. He turned back to Sproul's dossier and made a notation:

"Sproul's lawyer, Em. Burkholdt, reports Sproul recently inquiring about steps to be taken to get divorce. Indicated would go on with later."

That would remind Weigand, when he looked at it again, that Mr. Burkholdt, anxious to help the police as a sworn officer of the court, and noting that nothing had been said about Sproul's having been married, had thought the police might be interested in knowing that Sproul was talking about getting a divorce. Sproul had inquired how long it was likely to take, what specific evidence was necessary in New York State and whether Burkholdt would want to handle the action for him, if he decided to bring it. Burkholdt had said he would want to. Sproul had said he would let him know in a few days. But instead of letting his lawyer know, Mr. Sproul had died of an overdose of morphine.

13

Mrs. North had ordered Spanish lobster for lunch because she liked it and it agreed with her perfectly, and Jerry liked it and would be home. But it showed, she thought, how really very little I know about children, because probably it isn't good for them. Mrs. North sighed and thought how odd it was that so many things were not good for children, but were presumably all right for grownups, who were simply, when you came to think of it, children who had begun to wear out. After the children got to be a certain age, of course; not very young children, who were obviously intermediate.

"Of course, dear," Mrs. North said, looking at Beth's plate. "You mustn't forget it is very rich."

"Oh," said Beth. "I like things rich. This isn't very rich, Aunt Pam. And we never have it at home."

This did not do a great deal to assuage Mrs. North's doubts. Probably there was reason for that.

"We don't want you getting sick while you're here," Mrs. North said, thinking as she said it that it was something rather special in the way of understatements. If they get sick, I'll die, Mrs. North thought.

"If you don't think things will, they won't," Margie said, rather suddenly. Mrs. North, to whom the remark sounded curiously familiar, looked at her with doubt. Mr. North looked at Mrs. North, who shook her head slightly, and smiled.

"Experience, darling," he told her. "You don't live with yourself, so naturally it's beyond you. She means that if you don't think things are going to make you ill, they won't make you ill. Very succinct she was too, I thought. Weren't you, Margie?"

"Succinct?" Margie repeated.

Mr. North looked as if he wished he had not brought it up. He also looked puzzled.

"Oh, direct," he said. "To the point. Condensed."

"Was I?" Margie said. "Anyway, I don't know if it's true, but Miss Norton said so. In physiology. At school. Anyway, she said it was a little true. I think I'll have just a little more lobster, Aunt Pam."

Pam gave her a little more lobster.

"Do you go to a nice school?" she said. It seemed somehow the proper thing to ask.

"Oh, we go to high school this year," Beth said. "Because of Daddy being in the army, except this week. But we brought our books."

"Did you, dear?" Pam said, looking a little helplessly at Jerry. "To study, you mean?"

"Oh, yes," Beth said.

"But you haven't studied," Pam pointed out.

"No," Beth said. "Not yet. We'll study on the train going home. When there isn't a murder."

"Oh, yes," Margie said. "How is the murder? You know, New York is so big, and exciting, that I keep forgetting the murder."

"That's a very good plan," Jerry said. "I wouldn't think about it if I were you, Margie. Or if I were you, Beth. It's—well, you can leave murders until later in life."

"Jerry!" Pam said. "That certainly sounded funny." She looked at him. "Sometimes, dear," she said, "I don't think you're as clear as you used to be. In saying things. You don't think, sometimes. I—"

"I'm sorry," Jerry said. "It must be carelessness." He looked at her. "Or something," he added. "I meant they could leave interest in murders until later in life. Murders are for the mature."

"Oh," Beth said. "We both like murders. We always read about them in the papers. Out home a man killed his wife and another man with an axe and it was very interesting. That's one thing about going to high school."

Both Mr. and Mrs. North looked blank, this time.

"Because we live at home," Margie explained. "Sometimes Beth isn't very clear. In boarding school, we didn't have the papers. We just had current events." Her expression became reminiscent. "It wasn't the same," she said. "And only selected things on the radio, like forums and symphonies."

"Except the little one like a camera Vee-dee had," Beth said. "The one Miss Ryder thought *was* a camera. We used to get Cugat." They also remembered. "Very small, of course," she said. "As if they were whispering. Particularly when Vee-dee kept it under her pillow so Miss Frantz wouldn't find it."

The conversation seemed a little private to Pam, but she remembered that she was hostess and should show an interest. If possible.

"Vee-dee," Pam said. "That's an odd name. Was she one of the girls?"

"Oh, yes," Beth said. "Vee-dee Thompson. Or *was* it Thompson?"

"I don't think so," Margie said. "But it was something like Thompson."

"Thomas?" Mrs. North suggested.

Both girls shook their heads.

"Tompkins?" Mr. North offered.

"No," Beth said. "More like Thompson than either. Campbell, maybe."

Mrs. North looked puzzled a moment and then her face cleared.

"Oh," she said. "Like Thompson *that* way. Not

sounding like Thompson, but being like Thompson. I thought you meant *sounding* like Thompson."

"Really," Mr. North said. "Really." He looked at all of them. Evidently, he decided, it ran in families.

"Of course," Beth said. "Like Thompson that way. Like Franklin or Turner or Williams or one of those names. Or Jones."

"Not Jones," Pam North said. She said it over. "Jones." She shook her head.

"Jones isn't one of them," she said. "I'll give you Turner and Williams." She stopped suddenly. "Williams?" she said.

"It was Williams, Beth," Margie said. "I remember, now. And she had a daffy sister."

"Listen," Mrs. North said. "Was Vee-dee really her name? Vee-dee Williams?"

"Everybody called her Vee-dee," Margie said. "It must have been. Although it does sound like a nickname."

"Oh, I think her name was just Vee," Beth said. "Somebody added the rest. It was just Vee to start with."

"Nobody's named just Vee," Margie objected.

Beth said oh, she didn't see why. "You can be named anything," Beth added. "Maybe her parents were crazy too. And it's better than—than—"

"Lizzie," Margie said. She listened to it. "I don't see what's wrong with it," she said. "I'd just as soon be Lizzie. Beth sounds like *Little Women* or something."

"Oh, it does not," Beth said. "It's ever so much better than Lizzie." She looked at Margie without affection. "It's better than Margie, when you think of it," she said. "Much better."

"Girls," Mrs. North said, with admonition. But her curiosity overcame her. "You mean one of the girls at the school—this Vee-dee's sister, was really—daffy?"

"Not at the school," Margie said. "She wasn't at the school. She was at another school. For backward children, I guess. But Vee-dee talked about her. She always said, 'My sister's daffy.' "

"Oh, always," Beth said. "She didn't mind at all. I mean, Vee-dee didn't. I expect the daffy one did, really. Except maybe she didn't know."

"Look," Mr. North said, "could we please talk about something else. Maybe about somebody we all know?"

"Well," Mrs. North said, "of course you got the coincidence. Williams. And Williams. *Mrs.* Williams."

"Yes," Mr. North said. "Coincidence with a very short arm, dear. Like finding two people named Smith."

There was that, Mrs. North had to admit. She agreed that it wasn't a big coincidence. Then said, "Ouch! Toughy! My stocking!"

"He wants lobster," Jerry told her. "Naturally."

"Well," Mrs. North said, "he can't—*Toughy!*"

The gray cat was in her lap. A gray paw licked out and circled a morsel of lobster and seemed to toss it into an open red mouth. And Toughy poured himself off Mrs. North's lap with a movement like milk pouring. Toughy crouched over his morsel of lobster, looked up at Mrs. North with a yellow eye, swallowed the lobster and gulped. He seemed surprised and sat for a moment, evidently considering the downward passage of the lobster. Then he looked pleased, saw Ruffy approaching, crouched and swished his tail, and leaped half across the room, landing where Ruffy's head had just been. Ruffy's head had removed itself. Ruffy looked bored and began to wash herself. Toughy sat down and looked at her, got the idea with a start, and began to wash himself.

"I wonder," Mrs. North said, "if that Scat stuff would keep them off me?"

Mr. North nodded. He said he should think so. He

said he imagined she wouldn't be troubled by the cats if she put the Scat stuff on her.

"Or by anything else," he added.

"Jerry!" Mrs. North said. The doorbell rang and, clicked past the barrier, Bill Weigand came in. He said, when asked, that he had had lunch. He looked at the almost empty plate which had held Spanish lobster.

"Which is apparently just as well," he added. "Is that that lobster stuff?"

"Yes," Pam said. "I didn't for a long time and then I thought, what difference did it make? So now I do. After all, that was a long time ago, and it wasn't just the lobster. You'd have got him anyway, in the long run."

"Probably," Weigand admitted. "Anyway, as you say, it's over. Whereas this one—" Weigand sighed. "These two, now," he told them.

"*Bill!*" Pam said. "That's dreadful. I wish people wouldn't."

"Right," Bill Weigand said. "Job or no job. I wish they wouldn't. But they do. This one was with a pillow."

He told them about Mr. Demming; pressed, he ran quickly over what he had learned since he saw them. It amounted, he said, to nothing that came clear. Where people used to live, who had insured whom, which two were about to marry and which were jealous of others—somewhere in all this there might be a solution. But, bluntly, he didn't see it.

"Usually," Pam said, "you have a point when you can make a guess. Or get a hunch, or whatever it is. Haven't you yet?"

"No hunch," Bill told her. "No major hunch, anyway. Some little, intermediate hunches, hardly worth the mind they're thought on. It doesn't jell."

He looked at the Norths and they looked at him. He shrugged.

"Well," he said, "probably it's all there somewhere.

Waiting to come out in the wash. There's one point, Jerry—"

There was one point on which Jerry North might help him, and for that help he had stopped by on his way to an interview. "With the Akron girl," he said. The matter of life insurance, written in favor of Burden, on Sproul. As a man who knew something of such matters—was Burden's agency in bad straits financially? Was it probable that interest in what Sproul might have had to say was subsiding to a point which would leave the tour unprofitable?

"No," Jerry said. "Two no's. Burden's got most of the big people; the people who get the big fees. Unless the whole lecture business is unsound, Burden is sound. I'd bet on it. And as for Sproul—I'll grant you he's been superseded here in the East. But the East isn't everywhere. He's still big stuff in the West and Middle West. And I could prove that by sales figures."

Weigand said, "Um."

"I'll grant that the insurance deal is unusual," Jerry said. "I mean, I don't suppose it is commonly done. But I honestly think, Bill, it would be foolish to build too much on it."

"Right," Bill Weigand said. "I'm afraid I agree with you. However—no stone unturned."

"You're full of aphorisms today, Bill," Pam said. "I don't think they're terribly becoming. But by the way—how do you feel when you're not feeling well? Both of you."

She said the last to the two men, who stared at her.

"Again?" Jerry said.

"How do you feel when you're not feeling well?" Mrs. North repeated. "Surely that's clear enough."

"It sounds all right," Bill Weigand admitted. "Words and everything; even a verb. Only it doesn't mean anything. When I don't feel well I just don't feel well. Sometimes I have a headache. Sometimes I've eaten something—"

"That isn't it," Pam said. "I don't mean that at all. I don't care whether you have a headache."

"Well, Pam," Bill said, "after all— Old acquaintance forgot?"

"Don't make a joke out of it," Pam told him. "Of course I'd be sorry. Have you got a headache?"

"No," Bill told her. "Not today. I had one yesterday."

"I'm sorry," Pam said. "How did you feel?"

"Terrible," Bill told her.

"No!" Pam said. "You keep slipping off. Jerry— how do you feel when you don't feel well?"

"Please, Pam," Jerry said. "You've got us. I haven't the remotest idea what you're talking about. Bill hasn't the remotest idea. The girls haven't. Have you, girls?"

"No," Margie said, and Beth shook her head.

"You!" Pam North said. "All of you. It's perfectly simple, and if I make it any simpler there won't be any point. *Think!* How do you feel when you don't feel well. What do you say? You say, 'I'm feeling— what?' "

Bill Weigand looked at her and then at Jerry and both men shook their heads. Pam looked at them, compellingly.

"Say it!" she commanded. "Say it!"

"I don't know," Jerry said. "I don't get it at all. I'm sorry, Pam. When I'm feeling sick I just—"

"There!" Pam said. She was excited and pleased. "You say 'I feel sick' or 'sort of sick,' depending."

"I feel sick," Jerry said.

Pam looked at him, and her expression was suddenly worried.

"Jerry," she said. "Oh, I'm sorry, dear. The lobster?"

"I feel fine," Jerry said. "I was just saying it over." He looked at Pam a little desperately. "Are *you* all right, Pam?" he said.

Pam said she was fine.

"Now, Bill," she said. "What do you say? Do you say, without thinking, I feel sick? Without thinking?"

"I don't know," Bill Weigand said. "Maybe I do. Or— I suppose I really say, 'I feel ill." Unless I do feel sick—nauseated, that is. But I don't see that it makes any difference."

"Neither do I," Jerry North said. "Sick—ill. Probably I'd write 'ill' although I'd say 'sick.' And what possible connection this has with anything in the world—"

He broke off because there was an odd look, something like triumph, on Pam's face. She nodded and seemed very pleased.

"You were born and grew up in New York, Bill," she said. "Right?" Bill nodded. "And you came from the middle west, Jerry, middle west and south."

"Of course," Jerry said. "And of course it's regional. You sound like a radio quiz, or expert or something. The man who tells where you came from by your accent. Anybody can do it, after a fashion. It depends on ear and training."

"Naturally," Pam said. She still seemed pleased. She looked at the two men, as if waiting for them to make some comment. But the men looked at each other and shook their heads and Pam looked somewhat disappointed. She was abstracted then, for a time, and nodded abstractedly when Bill Weigand left. For a time after he had gone she still said nothing. Then suddenly, she said she had to run uptown and do some shopping.

"For—for stockings," she said. "Because the cats claw them so. I won't be long and then we'll go look at something. The Empire State Building or something."

She went, almost tempestuously. Jerry North looked, with a puzzled expression, at the door she closed behind her. He knew the symptoms. Pam North was up to something. He had been wrong to let her go alone, but she had gone so quickly; really she had gone before he realized she was up to something. He went to the front of the apartment and looked from a window down into the street. Mrs. North was getting into a taxicab. She looked up and saw him and waved, and before Jerry could open the window to call, the cab with Pam North in it had rolled to the corner.

14

Bill Weigand turned Pam's last few remarks over in his head, decided that they looked much the same upside down as right-side up and telephoned his office from a drug store booth. Mullins was back from Newark and reported himself full of news and was Weigand coming in? Weigand said that, on the contrary, Mullins was coming out. Weigand hung up and walked up Sixth Avenue to Charles and sat at the bar and waited for Mullins, taking time over a rye and water. Mullins came, by subway, sat on the next stool and said, by way of introduction:

"Damn it, Loot, I've got to go to Newark."

"You've been to Newark," Weigand told him. "Think, Sergeant."

Mullins looked at Weigand's glass, looked up at the clock and shook his head sadly. He said he oughtn't to, because he made it a rule not before five o'clock, but since the Loot insisted, Mullins ordered an old fashioned.

"I left the car," he said. "I thought I could get on and get off again, but by the time I'd proved it they'd closed the doors and we were out somewhere in the meadows. So I gotta go back and get the car." He looked at Weigand with sudden hope. "Unless you want to send somebody else, Loot?"

"Right," Weigand said. "I'll send somebody else—maybe. You got on all right?"

Mullins told him about getting on the train all right and said that anybody could do it. Weigand listened and nodded slowly.

"Without being remembered?" he asked. Mullins thought it over and nodded. With luck—with a heavily loaded train, enough people getting out at Newark, an air of assurance which raised no questions which might later rankle in minds. Weigand nodded again.

"Assuming," he said, "that nobody recognized you as a cop. Defense counsel could raise a doubt there." He looked at Mullins, looming beside him. "Quite a doubt," he added.

"O.K.," Mullins said. Mullins was equable. "I look like a cop. So what? I *am* a cop. Only I didn't bull my way on the train. Didn't have to. It's a cinch."

"Right," Weigand said. "I think it is. I think that's the way it was done. And when we know a little more, maybe we can prove it. Maybe we can dig around and find somebody who will remember seeing the guy who did it."

"Guy!" Mullins repeated. "It was a guy?"

Only, Weigand told him, in a manner of speaking. In other words, he was still guessing.

"Guy or gal," Mullins said, and Weigand nodded and said, "Right." Mullins thought.

"If it was a gal," Mullins said, fishing out a piece of orange and nibbling at it, "would she of dressed up like a man?"

"Why?" Weigand wanted to know.

Maybe, Mullins suggested, so that if somebody saw her coming out of Bedroom C and remembered that the occupant of Bedroom C was a man, that somebody would think she was the occupant. It sounded more complicated as Mullins put it. Weigand thought it over and shook his head.

"I don't think so," he said. "It would be an unnecessary refinement; it would amount to doing it the hard way. The chance of a woman's raising questions merely because she was dressed like a man would be greater than the chance of raising them because she was the wrong sex to come out of the bedroom. If it was a woman, I think she looked like a woman. And—" he broke off, thought, emptied his glass, shook his head at the barman, and continued.

"Maybe," he said, "Demming expected whoever it was. Maybe he wrote a letter to the guy or girl in question, saying he was coming east to spill the works. Maybe the murderer wired back, arranging to board the train in Newark and explain how Demming was all wrong. So then, when the train was slowing down at Newark, Demming stood up and waved or made some sort of motion so that the person who was meeting him would know where he was."

"Sure," Mullins said. "Just sort of beckoned—come on in and kill me."

Weigand stood up and Mullins, looking a little wistfully at his glass, obeyed. As they went to the door, Weigand said that Demming had been, obviously, too trusting. But he had not thought he was being too trusting; he had merely underestimated. Weigand led the way to the Buick and slid under the wheel.

"And," he said, starting his car, "what do we know about Demming? Has Pittsburgh come through?"

Pittsburgh had, to a degree. Demming had lived there for about ten years, working as the assistant head of the bond department of one of the banks. He had come from a bank in Chicago and, preceding that, had worked in a bank in Des Moines. During the last two years of his life he had been a semi-invalid and, although he sometimes went to his office, he was constructively on pension. He was a widower, his wife having died before he came to Pittsburgh from Chicago. He had been in his late fifties when he died—the bank records listed him as fifty-eight. He had lived in a hotel in Pittsburgh and his social life had been limited. It had proved difficult to find anyone who knew more about him than the bare facts which were on record.

Weigand listened, guiding the car northward. He nodded slowly when Mullins finished.

"Des Moines," he said. "That's the tie-in."

Mullins repeated the name of the city and there was a note of inquiry in his voice.

"Des Moines," Weigand repeated. Mullins said, "Yeah."

"Where the WAACS come from," he said. "Only I don't get the tie-in."

"Iowa," Weigand told him. "Des Moines, Iowa. The metropolis of the state. And Sproul came from Iowa."

"O.K.," Mullins said. "You call that a tie-in?"

Weigand admitted that it tied nothing tightly. But it tied a loop around at least two of the people involved—the two people who had died. They both came from Iowa; one was coming to tell something about the other's death when he himself was killed. It was tenuous, but perhaps it helped. It might indicate that the motive for Sproul's murder lay in Sproul's past. If they could find another person, still living, who also was tied in with that past—well, they would have something to think over. So—Weigand called on his memory. It would be pleasant if memory recalled that someone else had come from Iowa.

It did not. The Akrons came from New Jersey, south of Atlantic City. Schwartz came originally from Minnesota; Ralph White was born and grew up in Rhode Island and Mrs. Williams also was a New Englander. Y. Charles Burden came from— Weigand's memory pricked up its ears. Mr. Burden came from Nebraska, which was close to Iowa. As was, on second thought, Minnesota. Loretta Shaw came from the south and, as he remembered that, Weigand noted that it showed not at all in her speech. She came from Georgia, where the climate has an extreme influence on the English language. But it was no longer evident when Miss Shaw spoke. Bandelman Jung had been born in Java, by his own report. But the birthplaces of all concerned were, so far, by their own report. It might be worth checking on the accuracy of these reports, Weigand thought. It would take time; it would be neater to know first and prove afterward, if for no other reason than that, if you knew already, you would have to prove only what you knew; you would seek only corroboration, not illumination.

It would be pleasant if things were neater, Weigand agreed with himself, crossing through Fifty-seventh Street to Park, left-turning there and continuing north. The Akrons lived on Park in the Sixties. Weigand wheeled into the space immediately in front of the apartment house and looked blandly at the doorman who was keeping it open. He promised not to be long and mentioned that he was police. The doorman looked shocked and worried. He was relieved when Weigand let him announce them to Miss Jean Akron. At any rate, his manner said, it was not coming to the battering down of doors.

Miss Akron was at home and would see Lieutenant Weigand. Weigand and Mullins waded through carpet to the elevators and went up. The Akrons lived handsomely in a penthouse at the top, where the dim-out restrictions would cause them the most trouble. Weigand, waiting in the long, windowed living room, saw the blackout curtains waiting at each window, only partially hidden and marring the room. Some of the joy had gone out of living high, he suspected. Nervous people were already climbing down out of penthouses. But the Akrons were not, it appeared, that nervous.

Jean Akron, when she came across the room and watched Weigand and Mullins get up, did not appear to be nervous in the least. She was only polite and distant, as if plumbers had unexpectedly come to call. It was an unimportant, although faintly perplexing, intrusion, to be met with poise. Jean Akron, looking very handsome, met it with poise.

She was built to show poise, Weigand reflected, watching her cross the room. She was fair and tall and slender and moved easily; her broad forehead was smooth and without trouble, her taffy-colored hair was relaxed and quiet in its braids. As she greeted them—but would you call it a greeting?—her eyebrows lifted just perceptibly. She told Lieutenant Weigand that he wanted to see her.

About odds and ends only, Bill Weigand assured her; about this and that and Mr. Demming—Mr. Robert J. Demming, the "J." being, not for James or John, but for Jasper. Mr. Robert Jasper Demming.

Jean Akron showed nothing; she did not even show that she was showing nothing. She shook her head.

"Should I know Mr. Demming?" she asked. "I don't remember. Is he somebody—important?"

"Now," Weigand said. "I don't know about earlier. Now he's important because he's dead."

The composed young woman said "Oh" in a tone which might mean anything and was grave enough to acknowledge Death. Then she shook her head. She said she didn't think she had ever heard of him. Weigand said, "Right." He added that it was part of his job to ask people such things; part of his job now to find who had known Mr. Demming in life. Because, he told her, somebody had; apparently the person who had killed Sproul had.

"He was killed, then?" she said. "He didn't take something himself?"

Weigand told her Sproul had been killed. That much, he said, they were sure of. If they had not been sure before, the removal of Mr. Demming made them sure now. And nothing they had discovered, in any case, gave motive for suicide. Or did she know of something? The last question was casual, almost random. It touched, Weigand's attitude told her, on a point entirely academic, but not without historic interest of a sort.

"No," she said. She was sitting, now, on a low sofa, pliant and relaxed. "I don't know of anything. Anything specific, that is. But poor Victor was always so involved." She paused, lighted a cigarette. "With things and people," she said. "He was—oh, call it restless." She was reminiscent. "Nothing was ever settled for Victor," she said. "Nothing assured."

Weigand said "hmm." But it was a mistake, because the sound was an interruption. She dragged deeply on her cigarette and exhaled the subject with the smoke.

"But somebody killed him," she said. "So it doesn't matter that he might have run into some involvement he couldn't solve, and killed himself." Her tone ended the divagation.

Sproul might, Weigand pointed out when she passed the conversation to him, have run into some involvement that couldn't be solved by someone else, who had as a result killed him. It was, he told her, interesting to find out what could be found out about Sproul from people who had known him.

"Men arrange their own murders," he said. "By being what they are, doing the things they do, meeting the people they meet."

She smiled a little, and told Weigand he was a philosopher. Mullins moved uneasily, the leather belt which aided his suspenders in the task of supporting the Mullins trousers creaking. The creak said that Mullins thought all this was pretty silly. Weigand smiled faintly to himself, and to Mullins. Then, to Jean Akron, he shook his head.

"A policeman," he told her. "Merely a policeman, asking questions. So—"

She had known Sproul well, he gathered. At one time she had known him well. How well? She shrugged to that one, as if the question were beyond answer. She looked at Weigand and answered.

"Not that well," she said.

"How well?" Weigand was patient.

"At one time," she said, "very well. Almost that well. We were—we thought we were—well, we talked about marriage."

"And something happened?" Weigand said.

She shrugged. Nothing had happened, in any tangible sense. It was merely that nothing did happen. She was very casual.

"We drifted apart," she said. "We—we each met other people."

Sproul, Weigand assumed, had met Loretta Shaw. She nodded. And she—?

"Other people," she said. "Just other people."

And now, Weigand thought, watching her, she is too casual; now she is showing that she is showing nothing. He was blunt.

"Were you in love with him?" he said.

A kind of blankness came in her calm eyes. She said she did not understand.

"I was quite clear," Weigand told her. "Were you in love with Sproul? Did he—well, to put it bluntly, did he drop you for Miss Shaw?"

She said, "Really, Lieutenant!"

"Because," Weigand said, "it would be interesting to discover that you had been very much in love with Sproul, Miss Akron. And that he had, perhaps, pretended to be in love with you and that he wanted to marry you. And that he had left you, suddenly, for Miss Shaw."

"And," she said, "that I killed him?"

It was, Weigand told her, her own conclusion to the series. To such a series, she would admit it was an apt conclusion.

"I don't know," she said. "I don't know people like that—violent people. I suppose such things happen."

Such things might happen, her tone made clear, among the people with whom Weigand associated; of whom, her tone almost suggested, he was one. Crude people.

"Such things happen," Weigand assured her. "To people of all sorts, Miss Akron. Violence is no respecter of persons." He looked around the apartment, making it obvious. "Or of incomes," he added.

The girl stood up.

"I think there is no point in this," she said. "I think you and"—she looked at Mullins—"your man had better go."

Mullins started to get up, but Weigand's gesture stopped him.

"We'll go," he promised. "Quite soon. When we've finished. Do you deny you were in love with Sproul, and that he left you for Loretta Shaw?"

"In love?" she said. Her tone rejected the phrase as sentimental. "I was fond of him at one time. At that time I might have married him, if he had been in a position to marry. But it was not a—not a violent attachment. When we lost interest—when we both lost interest—we drifted apart." She looked down at Weigand, who was still sitting. "You can't make melodrama out of it," she told him.

"Right," Weigand said. "I'm not trying to make anything out of anything. I'm trying to find out who killed Sproul. Why don't you sit down and help me, Miss Akron? If you want to help."

"I can't help," she said. "I don't know anything. And I don't kill people."

Weigand let that lie. It did not seem a point to bicker over. He smiled faintly, accepting that much as read. He let a pause punctuate, and began again.

"Why wasn't Sproul in a position to marry, Miss Akron?" he asked. She looked at him suspiciously, said that he probably knew already. However—

"He was married," she said. "He had married somebody when he was very young—back in the west somewhere. They were still married. She was some—

some sweet little thing from a small town. It was a mistake for Victor, of course. She was—oh, a homebody. At any rate, that's what I gathered. She wanted a house and a yard, and Victor mowing the yard, and babies and—and the Middle West. Victor used to talk about her, and laugh—laugh rather oddly. As if he were laughing mostly at himself."

Weigand nodded. He could see the picture Sproul had painted; the picture of himself as an impetuous youth, long ago, his youthful ardors stimulated by a pretty girl, of the home town, perhaps—and this hinted—a girl's premature surrender. And after that, by the mores of the community, marriage and respectability. And, for them both, maladjustment, as she did not "grow" with him. Weigand nodded.

"And she never divorced him?" he said. "I assume he deserted her?"

Jean Akron's shrug was detached. About that, it and her words told Bill Weigand, she did not know. She assumed certainly that there had been no divorce, since Sproul said they were still married. Possibly he sent her money; possibly it had been, through the years, merely a separation and nothing final. She smiled faintly.

"And, for Victor, a protection," she said. "In the old days. But lately he wanted to marry and—settle down. The small town boy was coming out, I think."

She was calm, again, and detached. Since the questioning had turned, finally, from her own relations with Sproul, she was detached. She was trying to be helpful. She did not recall that Sproul had ever said so, in direct words, but she had got the impression that Mrs. Sproul still lived back in the Middle West, where she and Sproul had met. With a little house and a little lawn and a little garden, but without Victor Leeds Sproul. It seemed the inevitable thing to happen to Mrs. Sproul, as described.

Weigand let the questioning drift from Sproul to others in the group—the Paris group, but his questions were idle and her replies were not freshly illuminating. It was lulling and Mullins stirred restlessly. He knew what the Loot was up to. He was listening to the girl's voice, watching her eyes and her hands, trying to decide how she felt and thought and how she might act. "What makes the wheels go round," Mullins thought to himself. The Loot was wondering if she was the sort of dame who would get sore at being ditched and knock off the guy who had ditched her; if she would pretend and smile and put morphine in the soup. Or, more likely, the drink. Mullins knew what the Loot was up to. Which didn't keep it from being, to Mullins, dull. He looked at the dame and wondered would she? and thought maybe she would. He thought she had nice legs and curved well where she should, and that in general he liked the little ones. You wouldn't, Mullins decided, call Jean Akron a cute trick, and cute tricks were the best in the long run. In the short run, however—Mullins found himself looking at Jean Akron with speculation and sighed. It was too bad, in a way, that she had so much jack.

Mullins' mildly pleasant day-dreaming was interrupted. Weigand got up and said, "Thank you, Miss Akron," and started to move toward the door. Mullins got up, and Weigand turned around.

"By the way, Miss Akron," Weigand said casually. "For the record. Where were you this morning? About eight o'clock?"

"When your Mr. Demming was killed?" the girl said. She was quick. Weigand nodded. "Here, Lieutenant," she said. "In bed. Just waking up and getting ready to ring for breakfast."

Weigand said, "Right" and nodded. It was the inevitable answer; probably the maid would confirm it; possibly both Miss Akron and the maid would be telling the truth. True or false, it was the story to be expected. He said, again, "Thanks," and again started for the door and again appeared to think of one more question.

"And your brother, Miss Akron," he said. "He lives here?"

She nodded.

"Do you happen to know where he was around eight o'clock?" Weigand said. "This morning?"

"On his way to the plant," she said. "He commutes—in reverse. He lives in town and works in the suburbs—his factory's in the suburbs. He leaves here every morning about seven-thirty and goes to the plant, and he comes home every evening. Usually fairly late. About eight o'clock he was—oh, I suppose on the train."

"Right," Weigand said. "Where is the factory, Miss Akron?"

His tone was still casual, indicating merely routine interest.

"In New Brunswick," she said. "Just outside New Brunswick."

Mullins' eyes opened and his lips parted. But Weigand looked at him and his lips closed. They opened again outside in the car.

"Well!" Mullins said. "There's a guy could of bumped Demming. He was right there, if he wanted to be. He gets his usual train to New Brunswick, gets off at Newark, rides back and kills Demming, gets another train to New Brunswick—hell, it's a setup."

Weigand nodded slowly, agreeing. But to Mullins, Weigand seemed a long way off. He watched the fingers of Weigand's left hand beating a tattoo on the steering wheel; noticed the moment of abstraction during which Weigand sat staring at the dashboard and making no effort to turn on the ignition; saw the sudden decision of movement which sent the lieutenant's lean right hand out toward the key on the dash and brought his foot down on the accelerator pedal. The motor started with a snarl. The car, suddenly alive, moved forward with a little jump.

Mullins knew the symptoms. The lieutenant had a hunch. So it was about over. Mullins shook his head and wished he knew how the lieutenant did it. To Mullins, he admitted reluctantly to himself, it was still just as screwy as it had been when it started.

The car turned left at the first westbound street; it crossed Madison and turned left again on Fifth. It moved right along.

15

Mrs. North paid off the taxi and looked at the building and remembered, belatedly, that it was Saturday afternoon. She might, she thought, as well have saved herself the trouble; she might as well have gone, after all, and bought stockings. Still, now that she was here—

She went into the lobby and the lobby looked like Saturday afternoon. Two of the elevators had cards on them which said "Not Running" and the third, although it opened indifferently to the world, gaping sleepily at the lobby, did nothing to encourage passengers. Mrs. North went to it and looked in and found there was nobody there. She looked around the lobby. At one side there was a straight chair leaning perilously against the wall and in it was a man who was evidently asleep. He had on part of a uniform and Mrs. North presumed he was connected with the elevator. She pushed the call button and the elevator buzzed angrily, and the man came down in his chair, clacking on the tile floor. The man looked at Mrs. North with sleepy hostility, and she said she was sorry. She told him that she wanted to go up.

"Nobody there," he told her. "This is Saturday, lady. Saturday *afternoon*."

"Please," Mrs. North said. "I think maybe the person I want is there. I'm sorry to wake you."

224

"You're wasting your time," the man told her. But he walked toward the elevator and said, "What floor?"

"I don't mind," Mrs. North said. "It won't be much time, really. Fourth."

The man closed the door and looked dully at nothing and ran the elevator up. He opened the doors and said, "Four" with weariness and clanged the elevator doors closed almost on Mrs. North's heels. It was only after the elevator had gone down, leaving her in a peculiarly deserted corridor, that Mrs. North began to wonder whether she was being very wise. Because if she was right, she was not going to be popular and the fourth floor of an apparently deserted office building was a lonely place to be unpopular in. But probably, she decided, looking at the arrow which pointed toward rooms 410 to 422, the elevator operator was right, and she was merely wasting her time. She began to hope she was, and told herself not to be silly.

She went along, looking for 418 and expecting to find that it, like the other doors, showed no light through ground glass. She came to 418 and read the gold lettering on the ground glass and found that there was a light behind it. And, furthermore, the door was not quite closed. Mrs. North was conscious of a sharp, unmistakable, disappointment. She was pretty sure, now, that she was being unwise. At the least, she should have told Jerry. Or Bill. Or even the nieces.

But if she went back now she would seem very foolish to herself, and that was always an uncomfortable feeling. And perhaps, after all, there would be merely a stenographer in the outer office. Mrs. North opened the door.

The door opened on a small room with a railing across it. There was a desk behind the railing, but it was a vacant desk; it was a clean, Saturday afternoon desk. To the left, as Mrs. North faced the railing, the wall was blank, but to the right there was a door. The door was closed, but there was a light behind it; and then Mrs. North heard voices. One was a man's voice, and she heard it first.

"I think you are not telling the truth," the voice, light for a man's voice, said. "There is no reason why you should not tell the truth to me. We are on the same side."

"I don't know what you mean," the other voice said. It was a woman's voice; it was Mrs. Paul Williams' voice. It sounded as if Mrs. Williams was nervous.

"Please," the man said. Then his voice got low. Mrs. North went to the door and put her ear to the ground glass. "—for the side we are both on," the man finished. "You must tell me."

"I think you've gone crazy," Mrs. Williams said. "I don't know what you're talking about. I'll call the police."

"Please," the voice said. "That would be very foolish. The police are stupid; they would not understand. I would show them—"

Mrs. North listened eagerly, but the man did not say what he would show them. Presumably he showed whatever it was to Mrs. Williams.

"You're making a mistake," Mrs. Williams said. "I don't know anything about it—about any of it. What country do you think you are in?"

That was puzzling. Mrs. North pressed tight to the door in order to hear what country the man thought he was in. She steadied herself by holding onto the knob, and she must—she realized afterward that she must—have turned it. Because the door opened and Mrs. North, swinging on it like a child on a fence gate, swept violently into the room. She brought up with a jar when the door struck a doorstop.

Mrs. Williams was sitting in her own office, at her own desk. The little dark man with the funny name was standing beside her, at the end of the desk, holding something. As Mrs. North crashed in several things happened.

The man whirled away from Mrs. Williams and faced the door, and as he turned something dropped from his hand. It dropped to the floor and broke with the thin clatter of glass. And in Bandelman Jung's other hand there was a pistol, and it was pointed at Mrs. North.

For a moment the three stared at one another and then Mrs. North, in a strange, alarmed voice, said, "Oh!"

"So," Bandelman Jung said, "they sent you. They are fools!"

"He's got a gun," Mrs. Williams said. Her voice was high and nervous. "He's got a gun. I think he's gone crazy."

"A woman!" Jung said, and there was surprised contempt in his tone. "They sent a woman!" He made a kind of snorting noise. It was almost, Mrs. North thought in a moment of alarmed lucidity, as if he had said "Bah!"

"Who sent me?" she said. "I didn't come to see you."

"You followed me," Jung told her, with contempt. "The other one I fooled, but I did not know they would send a woman. The softlings."

"What?" Mrs. North said.

"I tell you," Mrs. Williams said, "he's gone crazy. He was threatening to kill me. Like he killed—"

"Shut up!" Jung told her. "I have killed plenty. Watch out I do not kill you."

He was, Mrs. North thought, still a preposterous little man. The pistol was too big for him, the words were too big for him. He was a small, absurd gesture. She wanted to laugh.

"I don't believe it," she said. "You haven't killed plenty. You're—you're too little."

He glared at her, and the pistol was an immediate threat. Mrs. North looked at his eyes and they were small, frightening eyes. They were blank in a strange fashion, as if they were solid and opaque. It came over

Mrs. North, frighteningly, that she was making a
terrible mistake. Little Mr. Jung was not at all funny.

"You believe it," he told her. The words were a
command. "You better believe it. You are a softling."

There wasn't any such word, Mrs. North told herself. The fact gave her an odd, tenuous, feeling of
superiority. She looked again at Mr. Jung's eyes, and
again at the pistol, and the feeling vanished.

"All right," she said, "I believe it."

She tried to make it sound conversational.

"I could kill you both," Mr. Jung said. "She is a
traitor. You are from the police. I could kill you both
and get away."

"He's mad," Mrs. Williams said. "He's completely
mad. A traitor!"

"You," Mr. Jung told her, "you I would like to kill.
But that is not for me. If I am told, yes. I should like to
kill you."

It was, Mrs. North decided, entirely bewildering.
She had come here with a theory, and thinking to ask
two questions, and it had, at the last moment,
seemed as if there might be some danger in it. But
there was nothing in her plans about a little man with
opaque eyes, and a gun; nothing about a conversation
which seemed to be about incomprehensible things—
about "traitors" and killing people one was told to
kill.

She looked helplessly at Mrs. Williams, who was
sitting with both hands on the desk. It occurred to
Mrs. North that Mrs. Williams had been told to keep
both hands on the desk.

"He came in raving," Mrs. Williams said. Her voice
was less shrill than it had been. "He's like—like a bad
melodrama. He keeps accusing me of preposterous
things . . . of being an agent for the Nazis; of—"

"You will be quiet," Jung said. As he said it he
struck, snake-like, with his free hand. His open hand
struck Mrs. Williams across the mouth. After a second, blood trickled slowly from her mouth. She put a

hand up to it and brought the hand away again and
looked at the blood on it with surprised eyes.

"No!" Mrs. North said. "You can't—you—"

"She is a fool," Jung said. "She should keep her
mouth shut. Give me your gun."

Mrs. North shook her head.

"I haven't got a gun," she said. "Why should I have
a gun?"

"You're police," Jung told her. "You have a gun.
Give it to me!"

Mrs. North was still holding the door, but her first
swinging rush into the room had carried her a little
beyond it, so that now she was holding the knob
behind her. Jung came toward her and, involuntarily,
she shrank back. As she shrank, the door began to
close behind her.

"I haven't any gun," she said. "I haven't anything
to do with the police. I came to see Mrs. Williams. I
didn't know you were here."

She spoke rapidly, trying to reassure him; trying by
simple words about facts to reassure herself. And as
she spoke she continued to shrink back, closing the
door as she retreated. Then the door met pressure.

She was staring at Mr. Jung, advancing with his
pistol, and his face was a mirror suddenly, telling her
that somebody was behind her. Somebody of whom
Mr. Jung was afraid. Mr. Jung was not advancing
toward her now. He was retreating, slowly, the gun
leveled. The eyes were opaque as before, but the lines
around them made them change expression. Mr. Jung
was afraid.

"Drop it!" a voice said behind Mrs. North. It was a
fine voice for Mrs. North to hear. She stepped back
into the room, pulling the door with her, and let Bill
Weigand come in. Weigand had his own automatic
drawn and it was pointing at Jung. "Drop it!" Weigand
commanded. "Get it, Mullins!"

Mullins was behind Weigand. No, Mullins was beside Weigand.

"No!" Jung said. The word was like a scream. "No! You never get me. *Schwein!*"

The last was sibilant, like a whip in the air.

The gun in Jung's hand went up to Jung's head.

"You never get me!" he said, again. Pam North, frozen against the partly opened door, waited for the horrible thing to happen.

But the moment hung. It was too long; somewhere the timing had gone wrong. Jung stood with the pistol against his head and stared at Weigand and Mullins, and the moment hung. And then Weigand spoke and his voice sounded tired.

"Oh, get it, Mullins," he said.

Mullins was in front of Weigand now, although skirting the line of fire between Weigand's gun and the little dark man. He moved across toward the little man, and he was in no hurry, and he spoke without excitement.

"O.K., little man," Mullins said. "Give it to papa."

Mullins held out his hand for it, and the little man stared at him. And then, under the dark skin, there was a slowly increasing redness.

"For heaven's sake!" Mrs. North thought to herself. "He's blushing!"

And then she heard the words and realized that she had spoken aloud again, and the little man's opaque eyes turned to her with a kind of horrible embarrassment. And then he lowered the gun from his head and held it out to Mullins. And as Mullins took it, the little dark man did the strangest thing of all. He began to cry.

"Oh," Weigand said, "for God's sake!"

He looked at Pam North, and she could see contempt and pity in his eyes.

"All right, Mullins," Weigand said. "Take him along. Get him out of here."

"Come along, guy," Mullins said. "Come with papa."

The little man was even smaller than he had been, with the large Mullins beside him, with a large Mullins hand closed on his thin arm. He was disproportionately small. As he and Mullins went out she turned to watch him, and then turned back to Weigand.

"He seems so little," she said. "And helpless, somehow. To have done all that. Why did he?"

"He's an agent," Mrs. Williams said. "A spy. He must have killed Sproul because—oh, of something Sproul knew about spies in this country. Or something Sproul did in France. They must have had Jung follow him here. You heard what he said."

This last was to Mrs. North.

"Yes," Mrs. North said. "He could kill people if he was told to. That fits in. Was it that way?"

This last was to Weigand. He nodded.

"He was a spy," Weigand said. "A little spy, doing little odd jobs. It was—oh, half make-believe and half real. The people he helped are real enough—and dangerous enough, and they used him. For little things. But he made himself believe they were important; he—well, dramatized himself. He was—call him a borderline spy. And probably a borderline case, in addition. But part of it was real. But it wasn't real enough, finally, to make him kill himself. And then he realized, I guess, that the dangerous, desperate man he thought he was, was mostly make-believe. And so he was upset and embarrassed."

Weigand seemed to Pam North to be talking to fill in time. And not everything that he was saying made sense.

"But killing Sproul wasn't a little thing," she said. "And it wasn't a make-believe thing."

Weigand shook his head, slowly.

"No," he said. "Murder isn't a little thing. I suppose it was getting mixed up in murder that finally frightened Jung, and brought him here and made him talk wildly." He smiled suddenly at Pam. "Mullins and

I were outside quite a while," he said. "Listening." He paused again, and took up the thread. "He was like a boy playing Indian," he said. "Like a boy who suddenly discovers that one of the other Indians is really dead. That it isn't a game."

"You're generous," Mrs. Williams said, suddenly. She said it with a faint contempt in her voice. "You make a good many allowances—for murder. And murderers."

Weigand looked at her and shook his head.

"No, Mrs. Williams," he said. "I don't make many allowances for murderers. I can't, you know. Even if I appreciate their motives—understand a little of how they must have felt—I can't make allowances. Not and stay a policeman."

There was something puzzling in the way he said it; about the tone of his voice. Mrs. North looked at him oddly and with a half-familiar, unhappy feeling. It was as if pain which had seemed to be over had returned. Weigand was looking at Mrs. Williams still.

"But of course," he said, "Jung wasn't a murderer, Mrs. Williams. We both know that, don't we?"

There was a peculiar alteration in Mrs. Williams' expression. She was staring at Weigand.

"I don't—" she began.

"Oh, yes," Weigand said. His voice sounded tired again. "You know what I mean, Mrs. Williams. Mrs. Sproul."

"No," she said. "No! I didn't!"

Weigand nodded.

"Oh, yes you did, Mrs. Sproul," he said. "You killed your husband. With provocation, of a sort. And Demming, without provocation. To save your neck. It won't, Mrs. Sproul."

"Don't call me that," she said. "That isn't my name. You know that isn't my name."

Then Pam remembered what she had come to ask; remembered that she had been right, after all.

"Your daughters," she said. "One of them is named Victoria, isn't she? The older one, for her father. Victoria Leeds Sproul. And the other one is Daphne, after you. And they call one of them Vee at school, or Vee-dee, but that isn't a name. And it would be a nickname for Victoria, wouldn't it? And the nieces thought the other one was 'daffy,' but she wasn't. That was her name. Vee-dee really said, 'my sister Daphne.' Or maybe she called her 'Daffy.' Did she, Mrs.—Mrs. Williams?"

"He wanted—," Mrs. Williams began. Then she seemed to stiffen. "That is all lies," she said. "You're both as mad as little Mr. Jung. I didn't kill anybody."

Weigand shook his head. He said he thought she had.

"Jung stole the glass Sproul drank out of," he told her. "Out of the speakers' room. When Mr. North chased him. Probably he found it had your fingerprints on it. He knew men who would be able to bring the prints up and compare them with yours, if he had yours. And he could get them. So he knew you did it. But he was wrong, of course, about the reason."

"He was wrong about everything," Mrs. Williams told him. "You're wrong about everything."

Weigand appeared not to hear her.

"It was part of his romantic notion about spying," he said. "He had set himself to watch Sproul; perhaps he was told to watch Sproul; perhaps Sproul had, when he was in Paris, learned things the Nazis didn't want him to know. The men Jung was working for might have told him to keep an eye on Sproul—follow him, learn if he planned to give any information to the authorities. So Jung was watching him. Then Sproul died. And that was a surprise to Mr. Jung—a great surprise. Because, you see, he probably thought that the men he was working for, the men from the Axis, had had Sproul killed. Without telling Mr. Jung. And that worried him, naturally; it was by way of being a slap in the face. So he—well, he began to do a little detecting on his own to find out what went on. He stole Sproul's notes and then—''

Weigand broke off. It occurred to him that there was no use telling everything.

"Then he did other things," he continued. "By way of investigating. Including getting the glass Sproul had drunk from. Which led him to you, Mrs. Sproul.''

"Don't call me that!" she commanded. But the command was, in some fashion, also a plea. "Don't call me that.''

"And so," Weigand said, "he assumed you were an agent too, and had been the one instructed to kill Sproul. And he wanted you to know that he had been underestimated, that he couldn't merely be brushed aside. That he could find things out. And so now he'll go to the Feds, and to prison. Unless some psychiatrist—"He broke off. "However—" he said.

"Your real motive was much simpler, of course," he told Mrs. Williams. "You may as well know what we know. You killed Sproul because he was your husband. He married you a good many years ago in Iowa and—''

Mrs. North broke in.

"If I knew she did," she said, "that was the other discrepancy. Besides her being out with this other man. When—when the poison began to work on Sproul she said to Jerry, 'Is he sick?' But if she'd really been what she pretended to be, she would have said, 'Is he ill?' Because she came from the east, if she was really who she said she was.''

"I think," Weigand said, "that you build a good deal on very little, Pam. But you get to the right place. And it was quick of you—about the girls, I mean. Vee-dee and Daphne.''

Mrs. Williams said nothing. She stared at them.

"He married you in Iowa," Weigand said, returning. "After a couple of years, and two daughters, he left you. Later you came east—looking for him, perhaps?—and when you didn't find him you—well, decided to burn bridges. To start all over. Even with a new name. As a widow. You were still very young. You—what? Went to night school for law?"

"That's true," Mrs. Williams said. "Anyway, that's true. And kept the girls alive by working as a waitress. After—after my husband died. After Mr. Williams died."

Weigand shook his head, almost gently. But he did not answer otherwise.

"And finally," he said, "Sproul came back. A few months ago. And then he was going to divorce you. He talked to people about it, without even using your name. He was saving that—it was like him. Until he sued in New York, where there's only one cause. I take it he could have proved his case, Mrs. Sproul? That you had—men friends. That his detectives could have got evidence?"

She did not answer.

"That was Mrs. North's other discrepancy," he pointed out. "You weren't as—as unrelaxing as you appeared, Mrs. Sproul. And your husband discovered it, and told you he was going to divorce you. For cause, in New York State. And if he could prove his case, he would be awarded custody of the children. That was really it, wasn't it? That was the motive I mean that was—understandable. He was going to take the children. Not because he wanted them, particularly. But to hurt you. He was a malicious man, everybody said. A very malicious man. And, of course, he wanted to marry again."

"You can't prove any of this," Mrs. Williams said. "It isn't true—and you can't prove it."

Weigand said he thought they could. Given time. They could, for example, prove things about Mr. Demming. Probably they could prove that he knew of the marriage, which must have been kept secret, or fairly secret; probably they would find out that he knew her identity as Mrs. Sproul. They would find out,

236   *Frances & Richard Lockridge*

when they looked—now that they knew what to look for, and where to look—that in the old days Demming had been in young Sproul's confidence, and had remained in his confidence.

So, although probably they would never need to, they might be able to prove that Demming had read of Sproul's murder, seen Mrs. Williams' name mentioned in connection with it, and become suspicious because she did not disclose her real identity. It was, he must have thought, something that the police ought to know. So he wrote the police a letter which, because of a rain-storm, they received too late, and took a train for New York.

"But he telegraphed you too," Weigand told Mrs. Williams. "He wanted to give you a chance to explain. He was going to you, to see if you could explain, before he went to the police. Because he knew about your life, and was sympathetic. So you met the train he was coming on, got on it at Newark, smothered Sproul's old friend—and your old friend, Mrs. Sproul?—and felt safe again. You told your secretary, as you told me, that the telegram was from an out of town client making an appointment. And such a client had made such an appointment, which bore out your story. But he had made it earlier."

Weigand paused.

"We'll prove those things, Mrs. Sproul," he told her after a moment. "When we get around to them. We'll prove that you had motive for killing Sproul, that you had the opportunity to put something in his drink in the speakers' room, probably that you knew his peculiar susceptibility to morphine. And we'll let little Mr. Jung tell us about the glass. If—"

"There!" Pam said. "On the floor! He was showing it to her and dropped it and her prints will still be on the pieces and—"

She did not finish. Because Mrs. Williams was no longer contemptuous, inflexible in her protestations of innocence. She had whirled her chair and was out of it, and her right foot was raised to stamp on the shards of broken glass on the floor. But Weigand was quicker than she, and before her foot fell he pushed her back, and then he stood over her and looked down at her, and his face was without triumph.

"You should have stopped with your husband, Mrs. Sproul," he told her. "People would have been—sorry for you. Seen your side. You should have stopped then, you know. If you had stopped then, it might have been second degree. You shouldn't have killed Demming, Mrs. Sproul. The jury isn't going to like your having killed Demming."

He looked down at her for a moment.

"I don't like it myself, Mrs. Sproul," he told her. "He was sick, you know. And weak—and sort of old. And he was trying to give you a chance."

She said nothing more, and she went with Weigand in a kind of daze.

16

The Norths sat side by side at Charles' bar and Bill Weigand came in and they moved so that he could sit between them. The Norths looked around for Mullins, and Weigand, who looked tired, smiled and shook his head.

"He's gone to Newark to get something he forgot," Weigand told them. "Where are the nieces?"

"At home," Mrs. North said. "It turned out they are supposed to study and they're studying. I think. I've told Jerry."

"About the murder," Jerry amplified. "About Vee-dee and Daffy and the use of 'sick.' " He paused, doubtfully. "Which," he added, "I still think anybody might have used."

"Well," Mrs. North said, "it worked. I knew. And, of course, there was the discrepancy about the man in the restaurant and the way Mrs. Williams was looking at him. That worked, too. But the little dark man did throw me off for a while."

Weigand agreed that the little dark man had been a nuisance. Thinking how much of a nuisance, Weigand rubbed his head thoughtfully. There was still a faint bump. It made him think of Dorian, who also had a faint bump, and he said that Dorian was coming along presently, and why didn't they all have dinner?

238

"Of course," Pam said. "Martha can feed the nieces."

There was a little pause while glasses were filled. Then Jerry North said that it was all all right, of course, but that he still didn't fully get it. What happened, yes. He got that. But how Weigand knew, that he didn't get. Granting the discrepancies—even granting the girls and their names. Mr. North looked at Weigand darkly and said it still wasn't enough.

"It sounds to me like intuition," he said. He said it with disapproval. Bill Weigand shook his head. He said that the pattern was obvious. Once the outline came clear, it was easy to fill in.

"The Iowa pattern," Weigand said. "And the divorce pattern. Sproul was not supposed to be married; he was married and he was getting a divorce. In New York. Nobody had heard of his having been married in the east; it was a good guess that he was married in the Middle West before he came east. Demming knew something; Demming's connection was that he came from Iowa. Hence—he knew something which had its origin in Iowa. The person who killed him, however, lived here, which indicated that one of the group here had his origin in Iowa, and that what he—or she—wanted to keep secret had happened there. Hence, it had happened a long time—a pretty long time—ago. So then—"

"So then," Mr. North said, unforgivingly. "You used intuition."

Weigand smiled.

"I guessed," he said. "A marriage which had happened a pretty long time ago, interest by the murderer in something which had happened a long time ago; the New York divorce law and—well, the determination of a mother not to lose the children she had given her life to; to lose them to a man who had never shown he cared anything for them or would, if he got them, give them a second thought. Except, perhaps, to put them in schools somewhere and pay their bills. And you could guess that Sproul's wife, if he had a wife, wouldn't be fond of him—might, if she were that kind of woman, hate him. And, if she were hard enough and confident enough, kill him out of resentment, which might by now be hatred, and a desire to protect the things she had worked for—and got. And a determination to keep the children out of his hands. That more than anything."

"He would have been bad for them," Mrs. North agreed. "Terribly bad. You can—you can almost see how she felt."

"Listen," Mr. North said. "You just guessed this. Right?"

"Right," Weigand said. "If you want the word, Jerry. I guessed. I thought—suppose Mrs. Sproul isn't the sweet, deserted little homebody tending flowers out in Iowa. Suppose she is here. Then it was Mrs. Williams. It had to be."

"I—" Jerry began.

"Because," Bill Weigand told him, "she was, if nothing else, the only woman the right age. The only one with children. The only one—"

He broke off, because Pam North had turned in her chair and was staring at the door. The men turned and stared with her.

Beth and Margie both looked radiant as they came in. They both had sailors.

"Those girls," Pam said, "are unfair to the army. They ought to be—they ought to be picketed."